The Amber

B.A. Chepaitis

To My father,

who loved the land.

Prologue

Early 21st Century - USA

The dining room was silent, and dark.

Thick velvet curtains covered the windows, closing out the light of day. In the center of the mahogany dining table, big enough for two dozen guests, there was only a bowl of summer roses, and a violin case, open.

An old and honorable instrument rested inside, sleek and golden as a dozing cougar, its surface smooth as a woman's flesh. If someone dared to draw a bow across the strings, it would sing of ancient trees, the pulse of human blood, the fall of moonlight across an open meadow in a distant land.

Soon, someone would dare.

The door to the room opened. A brush of air jogged the curtains, and the evening sun of the summer solstice poured over the violin, transforming it into a shining thing, a source of light. Soft footfall moved across the thick carpet, to the table.

A hand took the bow from the case and tightened it. An arm lifted the violin and drew the bow across the strings, tuning it to perfection. A brief pause, as the player considered what song to pull out of this living thing.

Another moment to gather thought.

Then, music.

Chapter One

Early 21ˢᵗ Century - Upstate NY

Stacey V. moved her pencil on the notepad she held on her lap. For all anyone could tell, she was taking notes on the meeting, but since her presentation was over and the bosses droned on, she was doodling.

Jonathan Seele, senior partner in Accent Marketing, exuded confidence and positive energy as he talked about profit margins and teamwork. He focused the red dot of his laser pen on the Power Point graphs at the front of the room.

Stacey, who'd heard it all before, kept doodling, until a storm-tossed ocean grew under her pen, with two men on horseback rearing back from its waves. She wondered if someone left a radio on, because she heard a violin playing somewhere. Sibelius, Violin concerto, the first movement. The waves on her notepad curled with increasing complexity, the faces of the men on horseback taking rugged shape.

When Jonathan was done, he turned the meeting over to junior partner Ed Horn, who said the same thing with even more confidence. Stacey smiled at the right moments, and continued to draw in time with the music, adding the face of a woman who was being pulled into the waves. She had no idea where the images came from. Like most of her drawings, they seemed to live in her hands, emerging beyond her volition. She continued to draw, until Horn said the magic words.

"That's it, folks. We're done. And we can still make Happy Hour."

The men and women of Accent Marketing sighed with contentment and rose from the gleaming conference table. A few who had agendas to push made their way to Jonathan. The others began to pack up and head out. Stacey did the same.

The meeting had gone well for her. They'd hammered out the busline proposal, a big account that raised a lot of competitive hackles, and no one bit or scratched. They'd divided the Syrius Restaurant budget between air, print, and internet, and everyone responded with enthusiasm to Stacey's graphics for the campaign. Grant clearly appreciated her support for his Mercy Hospital copy, because he was the first to applaud when she announced she'd landed the upstate *I Love NY* account.

Laura had made a cattie remark about her expertise with liquid sales – meaning she'd buy as many drinks as necessary to push a potential client into submission – but she didn't care. Grant admired that skill in her, and he was more fun than Laura. As she pushed herself back from the conference table, secure and sleek as any woman contending for partner in the firm, he turned a glance to her. She ran a hand through her long honey hair, stood and moved to him.

"You heading to Janus?" he asked.

That was the favorite watering hole for young executives on a Thursday evening. Normally, her answer would be yes. Tonight, she had other obligations.

"I wish I could. I'm house-sitting for my sister. Out in the country. I have to walk the dog, feed the cat."

"Ouch," he said.

"It's not that bad, if you like peepers."

He frowned. "I thought those were only sold at Easter."

"Not Peeps. Peepers. The frogs?"

"Oh. Frogs. Right. Did you want company? Besides the peepers," he asked.

She heard his reluctance, and figured it stemmed either from his distaste for anything in nature beyond sushi, or his recent interest in the new copywriter, Erin, who was blonde, thin, and had fantastic cleavage. She tried to work up some feeling about that, and found she couldn't. Their commitment to not committing was her idea.

"I won't ask you to drive up those roads," she said. "Go to Janus and have a drink for me."

Grant smiled. "You're a good woman, Stace," he said.

"So I've been told." She looked around. "Who's got a radio on?"

"What?"

"I still hear that violin. Or is it singing?"

Grant patted her shoulder. "Maybe you need quiet time. I don't hear a thing."

When he left, absorbed in the general milling, she heaved a sigh of relief. Grant was California beach-boy good looking, and he was fun, but she was tired, and didn't relish the thought of dealing with him and a Labrador retriever. Though she'd never admit it to anyone in the room, she looked forward to the time alone, and the peepers. She left the office with a briefcase full of accounts to go over, got in her car and drove away from the city where she worked, the capital of New York State.

It wasn't a hopping town, but there was government money here, and it was close to New York City and Boston. Since Accent had offices in both those cities, she might make her way to either one someday. In the meantime, she avoided the cutthroat competition of Madison Avenue, and appreciated the reasonable housing costs here, which allowed her to buy her own small house at the age of 28.

Part of the money for that came from her parents' will, split between her and her brother and sister when both mother and father were killed in a car accident three years ago. Martha built a house in the country with her share, and Vince – well, they weren't sure what he did with his. Drank it, Martha said. Stacey said no. At least he got a new car. She didn't tell Martha what he said about their parents being worth more dead than alive. That was just bitterness, and later he admitted he meant it only about their father, really. For the most part.

Fifteen minutes west of downtown the city dropped away, and Stacey drove a road that had more cows than people. She took the turn up the hill to her sister's house and anticipated the upcoming thrill. She wasn't disappointed.

As she crested the rise, the land spread itself out in front of her, hills and hollows illumined by the westward dropping sun. Rolling green of deep summer, grass long and soft in the fields and trees burgeoning with emerald leaves dripping sweet golden light. She sighed.

Though she was now an account exec, pushing her way toward partner, she'd started as a graphic artist, and she still appreciated a good visual. She'd thought of trying to paint this view, but wasn't sure how. As she considered possibilities, sun glare temporarily obscured all vision. She had a flash image of a startled face behind the steering wheel of a car, driving into a beautiful and blinding sunset. It would be an interesting task in perspective, light and pain.

Maybe she'd make a sketch tonight, she thought, but then she remembered the *I Love NY* account. She had to work on that. Work paid her bills, art did not. Maybe when she retired, she'd paint more. For now, she had a life to live.

She pulled into her sister's driveway, turned off the car and listened for a minute. The high call of tiny tree toads and peepers filled the air, underscored with the bullfrog's bass notes. She'd once found a tree toad on one of her sister's tomato plants. It was tiny as her thumbnail, its translucent flesh-colored skin veined in bright red. She'd been amazed that something so small could produce such a large sound. That was another painting she hoped to make someday.

She got out of the car, lugged her stuff onto the front porch and looked to the west. It was late June - the solstice in fact - and the sun had hours of light left to shed. Time enough to take the dog for a good long walk in the woods.

She dug the key from her pocket and went inside. Tamsa, a black lab who was sleek and happy as an otter, stood at the entrance to the kitchen, a ball in her mouth, her butt wiggling a mile a minute. Her name was Lithuanian for dark, a word they'd learned from their Lithuanian immigrant grandmother. Chaos, the family black cat, wandered over and wrapped his tail around Stacey's leg, a request for some petting.

"Hey, you two," Stacey said. "Happy to see me?"

Tamsa made the small whine that meant either great joy, or an urgent need to find a patch of grass.

"Yeah," Stacey said. "Just gimme a minute."

She put down her bags and glanced at the note Martha had left on the kitchen counter. It gave detailed instructions on walking, feeding, and taking Tamsa out to pee, along with who to call if the water turned brown, what to do if she smelled gas, the best way to get Tamsa back if she ran away, what canned and dry food to give Chaos, how much to feed the goldfish and hamster that belonged to Stacey's niece, Alicia, and six separate emergency numbers to reach her. At the bottom of the note was a picture Alicia drew of what she expected from their trip: A fairy with crooked pink wings, and sparkles sprinkled on top.

Martha and her husband rarely went on vacation, but they'd promised Alicia a trip to Disney World as soon as school was out. Martha, a high school English teacher who liked everything safe and predictable, prepared for it rather grimly, as if she was going to a Siberian prison camp. Stacey encouraged her to be more adventurous, but on the other hand, she appreciated the stability of her sister's life. They made up for each other's deficits, the way sisters often do, she thought. Stacey was the independent single woman, climbing the ladder of success. Martha, six years her senior, kept the home fires burning. They got a vicarious charge from each other's lives, and managed not to be jealous except now and then.

Tamsa nudged her elbow with a wet nose while she read. "Okay," Stacey said. "Let's walk. Then we'll see what kind of wine your human has around the place."

She tossed some catnip to Chaos, who rolled onto it and was content. She put her briefcase and bag in the spare room, and changed into jeans, t-shirt and sneakers. She stuck one of Alicia's baseball caps on her head to prevent tick infestation, which Martha said was bad this year.

In spite of that, she was looking forward to the walk. The evening was warm and fine, and there were hundreds of acres of woods behind the house to roam in. She tucked her pants into her socks, sprayed herself with organic tick repellant, and set out, Tamsa leaping with doggie joy.

Strolls here were strictly off-leash, and Tamsa scampered ahead, tracking good sniffs while Stacey walked at a leisurely pace, stopping to peer at interesting stones or fallen trees pocked by woodpeckers, thinking of other paintings she might make someday. She followed an open trail across the meadows behind the neighbor's house, which led to a path into woods where tall fir trees shadowed the ground, and patches of moss created a quilt of varied greens under her feet.

They took their time, arriving at the woods just as the sun sank to the western horizon. Once within that shadowed space they climbed a steep hill into the heart of the trees. Stacey stopped here to catch her breath. She needed more time at the gym and less at Janus, she thought, if that left her winded. Tamsa snuffled around, and Stacey bent to touch a patch of light green moss that formed a small pillow at the base of a pine tree.

When she did, her eye caught the colors black and yellow. She stopped, squatted down, looked more closely. Nestled in the moss was a tiny toad, its rough skin black and deep brown, with bright yellow outlining its mouth. It was narrow in the jaw, more elegant than she thought a toad could be.

She thought of her grandmother, who had kept a toad in her house one winter. It had hopped into her cellar after the ground was frozen, and she'd built a shelter for it, filling an old glass fishbowl with dirt from the garden shop, letting the toad burrow into it and rest there through the cold months.

"It's a blessing to have a toad in the house," she told Stacey. "A toad or the zaltys snake. If you ever find one, take good care of it. If you see a dead zaltys in a field, bury it. The sight of a dead zaltys would make the sun cry."

That was just one of many old Lithuanian beliefs their grandmother taught them. She never explained their origin, but when she spoke of them her voice was solemn and her blue eyes piercing, so Stacey knew it was important. To this day, she appreciated toads and snakes.

She was in grade school when her grandmother died at the age of 65, worn out from war and hardship and cancer. Still, she'd left vivid memories behind. She told stories of bees and trees, devils and creatures she called veles, ghost-like beings, sometimes devilish beings, she said would chase Stacey. She told stories of her own grandmother, whose name and slanted silver-grey eyes and high cheekbones Stacey had inherited. And she told stories of toads.

Now Stacey touched this small specimen on the head as a blessing of her own. It puffed its throat at her and hopped away toward the largest tree at the center of the hill. She followed, and saw it disappear under the roots. She squatted down to see where it went, images of glittering fairy houses appearing in her mind. In reality, what she saw was loamy earth, but what she heard wasn't peepers or toads. A new sound entered the woods. One that didn't belong there.

"Violin," she murmured, picking her head up and listening.

A violin playing the Sibelius, just like she'd heard earlier. And singing. A woman's clear, high voice. She couldn't quite make sense of it because it was muted, as if it reached her from far away. Was it a radio on in a house nearby? If so, it was blasting. She'd walked pretty far into the woods.

She pushed herself to stand, hoping to hear better. She tipped slightly on the uneven ground and pressed against the tree to rebalance. Her hand felt thick sap. She saw its congealed stream on the bark, golden brown and red.

Then, suddenly, she didn't see a thing.

"What the hell?" she asked. The sun had fallen quickly away from the earth, leaving her in velvety thick night. Jesus, she thought, it gets dark quick here. She sat down heavily, uncertain what to do.

"Tamsa?" she asked, but as in a dream, her voice wouldn't raise above a whisper. "Tamsa?" She tried again.

No response. She blinked around. Fireflies whizzed by, silent and frantic in their mating dance. Far away, coyotes howled, their voices punctuating the fireflies' dance.

Had she imagined she liked the country? She wished fervently for streetlights, a bar, a cop - anything that said city living. She put her hand to the tree again, a point of reference in the darkness, and her finger dipped into something almost liquid, too thin for sap. Without thinking, she put her hand to her mouth and tasted it.

"Honey," she said.

Fireflies zipped past, one lone honeybee trailing in the wake of their light. She thought that was odd. Bees slept at night, didn't they? Had she hit a hive? She hoped not. She was allergic.

She tried to make sense of it and failed. She dropped her hand to her side and felt long grass beneath it, soft as a woman's hair. Somewhere, someone was singing and a violin was playing Sibelius.

And she heard another voice, male, speaking words she didn't understand.

"Mano," he breathed out. "Jus mano."

She turned to the sound. A few yards away she saw an outline of a male form, silhouette within shadow. He gestured, beckoning to her. He was hungry for her. His hunger was an animal stalking her, terrifying and beautiful.

She thought of all the TV shows she'd ever seen about serial killers. Quaking with fear, she tried to run, but her foot caught on a tree root and she fell hard, landing face down on the earth. Night reeled around her, dragging her into its folds.

Then, only darkness, thick with ancient dreams.

Beginnings

Inland from Nida, Lithuania, circa 1ˢᵗ millenium BC

His hunger for her would not end.

Seasons came and went, and still he hungered. Children were born and grew, and he hungered. Animals were hunted and eaten. Berries were picked, beehives were found and harvested, and as the sweet honey dripped from her hands, he hungered for her.

Her hair was the color of thick sap from the trees, with sun on it. Her hair smelled of the ocean, and of honey. And he hungered for her.

He and Razak were exhausted and famished when they rode into her village, set between forest and shore. His woolen shirt stuck to his skin in the warmth of the day, and his hair was thick with dried salt water. Razak's clothes were spattered with sand, his face drawn and tight, though his eyes were lit with their customary fire.

"Don't worry, Naktis," he said to his only remaining friend. "All will be well."

Naktis wasn't so confident. Not after what they'd just been through.

Their group had ridden far and long, two week's journey south from their village as they sought new land. They were all young and adventurous, and they wanted a warmer land, something more hospitable than the long winters they were leaving behind. They'd had no trouble the whole time, dealing easily with a pack of wolves that followed them, finding all the food they needed as they went. Then, just as they rode toward the abundance of an open shore where fish would be plentiful, they'd been overcome by a storm that rose from the sea like an importunate prayer. It came up suddenly as they reached a stretch of unimpeded sand, the driving wind and drenching rain taking them all by surprise.

Through salt spray and curtains of water Naktis saw flicks of images – Horses rearing. His friend Gared disappearing under a mountainous wave. Gared's woman screaming and disappearing after him. Two more swallowed, then more unhorsed, hands reaching and bodies carried into the sea until all were gone except he and Razak, who screamed to him above the relentless wind.

"Follow me, Naktis. Upland!"

He'd turned his horse and raced against the storm, stumbling up vast dunes of sand, willing his horse to continue as they moved toward a blur of dark green that looked like the shelter of trees.

They'd achieved safety in the forest above the shore, panting and huddling against the stiff bark of foreign trees. They stayed through the night, sleeping restlessly as Naktis tried not to think of what had happened to their people. The rising sea was an evil omen, a sign of the god's displeasure.

"It's the sun's day," he muttered. "We didn't sacrifice, so the gods took what they wanted."

"The gods should learn some patience," Razak replied. "We would have given them their due when we stopped."

Naktis said nothing. Razak was feared both for his blasphemy, and because he was never struck down for it. The people in their old village believed his own god gave him power. He was chosen to lead this group south mostly to get rid of him. Naktis went along because he was sick of the long winter darkness, and the old men who left nothing for the young. He wanted sun, and a little land for his own.

When the night thinned they mounted their horses and rode on, wordless in their hunger and fatigue. Their supplies were gone along with their friends, and soon they'd have to find more food. But they'd ridden less than a mile before they reached an open field, and ahead of them they saw small, squat houses made of mud and straw, built in a circle with a large open space at the center. Here a fire burned, and people dressed in finely woven linen with stripes of bright red and yellow danced around it. Naktis counted almost a hundred men and women, children and old folk, before he gave up. Yellow dogs hung nearby, panting wearily as if they, too, had danced.

"Should we go there?" he asked.

"Yes, of course," Razak said. "They have food."

"They might kill us."

"They might not," Razak answered.

So their horses clopped slowly toward the gathering. That was the first time he saw her, dancing with her people, lit by the rising sun.

She wore a necklace of polished amber that caught the light, and on her upper arm was a bronze band ending in a tightly curled spiral. When she saw them she stood still, her face curious and unafraid. One by one the other dancers stopped and turned to them.

"We were caught in the storm," Razak called out. "We're very hungry."

An old woman with a thin grey braid and flesh like rough tree bark cackled at them. She spoke in a language neither he nor Razak understood, but her gesture was clear. Come forward. Join us. The beautiful woman with the amber necklace nodded and gestured as well.

They got off their horses and led them forward. The dogs circled them. One of them sniffed at Razak, yelped and ran away. The others stayed near Naktis, nuzzling his hand. The beautiful woman walked toward them and spoke unfamiliar words. Naktis frowned, shook his head. She pointed to herself. "Austeja," she said.

That he understood. Her name. He pointed to himself. "Naktis," he said.

Razak did the same. She looked at them both for a long time, as if her eyes could drink their thoughts. The old lady called something out. Austeja shook her head, said something back. Then she took Naktis by the hand and led him into the circle. The singing started again, and she danced, everyone following her lead.

Though Naktis didn't know their language, their gestures made it clear they were praising the sun on the longest day of the year. The rolling sun dances in the sky and all things grow. In their old village, Father Sun demanded sacrifices today. He hoped these people had already made theirs. He and Razak had certainly done so, albeit unwillingly.

As daylight came on full they stopped dancing and passed around a sweet drink that tasted of honey and made the world spin like the sun. Then they walked to a nearby river and tossed in wreaths of pungent herbs, Naktis and Razak tossing theirs in with the rest. The people watched their progress along the currents, and when Naktis's wreath pressed against Austeja's, the old woman made a sound like a growl. Austeja turned to Naktis, her face blanched and serious. She put her slim hand in his and spoke to him as if she knew him. He felt fire burning in him, hotter than the sun.

After this, there was a good enough feast to satisfy any weary traveler. Wild boar was roasted on a spit over an open flame, and bread sweet with honey was passed around. If anyone dropped a crumb of it, it was immediately picked up and kissed, apologetic words spoken over it. Razak said they should stay here, since they were welcome, and well fed. Naktis did not argue.

℘

Austeja, he called her, though the word was hard on his tongue. He kept a watchful eye on her as he and Razak settled in to learn the ways of these people. She was clearly a woman of importance, but he didn't know why. She was beautiful, but beautiful women had no extra measure of power where he came from. Sometimes men fought over them, but that was all. Any power they had came from the man they belonged to.

Austeja seemed to belong to no man, though two honey-haired girls followed her about as if they were her daughters. Yet he never saw a man claim her, and she looked to no man for instruction. The only one she ever listened to was the old woman, who was often with her.

"Their ways are different than ours," Razak told Naktis. He picked up on the words quicker, and already understood much that was said. "The women have babies as they want, and everyone cares for them. No man claims any woman as his own."

"What? They sleep where they want?" He'd exclaimed, bewildered.

Razak only laughed. "Don't scorn it, brother. It works to our good."

"To your good," Naktis corrected, for he'd seen Razak with more than one woman already. Women liked him easily, though he didn't work as hard, nor was he as strong as many others, including himself. Still, he rarely slept alone. But Naktis wasn't envious. He wanted only Austeja.

That didn't change as summer passed into autumn, or as winter, milder here, turned to spring and Naktis learned the customs of his new home. Except for the women, it wasn't that different from what he'd left. They tended goats, hunted for deer and boar or fished the nearby shore and nurtured patches of berries and mushrooms. They wove cloth from flax, and built houses from earth and straw. They sang to their gods and raised children, grew old and died.

He and Razak taught them their way of making pots, using cords to bind and decorate them. They were taught to gather and polish the clear brown stones brought to shore by the sea, making small discs that the women wore around their necks or on their dresses. Austeja said that these stones, called gintaro, were the blood of the trees, and they held life. Encased in the stone she wore was a small bee, its wings eternally spread in flight. He learned that she was friends with the bee goddess, whose name she carried.

Naktis followed her as she went about her tasks, helping when he could. She was kind to him, even friendly, but she was like that with everyone. He wanted more.

One day, he followed her secretly through the forest to a great rock, grey and smooth with a surface like a bowl. He'd seen women stop here and gather rainwater from hollow, wash their faces with it and mutter a prayer. He watched from behind a tree as Austeja spoke quietly to the rock, her lilting voice like song. She took golden pollen from a cloth pouch she carried and sprinkled it into the hollow. When she was done, she sighed.

"Why do you follow me?" she asked, without turning to him. "Since you came here you follow me. Tell me why. I mean you no harm."

He gathered courage and walked to her, hoping he seemed easy, unafraid. "What are you doing?" he demanded when he reached her.

She let her gaze run over him. "I'm feeding Alkos," she said. "Our great stones. That way, the animals have young, and our children are born well."

He shuffled his feet. They had no such custom in his old village. "You already have children," he noted.

"Yes. But others want children, too."

"Would you like more?"

"I might." She tilted her head, her swift smile a song he wanted to hear again and again.

"I'll help you," he said, his head swimming, not even sure what he said.

Her face grew serious. She touched his hand. "You know what the old lady says of you? She sees a long road of trouble going out ahead of you."

"All the more reason to take pleasure now," he said hoarsely.

She considered this, her eyes unfathomable as water, silver as the sea. Then she moved closer. He pulled her to him, lifted her onto the stone, and took enough pleasure to make up for many lifetimes of trouble.

꩜

After that, he thought he'd lose his hunger for her. That's usually how it was with women and men. Instead, his appetite grew until it was a gnawing hole not even their pleasure could fill, because no matter what he did, she still belonged only to herself.

If she wanted him, she'd draw him into her house or the woods. If not, then she went about her day. He knew she was with no other men because he watched her, but that could change at any moment and he had no way to stop her. And there were all the things she did beyond his understanding. The stones she fed, the bees that followed her, the songs she gave to the moon and trees and sea – all that was hers alone.

Some places she wouldn't allow him to go. He tried to follow her to the grassy field beyond the forest where she went when the moon was full, but she sent him away. "This is for me to do," she said, kindly but firmly. "You cannot watch."

"Why not?" he demanded.

Her face was solemn, and a little sad. "You are not ready," she said.

He knew the others in the village laughed at him. What did they know? They had no gnawing hole in them. He couldn't even name what he wanted from her. Something she had that he did not, like a color he couldn't see. At the least, he wanted to feel what she felt inside herself when she sang. And she sang all the time.

She sang songs about deer, and the hunters came home with a catch. She went to the river and sang of rain, and the rains came. She sang for the bees, and a hive full of honey was found. He learned her songs and sang them, but nothing happened. He didn't know how they worked for her, and when he asked her, she only laughed. She existed behind walls of light and sound he could not penetrate.

She began to look at him with pity, which he could not bear. The hole inside him burned with fury, and he no longer ate or slept.

Razak took him aside and asked him what was wrong. "You grow thinner every day, and your woman is soft and round as new fruit," he said. "What troubles you?"

"Do you think she's carrying a baby?" he asked.

Razak shrugged. "What do you care?" he asked.

One day, he followed her into the woods to see if she met another man, but she only walked to an old oak tree, massive and burdened with leaves. She spoke to it, then scraped fresh sap from it into a small, light green clay jar she wore like a necklace, dangling from a leather thong. This jar, she'd told him, held the best honey, full of the queen bee's gifts. After she'd plugged it, she began to sing.

When she was done he went to her. "What are you doing?" he asked.

She turned, smiled. "Speaking with the ancestors, and the spirits who live here," she said. "And they are speaking with me."

"Teach me," he said.

She took his hand and sang again. He listened, but felt nothing different. "Is it a trick?" he demanded.

"I don't know that word," she said.

"How does it work?" he asked.

"It's - a feeling of the heart. Like water and light and stone and fire all at once." She put her hands to his heart. "You hear it here."

He pressed his palms against his own chest. "It's nothing," he said. "Empty."

"It's everything," she said. "Who we are, what we know, what we love."

He didn't understand. He put a hand up to touch the tree, to see if the answer was there, but she grabbed his wrist in a grip that surprised him with its strength.

"You cannot touch it," she said firmly. "You are not ready."

He jerked away from her hold, and left the woods.

After that, he'd go and stand by the old oak when all were asleep. He sang her song, but nothing happened. Defiantly, he put his hand to the trunk, but he felt nothing. He peeled back the bark to see what it hid. He found only more tree. Angry, he ripped at the bark, shredding it and tossing it on the forest floor.

He learned nothing, but he noticed that Austeja grew thin and sad. And though his hunger didn't abate, its fire no longer consumed him. Instead, it gave him power and strength. He went back to the tree, and ripped more bark from it. Then fewer deer came to feed the people and no honey was found. The people spoke of moving, and Austeja's little girls watched him warily, there eyes wide and impermeable, seeing everything, giving nothing away.

"Stop it," he yelled, shooing them away, but they only backed up and continued to watch. He saw that the older girl carried her mother's small jar around her neck. "Why do you have that?" he shouted at her. "It's your mother's."

She pulled herself up tall. "She gave it to me. It's mine now."

He moved to her, intending to grab and shake her, but the force of her glance made him stop in his tracks. That night he returned to the oak tree, tearing at its bark. As he did so, Razak found him. He crept up quietly, and Naktis only heard him when he laughed. He whirled about, bark still in his hand.

Razak smiled. "Friend, if you feel that way, why don't you cut the tree down?"

He looked at the bark in his hands, at Razak. "Her gods would be angry."

"Is that all? I know bigger gods than hers. They'd give you what you want."

"To have her?" Naktis asked. He already believed Razak had strong gods.

"To control her," Razak said.

"What do your gods want in return?" They always wanted something.

"Not much," Razak said. "Just your soul."

As far as Naktis knew, the gods always wanted that. "They can have it," he said.

Razak put a hand on his shoulder. Naktis felt a tingle at the touch. "Then cut the tree down," he said quietly.

The following night Naktis went alone and made a fire near the oak. He took a burning log and used it to scorch the bark at the base of the tree, circling the trunk. This would kill it, and later he could cut the massive thing down. For now he hacked at the branches, adding the fallen wood to his bonfire. It was hard labor, but he stayed at it until almost dawn.

Just when he was ready for a rest, he heard a cry of pain. He turned to see Austeja, staring at him in horror. Her long hair flowed loose around her shoulders, and she was dressed only in a thinly woven gown. The wind pressed it against her skin, showing the outline of the body that tormented him. He heard a strange sound, as of a thousand bees buzzing.

"You are cursed," she whispered, and she turned swiftly, giving him her back, leaving him.

Panic rose in him. She would tell her people. They would kill him, or they'd force him to leave which would be the same for he'd die if she pushed him away from her.

He grabbed her arm, pulled her to him. She was not strong anymore, but she was still lithe as a snake, twisting away from him. He caught up her hair and wrapped it around her neck like a rope. She clawed at his hands but he held on. This was what Razak's god promised. She was his, utterly his, her life in his hands.

He yanked the noose of hair tight at her throat and held it until she went limp and her breathing ceased. He thought it odd that he could barely tell the difference between life and death, it passed so quickly and easily. He lowered her body to the ground and held it in his lap.

"Mine. You are mine," he murmured over and over. "You are mine."

He stayed that way all day. When the sun set he took her body to the grassy field beyond the forest, the place she'd forbidden him to go. There, he buried her.

Nobody spoke to him or met his glance when he returned to the village. They kept their distance, muttering words of protection when he passed. Even the dogs, who once nuzzled at him, bent low and skulked away.

They knew. They all knew, and they were afraid of him. That pleased him. He was powerful. He'd taken the woman of his choice. So he told himself. But a day passed, and another, and he didn't feel powerful. He felt alone. He couldn't even gloat with Razak because he'd gone to the shore with a fishing party.

By the third evening, when the moon rose full and no sweet voice sang to it, he realized Austeja had escaped him. She still belonged only to herself.

In the middle of the night he went back to where he'd buried her. The grass, golden and moonlit, almost the color of her hair, had already grown to his waist, in a hurry to cover her. He walked through it, running his hand over it, feeling its sibilant warmth.

The breeze moving through it sounded like her voice in soft laughter. It hissed against his fingers.

"You should not have hidden from me," he said angrily. "You would bind me to your tree, but tell me nothing. This is your own fault."

The grass laughed under his hands. One thin blade curled over his wrist. He tried to lift his other hand to brush it off, but found that was held by another silken cord. He pulled against them to no avail. They would not release him. He felt motion at his feet like the writhing of a thousand snakes and saw the grass wrapping his ankles, swarming his body to pull him down to the ground, shackling him there. He was too surprised to even gasp.

Then a single blade, thin as a strand of hair, slid toward him, singing as it came. When it laid itself against his face and began peeling back the flesh, he caught the mingled scent of ocean and sweet honey, warm in the sun.

He screamed out only once before the slicing strand took his tongue. Somewhere, in the distance, he heard a woman singing.

∾

Razak returned from fishing a few days later, and learned that Naktis had disappeared. He observed that Austeja was also gone, and he needed no further explanation. He understood.

In the heat of the afternoon he went to the grassy field and stood sniffing the air. He caught the scent of honey and followed it, walking carefully until his toe touched something hard. He looked down. At his feet was a skeleton, human and new, bones glistening with dew. He squatted next to it, and saw that honeybees had made a hive in the ribcage. It was already filled, honey dripping from the bones like blood.

He waved his hand at the bees. "Go away," he told them. "This one is mine."

In a flurry of activity the bees rose into the sky and flew off. All except one, which stayed near him. Razak smiled at it. "Naktis?" he asked, and the bee buzzed at him.

"Well, my friend," he said, "I see you found a body to occupy, but you won't be staying in it. You cannot be one of Austeja's creatures. They don't like me and I don't like them. I'll get you a better body soon enough. Come here. We should talk."

The bee flew to a landing on his knee, where it danced about frantically.

"Why are you upset?" Razak asked. "I never said my master was kind. Only strong."

The bee buzzed low and deep, and Razak grinned. "No, you cannot die. You're a Vele now. A living ghost. More precisely, a Vaidilia, since you'll be doing my work. But we need not be fancy. Vele is good enough. And you have much to do for me. That is our deal."

The bee moved about, but more slowly now.

"Nonsense. You wanted to control her and so you did. I didn't say how long you'd control her for. At any rate, you made the deal. You'll serve me and my master for as long as I say."

The bee buzzed, lifted off his knee and resettled. Razak laughed. "A way out? Well, if you steal another soul to take your place that will change things. Or if you can somehow undo what you've done. How? I don't know. That's for you to figure out. Until then, you are mine." He grinned. "Be a man about it, would you?"

Razak lifted his hand and brought it down on the bee, crushing it. "That's a joke, my friend. Be a man. So you will be. Or something very near to it."

He flicked the dead bee away and went back to the village to gather his things. The old lady said the sea would rise and pour sands over their village. They were moving inland where they'd be safe from the vengeful water, the angry earth.

In the field, the bees returned and buzzed about the dead one, learning what they needed to know.

Chapter Two

Upstate New York, Early 21st Century

There were small, harmless fairies everywhere. They danced, or began to dance, and then forgot what they were doing and wandered away. Soon they forgot why they wandered away and came back, dancing again. Each one was a particular piece of beauty, some with darkly burnished wings and faces, some made only of light.

They were the fairies Stacey's grandmother had told her about. The *laume*, joyous, and incredibly absent-minded. Stacey found them lovely, but irritating. They danced wildly, randomly, ending up either balancing on her clavicle, which tickled, or prancing on her nose, which made her sneeze. Some kind of powder puffed off their wings, and apparently she was allergic to it.

When she'd had enough, she brushed them away. "Oh, for Chrissake," she snapped. "Cut it out." She thought she heard laughter, and with that, they were gone.

She lay where she was. She'd been dreaming. Dreaming of fairies. She felt sunlight streaming over her, but something dark obscured her vision. She focused until she realized what it was. Tamsa's face was in hers, licking at her nose. Stacey patted her and looked around. She was in the woods, and it was bright morning.

"Jesus," she said, then changed her mind. "Hell. Oh, hell."

She scrambled to her feet, relieved that she could stand with no trouble, though she felt mildly hungover, like she'd had too much wine instead of too much gin. Vague memories of other dreams, disconnected images of trees and bees and a strange man, recurred to her. Tamsa pranced around her happily. To her a night in the woods was an interesting excursion humans rarely offered.

None of it made sense. She must have fallen, hit her head. She put her hands to it, felt it gingerly for wounds and found none. She hoped she wasn't bleeding internally in some horrible way that would reach crisis in the middle of a meeting, but she had no time to worry about it.

"Okay, girl," she said to Tamsa. "We gotta get going."

She took the quickest trail back to Martha's house, jogging as fast as she could. Once inside, she glanced at the microwave clock, which said 8:45, and cursed vigorously. Chaos wove around her legs meowing, scolding her for her absence. She got food into his bowl and Tamsa's, then dashed to the bathroom. She'd had an eight-thirty appointment for a haircut, which she'd already missed. And she had a 9:45 with Edward to go over the I Love NY account, which she hadn't opened last night. Then an 11:30 with Mercy Hospital. No time to shower or get coffee.

She did a quick and clumsy toothbrushing, threw water on her face and checked herself in the mirror. It would be a make-up in the rearview mirror kind of day. She got herself into clean clothes, shook out her hair, and went. She forgot to grab aspirin for her headache, a dull thud that continued to make itself known behind her eyes.

ॐ

She got through her morning meetings by smiling a lot and improvising, something she was particularly good at. The headache only got worse, but she wasn't passing out or frothing at the mouth so she supposed she'd live. After her Mercy Hospital meeting, which ran an hour over, she had a teleconference with potential clients from a new car dealership, and then a team meeting on the new radio account. By the time that ended it was late afternoon, and she realized she was starving. She made her way into the staff room to hunt for donuts, muffins, anything high-carb and full of sugar.

She found some illicit twinkies in the cupboard – probably they were Annette's, the chubby temp worker who left a week ago, and therefore fair game. She was pushing one in her mouth when the staff room door opened and Grant walked in.

She pointed at the twinkies. "Missed lunch," she sputtered around crumbs.

He raised his eyebrows. "Partying hard out in the country?" he inquired.

"Hell, no. Why?"

He reached up, touched her hair, pulled out a twig. "This?"

No wonder they gave her odd looks at Mercy, she thought. "Oh," she said. "That." She gave him a quick, bright smile. "Early morning walk with the dog."

She patted at her head, wondered if she was also crawling with ticks, then decided not to think about that. "See anything else?"

He scanned her. "You're clean," he said. "Are you okay?"

"What the hell kind of question is that?"

"Just asking. You ready for the Busline meeting?"

"Of course I am," she said, snappish because she'd forgotten about it, then moderated her tone. "When is that?"

"In half an hour. Downtown, at Jack's Pub. Seele's going. You knew that, right?"

She growled out another curse and fled the room, thinking at least they'd have food there.

&

The meeting went well, though most of the time she was imagining ticks leaping off her hair into her boss's drink. But food was plentiful, and the clients stayed and stayed, relaxing into the end of their work week. She relaxed with them, keeping her smile on and doing her best not to worry about ticks, or strange dreams, or what might be happening inside her skull. Nobody stood to leave until after 6.

She shook hands all around, and accepted the wink Seele offered her as a good sign. She made her way to her car and started it up, but she didn't go back to her office as she often did on a Friday evening, to take advantage of the quiet and get some work done. Nor did she go to Janus to chat up potential clients. Instead, she drove around downtown, looking for a bar where she could get a quick drink, alone, and gather her thoughts. She didn't want to talk to anyone. She just wanted to regroup before she went back to her sister's house. She cruised along until she spotted a seedy looking pub called RALPH'S, with the 'L' missing from its neon sign.

"What the hell," she muttered. She found a parking space, pulled herself out of the car and headed toward the door.

She stopped for a moment after she'd entered to let her eyes adjust to the dim interior. Dusty venetian blinds were pulled down over the windows, and the panelling was dark. The place smelled of decades of cigarette smoke, embedded in the wood during the days when smoking was allowed indoors. An old TV played a Yankees game behind the bar, and men with gnarled hands and few teeth watched it.

Perfect, she thought. No one would bother her here, and she could nurse her confusion in peace. She grabbed a seat at the darkest end of the bar, far away from the other occupants. The bartender, burly and bald, came over and mumbled at her.

"Jack and Coke," she requested. "Light on the coke." This wasn't a Martini kind of place, or day.

When he brought it she drank it fast and let the warmth settle in before she lifted her glass for another. As she did, she felt a hand touch hers briefly. She turned quickly.

At her side was a tall, lean man in jeans and an impeccably tailored black silk shirt. She squinted at him. He looked like a younger, dark haired version of David Bowie. He had the same sharp nose and carved jawline, the same crooked grin. And he had bi-colored eyes, one almost black and the other a greenish hazel.

"I'll be damned," she whispered.

"Maybe, but not just yet," he replied. He lifted his hand to the bartender. "I'll get this one," he said, and she was relieved that he didn't have a British accent.

She segued back into reality. "I can buy my own," she said crisply, turning away from him.

His face worked on this, then showed a grin. "I was being chivalrous – and egotistical, I suppose. I thought you'd prefer my attentions to old Jake, who wanted to come over. I told him I saw you first." He nodded at the other end of the bar. "Jake's the one with the pork pie hat."

She looked, saw old Jake, wondered briefly about the stains on his denim shirt, and glanced back to the man at her side. He was right.

"He's a friend of yours?" she asked.

"No. Just temporary bar buddies, making man talk." He nodded at the bartender, who brought her drink and went away. She took a sip, ignoring the giver.

"You're welcome," he said. Then, "My name is Nick. Nick Vecchio."

"Italian," she noted.

"The name is. I'm not. I took it on some time ago, because I liked the sound of it. But I call all nations my own."

"And I'm a woman of the world," she said a little grimly.

He raised his glass, which was filled with something clear and had a lime slice in it. She didn't raise hers back.

"Obviously, you want to be alone," he said. "But if I leave you'll be flooded with other contenders. You're a rare sight in Ralph's, and Jake has friends."

She supposed he was right. Her skirt and suitjacket were forest green nubbed silk, and she wore designer heels, a good gold necklace and earrings. Ralph's probably didn't see that too often. She glanced at the other end of the bar. A man with many tattoos grinned at her. She was torn between being grateful for the protection, and resentful of the need for it. She turned back to her drink and said nothing.

"I won't ask if you've been here before because I can guess the answer," Nick said. "But I'm curious about what brings you to Ralph's instead of your regular haunts - I'd guess Janus, or maybe Parker's on an off night. Young executives mingling with minor political appointees and the occasional drunk senator? Brittle smiles, Martinis and cagey pickup lines like 'I don't think authentic intimacy requires long-term commitment, do you?'"

She thought about taking offense, then laughed instead. He was right. Janus was just like that. And halfway through her second drink, she was relaxing. What the hell, she thought. She'd never seen him before, and would probably never see him again. Most likely he was gay, cruising for a blue collar experience.

"Don't mind me," she said. "I got lost in the woods with a black dog last night. Weird shit happened. I needed someplace I didn't have to worry about my smile."

"Well, then," he said. "Don't worry about it. If you get sick of me, in about five minutes you can throw your drink in my face. I'll go back and tell them you're a lesbian. Or a nun, as you prefer. Meantime, trust me, I wasn't trying to pick you up with a three dollar drink. Your time isn't sold cheaply. I can tell by your shoes."

She hoped he meant that in a good way. Just to make sure she said, "I'm an account exec at Accent Marketing, and they bill me out at $200 an hour. My social time isn't for sale."

"Of course not. Sell your work, but body and soul remain your own." He raised his glass again. She once again deliberately failed to raise hers.

"Though some people," he continued, "believe that selling your work is the same as selling your soul. If they're right, that pretty much screws the pooch on capitalism."

She took a sip of her drink and said more nothing.

"Others," he said, "would gladly sell their souls to get out of work, if they could find a buyer."

"Most people," she noted, "don't really think they have a soul."

"Oh, really? What does our money say - In God We Trust?"

"Words. Social glue."

"A cynic. So you don't believe in souls?"

"I didn't say that."

"Then you do?"

"I didn't say that, either."

"Hmm. I'd guess you're a Gemini. Moon in Capricorn, with a Sagittarius ascendant?"

She frowned, about to ask him how he knew all that, but he laughed.

"Don't worry. I'm not here to cast your chart or make Jesus your personal savior. Just talking to pass the time while Jake drowns his sorrows. So if you believed you had a soul, what would you sell it for?"

She gulped down the rest of her drink. "What?" she asked.

"What would you sell your soul for?" He emphasized each word carefully.

If he meant to get her attention, he had it. She turned her head a quarter inch and scanned him through narrowed eyes. He made a deprecating gesture.

"This isn't my usual hangout either. I wandered in on a whim, to experience the ambience. And here I find an attractive woman of substance and class, seeking refuge. What, I wonder, would amuse her? Lift her troubles from her? No perfunctory conversation about weather would do. Only substantial questions would suit her. So I ask again – what price your soul?"

Definitely gay, she thought. And philosophical discussion about souls with a gay man was probably just what she needed. She mulled his question. She was raised Catholic and went to church for special occasions, and she was godmother to her niece and therefore technically responsible for her soul, but in fact she didn't give much thought to either souls or religion.

"Is it the same as what you'd give your life for? Or at least risk it by jumping in front of a moving vehicle?" she asked.

"Pretty close," he said, "only more so."

"I suppose," she said, "I'd do it to save my sister or her daughter."

He raised an eyebrow. "Not her husband?"

She shrugged. "He's okay. Good father. Good husband. But you're talking about my soul."

"Family first. But your sister doesn't need saving."

"How do you know?"

"One, she married a good man. Two, your face is relaxed when you talk about her. Three, your tone is speculative rather than urgent."

"Pretty good," she said.

"I pay attention. Any alternatives?"

She quickly found a compelling and irritating specter rising within her. She glowered into her drink, which was empty.

"I can't hear it if you just think it," he said.

She muttered into her glass, tipped it back and chewed on ice.

"What?"

"My brother," she repeated, too loud this time. She began to recognize she was at least mildly tipsy.

"That loser?" he asked.

She plunked her glass down hard on the bar. "You don't know him."

"I see your face," he said.

"My face doesn't say he's a loser. It says he's – he's complicated. He's a musician," she added defiantly, as if that explained everything else.

"Of course." He signaled the bartender for another round.

"I shouldn't," she said.

"But you will," he replied. "And I'll get you home if you can't drive."

"Don't get any ideas," she said curtly.

"None at all. There are taxis and so on."

"I need my car. I have to get to work tomorrow."

"Tomorrow," he said, "is Saturday."

"Oh. Right." Her drink arrived and she sipped it slowly, then eyed his glass. "What are you drinking?"

"Rum. Good rum, undiluted."

She whistled softly. "I'll be calling a cab for you."

"Unfortunately not. It's one of the curses of my life. I can drink anything in any amount and never get more than mildly buzzed."

She shook her head at this.

"It's true," he insisted. "A strange and expensive physiological anomaly. By the way, what's your name?"

"Stacey," she said.

"Just Stacey? Nothing else?"

She licked her lips to make sure they worked. "Stacey Vitautis."

He gave a short intake of breath that made her turn to him sharply, showing him her full face.

"Did I say something wrong?" she asked.

For five seconds he just stared at her eyes, his lips pressed together and his forehead knit hard. She would swear his pupils dilated. Then he went still, relaxing into a broad grin.

"Not at all. That's a Lithuanian name, isn't it?" he asked.

"Like every cell in my body," she said, mildly impressed. "Most people think it's Russian."

"Which most Lithuanians would find insulting."

"How do you know that?"

"I told you. I'm a man of all nations." He waved it away. "About your brother. What's his instrument?"

"He's a violinist. Why?"

"Just wondering. And you'd sell your soul to save him? Why?"

"Because he's family. And – and he had a rough time. And because I would. Do I have to give the devil a reason?"

"I think," he mused, "selling your soul has to be for personal gain. Isn't there something you want for yourself? Or are you a womanly woman, always thinking of the needs of others?"

She bridled. "I earn a six figure income, own my own house, drive a BMW that's paid for, and I like my work. I don't need a damn thing."

"Sad," he said.

"What?"

"There's nothing you want enough to sell your soul for. That means there's nothing you'd give your soul to. And so you're empty. Except for your brother."

"That's – that's a specious argument," she said, liking the word specious though she wasn't sure if it applied.

"How so?" he asked.

She opened her mouth, closed it again. She found she couldn't really explain. "It's been more than five minutes," she said.

"Oh. Well. Are you going to?"

She looked at her drink. Her glass was half full, and not finishing it would probably be a good thing. She never had before, and wondered what it would feel like.

"Yeah," she said.

He braced himself. "Ready when you are."

She stood. "Go to hell," she proclaimed, then tossed the contents of her glass at his face.

She turned and stalked out of the bar without looking back.

Chapter Three

Upstate New York, early 21st century

Stacey spent a quiet weekend at her sister's, finally getting through some of the work she'd brought with her, and keeping to the open trails in her walks with the dog. She avoided any further strangeness, and on Monday morning she was back at her desk, her smile on, its beams as high as those of the two clients who sat across from her. These were Carrie and Joshua, reps for a local Christian radio station, both squeaky clean and relentlessly upbeat. His brown hair was as perfect as her light pink lipstick.

The account was a good coup because they had lots of money to throw at the college crowd, a substantial audience in this listening area. And their local station was part of a network of nationals. Work locally, grow globally, Jonathan always told them.

But Stacey didn't like them. Buying new souls, she thought cynically, and they liked them young and fresh. In spite of that, her team had done its research and came up with a schedule of college campus promo events, which all met with approval. Free bagels and coffee at one college, free pizza at another, Frisbees and t-shirts for live music events, and a section on their website for college girls to meet boys who claimed they were more interested in relationships than lust and beer.

So far so good, but the clients weren't as pleased with the print campaign. Stacey had drawn what she thought were good sketches – a dove in contemporary style, wearing sunglasses and carrying a microphone instead of an olive branch in its beak, and two bright people clasping raised hands under an Hour of God sky, with sunlight streaming through clouds.

"God is the answer" was the copy under both, with the station's call numbers and URL. But the clients expressed concern that it didn't represent them properly, which confused Stacey.

"It's a Christian station, isn't it?" she asked, seeking to confirm reality as she understood it. "I mean, that's your listener base, correct?"

"We're so much more than Christian," Carrie said. "We're about a positive outlook on life. We don't want to limit our audience."

Stacey had spent three days listening to their morning, afternoon, and evening show, and didn't recall hearing any song that, for instance, a Jew or a Muslim would relate to. But she understood. They wanted listeners to fall in love with their station before they knew it was Christian, in the hopes they'd keep listening and convert. A lot of advertising was like that now. Guerrilla advertising, she thought. Terrorist marketing. She wasn't sure she liked it, but she knew it was effective. She worked her smile, reminding herself what a good account this was, reminding herself the client was always right.

"Okay, then," she said. She scratched out God and replaced it with Love. "How's that? And the sun motif - that's not specifically Christian."

"That's great," Joshua said positively. "Love is what we're all about. Except - well, we'd rather avoid nature metaphors."

Carrie nodded. "They're too . . . young."

Stacey frowned. "You're aimed at a young audience, aren't you? That's your demographic?"

"Yes, but not *spiritually* young. Not people who haven't evolved beyond nature based thinking," Joshua amended.

"Ah," Stacey said, catching on. "Pagans. But isn't that who you want to grab?"

They looked a little shocked, and she silently cursed herself. Sometimes her mouth got ahead of her brain. She spent a moment interpreting. They wanted to get people closer to their base - maybe disillusioned Catholics and agnostics and so on. Pagans were too much for them to deal with. She nodded at them, remaining cheerful.

"Then how about this – just hands clasping. Young and old – black and white?"

She began sketching out the thought on her pad, shaping it into a peace sign, which college students were embracing again. As she did, her phone rang. She didn't pick it up, because she'd told her assistant no calls, but it kept ringing. She glanced apologetically at her clients and reached for it, continuing to sketch.

"Accent Marketing, Stacey V. speaking," she said.

"Hello, Austeja Vitautis," a vaguely familiar male voice said on the other end of the line. A blip of time passed as she tried to place it, and couldn't. Only her grandmother had called her Austeja, her given name. Hardly anyone used her last name except telemarketers, who struggled to pronounce it. As far as anyone except family knew, she was Stacey V.

"Surely you haven't forgotten me. Not when we're in the middle of negotiating for your soul," the caller said.

She had to bite the inside of her cheek to stop from blurting out oh, hell. It was that man from Ralph's. Nick something. Nick Vecchio. She should know better than to talk to strangers when she was drinking. On the other end, she heard a soft chuckle.

"Say something meaningless and polite," he suggested, as if he knew her situation exactly.

"How nice to hear from you again," she said.

"That's good. Now maybe you can say you're surprised."

"I am," she agreed. "I didn't expect this at all."

"Of course not. But we didn't finish our conversation, so we need another meeting."

"I don't think so," she said cheerfully.

"I do. I'll be at your office at six. In time to introduce myself to your boss."

"No. Um . . . Let's try elsewhere."

"I thought you'd say that. How about Janus? Eight o'clock, so you can get some supper first. If you don't show up, I'll assume you need a ride and come get you at your home – 636 Manning, isn't it? Not as trendy as the brownstones on State Street, but nice in its own way."

She smiled at her clients. "I'll meet you there. Good to hear from you."

"See you soon," he replied.

She hung up, apologized for the interruption, and continued the meeting.

She went to her sister's to take care of Chaos and Tamsa, grabbed a quick bite to eat there, and arrived at Janus before eight, just to be certain he didn't go to her house. The last thing she wanted was to have him skulking around her home. When she got there the parking lot was still full, the remnants of Happy Hour hanging around. That wasn't unusual for this time on a Monday. By ten it would be empty.

She parked, walked around to the front and stepped inside, into darkness and blaring music and clusters of well-heeled men and women, the small chrome tables with high seats all full. She looked around for Nick, bracing herself for a fight. She was angry, and ready to tell this wacko that if he bothered her again, she'd call the cops. Also ready to make him say how he got her name and her address.

She spotted him at the bar, standing in front of a man and woman seated on stools, in happy conversation with them.

"Okay, big boy. Here I come," she muttered, and took a step forward. Then, she stopped.

Nick moved to one side and she saw who he was talking to. June and Richard Ekhart. She knew their faces from her own research. They were from New York City, executives with Triton, a global nanotech company that was moving a branch upstate. She'd been trying to get to them for weeks, putting in calls, sending emails, and getting no response. And here, on a silver platter, they were. With a wacko. Her wacko.

Nick saw her, and waved her over. He turned back to the couple, gesturing toward her. She rapidly sorted her options, made an executive decision and reset her emotional barometer. She moved to them, her face back on.

"Hello, gorgeous," Nick said, and slung an arm around her shoulder, kissed her cheek. "I wondered if you'd make it."

"I said I would, didn't I, handsome?" she replied, extricating herself from his embrace. She put her hand out, toward June. She'd learned that when dealing with couples it was best to offer your hand to the woman first. "I'm Stacey V., from Accent Marketing."

Nick leaned close to June. "She's an absolute genius, like all my friends," he confided.

June took her hand, looked her up and down. She was assertively blonde, tall and thin, with a narrow jaw and wide eyes she liked to emphasize with blue liner. She was also about ten years older than Stacey, who suddenly wondered if she'd look that brittle by then.

"Nice to meet you," June said. "I've heard good things about Accent."

"From Nick?" Stacey asked.

"And other sources. But I trust him most." June gave him a smile that was not at all brittle, and Stacey could imagine the rest. Rumor said she and her husband had an open relationship.

"Drink?" Nick asked Stacey. "The usual?"

She nodded, though she wanted to say Martini. Jack and Cokes were for dive bars. He smiled mischievously and made his way to the bartender. She cursed him silently and worked her smile.

"How do you know Nick?" she asked June, casual, conversational.

"I can't even remember how we met. Do you remember, Richard? What were we working on then?"

The man with her was a visual nonentity. Dark haired with receding hairline, a face whose structure was ready to collapse, and the beginnings of a paunch. When he spoke, Stacey was reminded of a computer voice, dull and toneless. "Capital development for med-pac," he said. "Emphasis on capital. Nick's specialty. Midas touch and so on. We often stay with him when we come upstate. A fine house."

Interesting, Stacey thought. June had chosen a tool for her mate. Someone who knew all the facts, and not much else. She'd often considered that option herself, but just couldn't bring herself to do it.

Nick returned with his own rum and a Martini for her, which he offered with his grin still on. "They were out of your favorite," he said. "Will this do?"

"It's perfect," she cooed, hoping her eyes said what she really meant.

Richard continued talking about Nick as if he weren't there, saying something about how he knew everyone, had a finger in every pie. He trotted out a few more clichés, then subsided.

"They think more of me than I deserve," Nick told Stacey.

"Not true," June said meaningfully. "Not in *any* way at all."

The sizzle in her words was unmistakable. Nick remained unabashed. "My sweetness, you embarrass me," he said demurely.

She preened a little, then turned to Stacey, running her gaze up and down her form, evaluating possibilities. She put a small purr into her voice. "So what's new at Accent these days?" she asked.

Stacey didn't purr back, but neither did she hiss or spit. If lust got June to her office that was fine with her. She talked work, waxing enthusiastic about Accent's policies and clients, how much she loved being part of such a creative group with such a global outlook. June listened, but her eyes were focused on nonbusiness opportunities. Stacey did a quick assessment and turned the conversation to fashion, admiring her necklace, touching it lightly as she did. That satisfied her, and they launched into girl talk, clothes talk, hair talk. They'd made their way from shirts to shoes when Nick took her arm.

"June, I hate to break up the fashion conference, but I'm afraid we have to leave," he said. He nodded at Stacey. "We have business to discuss."

Stacey was ready to give him a nasty look, then realized he was right. Always leave them wanting more. She dug into her purse and handed over her card to June. "If you're looking for some upstate help, give me a call," she said.

"Oh, I will," June said. "How's Wednesday morning, for a quick phone conference?"

"I'm in at 9."

"Then I'll call," June said.

Nick steered her away from the bar and toward a table at the back of the house. She sat down with a hefty sigh of satisfaction.

"Sorry to interrupt, but you know. . ." he said.

"I do," she replied. Then, with reluctant admiration. "You have good timing."

"It's one of my skills. Did that go to your liking?"

"Yes," she said. "Very much so. A – a real piece of luck. Quite a coincidence."

"Was it?"

"Well, yes. I mean, I've been trying to contact them for some time." She saw him subdue a smile. "You couldn't know. How could you?"

"There's a few ways I could find out, but we can stay with coincidence if you prefer. Anyway, I'm glad it worked out for you."

She sipped her drink, rearranging her thoughts about him, moving him from crazy stalker into the wealthy venture capitalist/pirate category. "If you know everyone and – well, what they said – how come I never heard of you?"

"Do you hear about everyone?"

"For business? Everyone who matters. But I've never heard of Nick Vecchio."

"Nor will you find me on Facebook or Twitter," he said. "In fact, the last man who mentioned my name there lived to regret it. I'm known by those I want to know. A better topic is how we finally did meet - because a black dog led you astray in the woods and you went to Ralph's to regroup. Did you want to say anything more about that?"

"Not really."

"Well, maybe when you trust me better. But I'm impressed by your quick turnaround time. I'll bet when you came in you were ready to tell me to go to hell. You must've done some determined emotional realignment when you spotted your prey."

She was embarrassed enough to consider lying, but changed her mind when she realized that would please him even more. "Something like that," she admitted.

"So you value Jane and Dick – I'm sorry, June and Richard's opinion – that much?"

She thought about it. "I've actually heard they're pretty slimy. All kinds of rumors about her recreational habits, and he's been known to stiff people on accounts."

"The rumors," he said, "are all true. You did catch on to her interest in you?"

"It'd be hard to miss. But her fantasies can only work to my benefit. And they know you. That means you're probably not an axe murderer. Right?"

A muscle in his jaw twitched. "Not lately," he agreed.

"Good. And it means you're accountable in some general public way, so if you try anything stupid, I'll be able to talk about you."

He twisted his lips around while he thought about this, then gave a grunt of assent. "Then do you feel safe enough to take a walk in the park with me? It's a fine night, with a good moon."

"Sure," she said. When he reached for his wallet, she stopped him. "I'll pay."

"Of course," he murmured.

Chapter Four

The night was fine and mild, the scent of lilac in the air, a burgeoning moon coming up over the horizon as the sky darkened from deep blue to soft black. They made their way to the nearby park, Nick entertaining her with more June and Richard stories and historical facts about local architecture as they went. She had no idea what he wanted, but she was content to let it play out now that she knew he wasn't a bum, and even if he was a wacko he might be a useful one.

When they entered the park he grew quiet and she didn't work to change that. Let him make the effort, she thought. They passed through a row of large old oak trees the city had the wisdom to nurture. Something about walking among them soothed and settled her mind. They required no strategizing from her, and offered only silence. The moon shed soft light on the backs of their leaves, turning them silver. She stared up as they walked, admiring the view.

"You like trees?" he asked.

"I like their structure. Their composition. However they're shaped, they always look right."

"Your Lithuanian ancestors worshipped trees. They were known to kill priests and kings who tried to enter their sacred groves. In fact, one of the earliest written mentions of Lithuania outside the country is about them killing a priest – 1009, St. Bruno of Querfert. I think his crime was baptizing someone named Netimer."

She startled. "Netimer?" she asked.

"Yes. Why?"

"It's just - familiar," she said, a little hesitantly. When he'd said the name an image of a man in robes and furs occurred to her, as if she knew him. As if she'd seen that somewhere. "Is it a common Lithuanian name?"

"Not that I know of."

"Oh. Well, maybe I'm confusing it with something else. Anyway, I'm not at all surprised. Especially about the trees. My grandmother used to sing to them."

She would place old crusts of bread under the maple tree in their yard, singing in Lithuanian and touching the tree lightly. "Always plant a tree," she told them. "When a child is born, plant a tree. When someone dies, plant a tree. Thank the trees, and your prayers will be heard."

Though Stacey didn't really believe all that, she did appreciate that life on the planet was inextricably intertwined with trees, which made the oxygen necessary for other creatures to flourish. She owed them her breath. They drank hers. Her grandmother was right to honor them.

She had a sudden, unbidden memory of that old woman as she lay dying, her body shriveled by illness into something terrifying and grotesque. Stacey was brought in to her hospital room to see her. She'd grabbed Stacey's wrist in a talon's grasp, her long nails slicing into her flesh. She wouldn't let them be cut, saying she needed them to climb the ice mountain to heaven.

She'd looked at Stacey fiercely and rasped out, "Remember to plant trees. Make homes for the bees who protect you."

She didn't know what that meant, so she only whispered, "Yes, grandma," and gently tried to move away. But her grandmother's clasp grew tighter, and she leaned closer.

She'd stared into Stacey's eyes. "The devil will find you," she said. "Don't be afraid. You'll know what to do, when the time comes."

After this, she'd released her, and her parents took her home. "Don't worry about what Grandma said," her mother told her. "It's the morphine talking."

Stacey didn't worry, but she remembered. The fierce eyes, the spittle that formed in the corners of her mouth, everything she'd said about ghosts and devils and trees and bees and toads, all were imprinted in her memory.

Now she put her hand on one of the old oaks, humming the song her grandmother once sang. Behind her, Nick gave a small gasp, and she turned to him.

"What?" she asked.

"Look out," he said, shifting his gaze to her left. She followed where he looked. A large dog – Rottweiller – was moving toward them fast, off leash.

She was about to say 'It's just a dog,' when she saw a man lolloping up behind it, calling frantically, "Dolly. Here, Dolly. *Here.*"

The dog ignored him, raised its hackles and charged directly at her. More perplexed than frightened, she stood still.

Nick moved, putting himself in front of her. "Stok!" he commanded.

The dog tucked its ears back and got down on the ground, rolled over and showed its belly. The frantic owner came rushing up behind, scolding as he came.

"Bad Dolly," he said. "*Bad* dog."

He got a leash on her, then looked up at Nick. "Thank you. She – she sometimes gets a little overprotective of me."

"You shouldn't let her think you need protecting," Nick said impatiently. "For God's sake, go home and watch the Dog Whisperer."

The man dropped his jaw, closed it, took his dog and left. Nick touched Stacey's elbow and they moved forward, to the bridge that crossed the lake at the center of the park.

"Well now," Stacey said. "I guess that's another one of your skills. You're good with unscrupulous business people and crazy dogs."

"It's nothing," he said, still irritated. "Really, it's simple enough to control them. They crave control. I don't know why people have to be so stupid about it."

"What was that word you said?"

"Stok? It means stop. In Lithuanian."

"Oh. You speak Lithuanian?"

"Lithuanian, Urdu, Russian, Mandarin, Italian, Mohawk, and six others fluently. Ten others less fluently. I suppose, given my company, Lithuanian came to mind first." He stopped on the bridge, leaning his arms on the rail. "Do you know any?"

"A few words." She pointed down to the reflection of moon on water. "Menulis."

"The moon, which is male to Lithuanians, while the sun is a mother," he said. "Any others?"

"Not enough to make small talk with."

"Then we'll stay with English."

She stared down at the lake, saying nothing.

"Or not, as you prefer," Nick said.

Once more she thought of her grandmother, who told stories of the moon and sun, and had songs for both celestial bodies. She hadn't thought of her this much in years, and wasn't sure why she was so present now. She stayed silent, staring at light reflected in water while she waited for her companion to get to his point, whatever it was.

"Even if you don't know the language, your sensibilities aren't far removed from your ancestors," he said after a while. "It's said that you know a Lithuanian best when they're working or daydreaming. And here I thought you were a twenty-first century city girl."

She gave him a sharp smile. "I started my career as a graphic artist," she said. "Visual thinker. I - see things."

"Ah. Unlike your brother, who's a musical thinker."

So, she thought. They were back to that. Certainly not his real interest, but she'd play along. "That's true," she said. "He thought in sound when he was a toddler. Always noticed bird song, that kind of thing."

"You're the big sister?"

"I am."

"That explains why you want to save him. What's his problem, exactly?"

"It's really not – "

" – My business?"

"I was going to say not something I like to talk about."

"But what if that's the only way to save him?"

"I don't see how it could help."

"Neither do I, unless you tell me more."

"Maybe we should just get acquainted first."

"You'd rather go through the standard litany? Where are you from, where did you go to school, what was your childhood like?"

She scanned him, and realized the futility of that. "You already know, don't you? Like you knew my real name and address. What else do you know about me?"

"Enough. For instance, you didn't start as a graphic artist. You went to NYU for fine arts, then transferred to a local college for a program in graphic design and communications. Much more practical. After graduation Accent grabbed you, and now you're clawing your way up their ladder. You're second generation Lithuanian-American, mom and dad both dead in a car accident. They left life insurance and a house to sell, which you used for some good investments and a house of your own, so you're doing fine. Financially, at least."

"That's all? What about who I'm sleeping with? What I search for on the internet?"

"I like to leave room for surprises. Besides, the facts of your life aren't as important as how you feel about them. Your casual relationship with a man at your office named Grant isn't half as interesting to me as what you see when you stare at the water."

She realized he was very close to her, his voice a breath of whisper near her hair. It reverberated within her, asking her for something she couldn't name. She stared at the water. Small ripples ran through it, creating patterns perfect in their symmetry.

"I see motion," she said. "Shifting patterns giving the impression of intent. Beautiful, compelling and meaningless."

"Like our lives?" he suggested. "Yours, mine, your brothers. If that's so, it shouldn't be painful to talk about him. He's just another ripple in the lake."

She wanted to turn and look at him, but he was too close, and she was afraid he'd make a move. He was potentially too valuable as a business connection, and she didn't want sex to get in the way.

Perhaps sensing that, he pulled back from her. "Tell me about your brother, Austeja," he cajoled.

She sighed. He was persistent. But why not, she thought. Why the hell not? He probably already knew it, and just wanted to hear her say it. "My father drank too much," she said. "He was great when he was sober, but he was a mean drunk. Mostly he took it out on Vince."

"Not you or your mother or sister?"

"My mother caught a lot of it, too. Me and my sister were pretty much ignored."

"How insulting. Why?"

"Boys were more important, I guess. And Vince was like him. They both played the violin, but my father gave it up to support his family."

"And made them pay dearly for it. So now Vince – what does he do? Drink? Drug? Make bad choices in women?"

"Gambling, mostly. Drink is second on the list. No drugs that I know of, and only the occasional woman." After that she was quiet, watching the water.

"There's more, isn't there?" he asked very softly.

She shook her head. Information was power and he already had enough. "Nothing you need to know," she said. "Except he's not a bad person. I mean, he has a good heart, and if he could climb out of his past, he'd be okay."

She waited for him to say something cynical, but he didn't. Instead he asked, "what would help him do that?" His voice was detached, almost clinical, and she found that comforting. It took the conversation outside her personal pain, into a realm where change was possible.

"I think," she said, "if he could get the Amber back, that'd help."

"The Amber? Would that be the family jewels?"

"You don't know already?"

"I don't know how you describe it, and that might be important."

"Right. It's a violin. A rare one. It belonged to my mother, who got it from her mother, though I never saw either of them play it. I think my grandmother did when she was younger, but she gave it up. Anyway, my father thought it was pretty special." She laughed lightly. "Sometimes my mother said he married her for it. After he quit playing it went to Vince. Then, when my parents died, he - well, he lost it in a poker game."

"Ouch," Nick said. She looked at him quickly and saw he meant it. "For how much?"

"Ten thousand dollar bet. It was just a family thing to us. He – he'd stopped playing, and was gambling a lot by then. None of us knew what it was worth until he lost it."

"How much?"

"A couple million."

Nick whistled long and low. "How'd you find out?"

"A dealer called, out of the blue, really. He'd found some reference to it in an old Italian book, and somehow tracked it to us. We thought it was Lithuanian, kind of homemade, because it has an oak scroll and it's lighter in color than most violins."

"Hence, the Amber."

"I guess. The dealer believed it was from the Guarneri family. One of a kind, tonal purity and clarity, that kind of thing. It has the signature, but we thought it was fake. He said not."

"And now your brother has to live with his shame, the last of many."

"Exactly."

"Do you play? The violin, I mean. Or any instrument."

"No."

"No music in you?"

"Visual thinker, remember?"

"Do you still draw or paint?"

"Not too much."

"Why not?"

"Like my father, I guess. I wanted a life."

"And do you have one?"

"I told you –"

He waved it away. "You did. And if you had this Amber, would you sell it? Keep the money?"

"Vince would decide what to do with it."

"But if you sold it, you could paint."

"I don't need money for that. I can paint now, if I want."

"Money," he noted, "buys time. So you could *only* paint."

She thought about it. That would mean commitment of a larger kind. Facing all those questions about whether or not she was any good. Facing the kinds of things she wanted to paint, and what it did to her to paint them. But it didn't matter. The Amber wasn't hers.

"It belongs to Vince," she said firmly. "I can help myself. He can't."

"Then maybe you should let him drop out of the genetic pool before he breeds."

"That's rude."

"Honest."

"Rude. You don't know him. You have no idea what's good about him."

"I apologize. What if I could get it for you? This Amber."

"I don't see how. Vince didn't get a name for the guy who won it. He probably sold it to someone who sold it to someone who sold it again. It could be sitting in a flea market, or maybe someone's using it as a door decoration, with dried flowers in it."

"Take it as a hypothetical question. If I could get it, what would you do?"

"I – I don't know. I can't afford to buy it back for what it's actually worth."

"What if you could negotiate some kind of barter?"

Christ, she thought. There it is. Trading power for sex, just like any other man. She spent a moment being disappointed in him, then asked herself if she'd do that, for Vince. Well, she thought, why not? She'd slept with men for stranger reasons.

"You'd have to use a condom," she said.

To her surprise, he laughed.

"What?" she asked. "Is that funny?"

"Amusing. I was just realizing how the world looks to you. So you really would trade your soul to help your brother, wouldn't you?"

"No. Just my body."

"What makes you think there's any difference?"

"Besides a few thousand years of Western thought?"

"Besides that."

"Oh, come on."

"Don't get me wrong. I've got nothing against casual sex. I've had enough of it, God knows. But we might as well admit that who you sleep with and why is a reflection of who you are. And certainly in this case, your body would be proxy for your soul. Unless . . . do you find me attractive?"

She thought about it. "In a weird and mildly repulsive sort of way."

"Oh, really?"

"Yeah, really."

"So you'd only have sex with me to get your brother his precious violin?"

"Pretty much."

"Well, then. There it is. You see what I mean."

"No," she protested. "The opposite, in fact. I'd rather let you borrow my body than let the devil take my soul. Isn't that a better deal for me?"

"Only if you assume they're so easily separated. That the action of one doesn't have an effect on the other. Or at least that they don't communicate with each other."

"And if you believe in souls," she said.

"Which you're still not sure about."

"Right. But all this philosophical bullshit aside, could you get the Amber?"

"There's lots I can do."

"Then would you give it to me if I had sex with you?"

"I'm bargaining for your soul," he said blandly. "I'd have to decide which is worth more."

She took a step to one side to put space between them. His face was smooth and neutral. She didn't have a clue whether he was serious or not.

"You've got a great deadpan," she noted.

"It's an asset," he admitted.

She grinned. "Let's put it this way. I'm a realist."

"When you're not singing to trees or black dogs aren't dragging you into weird shit in the woods?" he asked.

"Those," she said, "are anomalies in an otherwise practical life. So show me the violin and we'll decide what's next. Until then, it's all just talk."

He ran his gaze over her. "Austeja, it's a pleasure doing business with you."

When they parted, he didn't try to kiss her, and she didn't know if she was relieved, or disappointed.

❧

Once Stacey returned to her sister's house she took out her laptop to get some work done on the *I Love NY* account. But she was distracted, a niggling thought at the back of her mind sending her away from work. Something Nick said.

Netimer. A Lithuanian named Netimer. Why did she know that name? What did it matter?

She did a google search on it, and learned that he was a Duke of Lithuania, circa 1009. He was converted to Catholicism by St. Bruno, who was killed by Zebeden, Netimer's brother. Zebeden apparently objected to the Pope and all his minions, as did most of Lithuania.

Interesting, but it meant nothing to her personally. In spite of that, it contained an emotional resonance she couldn't explain. Was it a story her grandmother told her? She had vague memories of it associated with childhood dreams of pine forests, images of ancient men whose cold breath was frosty white in the cool morning.

"Jesus," she muttered to herself. "Who cares? Get some work done or go to sleep."

She chose the latter, shut down her laptop, and tucked herself into bed. But for some time she tossed and turned, feeling as if the participants in the oldest dramas of her ancestors were watching her, seeking the only place she could not deny them access.

 Day of Dews

Near the Neman River, Lithuania, circa 1009 AD

The men crept through the trees slowly, stopping to listen now and then. Cool mist swirled around the dark trunks and over the frosted earth, the breath of the spirits who sang in this forest. The sacred groves were just ahead, and here they expected to find the men in dark robes, who said they worked for someone called The Pope. These strangers would bring a new god into the woods to disturb the ancient gods already residing there. They meant to destroy the trees, because The Pope's god allowed praying only to him, and only in his own houses.

Aras, who was cousin to Netimer, their southern chief, led them. At his right hand was Naktis, the man he valued most. Naktis knew all about this Pope and his priests. He'd been with Netimer when the priests poured their water on him, washing away his gods. He'd heard Netimer promise that his people would do the same. The people objected, and Netimer and the priests were killed, but more were coming. Naktis found Aras on his own lands to tell him about it.

"Why would my cousin do such a thing?" Aras asked, horrified.

"The priests promise eternal life if you give your soul to their god," Naktis said.

"They take your soul?"

Naktis smiled. "Yes. They always do. But we can end their work. Some are headed this way, to kill the sacred trees."

They gathered a group of Aras's best men and rode through late night and into morning until they reached the edge of the forest, a place not even their greatest chief dared violate. Here they got off their horses and crept to where Naktis said the Pope's men would be killing the trees.

As they crouched behind a group of pines, clutching their woolen cloaks against the cold with one hand while keeping the other on their swords and knives, they saw the priests in their dark robes, who knelt on the ground and spoke with their god near the oldest oaks, their breath making mist in the cold air.

"They have no weapons," Aras whispered to Naktis.

"Their words are their weapons," Naktis said.

"I can't understand their words."

"I can. They ask their god to destroy the forest, so our gods will have no place to rest."

Aras considered. "We can't kill them when they're weaponless. We'll take them prisoner." He drew a sword and marched forward, signaling his men to follow.

The priests continued speaking to their god as Aras and his men surrounded them. Then one of them stood, faced Aras, and spoke in his own language. He lifted a skin full of water and poured some into his hand.

Naktis called out, "that's for washing away your gods. It will burn the trees!"

The other men stood frozen, not sure how to defend themselves against water. The priest boldly moved to the oak tree.

"Do not touch it!" Naktis cried, and he stepped forward, swinging his sword. The priest's head fell from his shoulders as his lips still moved in prayer.

The other priests drew together, and Aras's men sprang to life, cutting them down until the ground around the trees was wet with blood.

When it was done, Aras's men dragged the bodies back to where they'd left their horses. They debated whether to bury or burn them, and finally decided a shallow grave mounded with stones would be enough.

"Even men such as these should be united with the earth," Aras said. "We don't want their veles troubling us." Then he clapped Naktis on the shoulder. "My friend, I thank you for your help. How can I repay you?"

Naktis considered. "Land would be good," he said. "Land is always good."

"You'll have it. Maybe you'd like a woman, too? Women and land go well together."

"No," Naktis said. "I got in trouble with one once. I don't think I'll try again. Unless . . . . well, if you know one with an old soul, and silver eyes, I'd like to meet her."

"You know, I've heard of such a girl," Aras said thoughtfully. "She's still young, but she lives with her family just beyond the river on some good land."

Naktis tilted his head. "Do you know her name?"

"Austeja they call her, because she knows the bees. You should get to her in less than a week, and her people would welcome you."

Naktis smiled. He knew she would return, her spirit to strong to rest. He'd been looking for her in the years since Razak took his soul. He'd done good work for him, corrupting many men, but Razak said he hadn't done enough to earn back his own soul. He remained in thrall. That would end if he could make Austeja agree that he'd undone his wrong to her. Surely he'd done that by protecting her trees.

"Then that is where I'll go," he said.

He found the place and the girl easily, and was welcomed by her family, just as Aras said. But he did not find it so easy to win Austeja's confidence. Still he stayed, letting spring turn to summer while he sought the right way to make her return what was rightfully his.

๙

Austeja sat on a wooden stool, kicking her heels against it while her grandmother bent over the big clay pot that rested on the table nearest the narrow, unshuttered window, muttering to it, to herself. The small, dark room where food was prepared smelled sweet, sticky and thick from the midus her grandmother was spicing and the honey loaves that were rising, waiting to go to the oven outside. The evening was hot, and the sky still silver with a sun that would linger for many hours.

Today was Rasa, the longest day, the Day of Dews. The celebration had started at dawn, when she and her sister Daina went out to the riverbank to wash their faces with dew. That would make them beautiful, something most important to Daina, who was old enough to seek a husband.

Then they went to the fields with their mother and father, aunts and uncles and cousins, to ask Zemyne and Perkunas to bless the land. They ate and drank outside, raising bread to their lips and kissing it before they savored its goodness. And they sang to thank Saule, the sun, a goddess who cared even for those whom fortune had abandoned. The world itself was here under her motherly warmth.

Austeja's grandmother told her that Saule had even given them honeybees. She looked down at the people who worked so hard, facing hunger and sickness and hurt, and she thought they needed more than warmth. They also needed sweetness. So she allowed small pieces of herself to fly down, little creatures as golden as she was, and these were the honeybees. They made the fruit and flowers grow, and they shared honey and wax and the sticky glue of their hives. They kept some of Saule's fire in them, and that could burn you if you weren't respectful, but mostly they were peaceful creatures, calm under the sun.

Austeja was named for the bee goddess Saule sent to protect her creatures, and that suited her. She knew the dances of the bees, and the songs they liked best. No one taught her. She was born knowing. She understood how the bees fed each other, making honey and wax in the feeding. She knew which hives had dark honey, and which had the light. Those they shared hives with, their biciulis, spoke with her about it, and she helped them by singing, and then the bees would show their homes. The bees, who protected the houses from lightning when Perkunas raged in storm, would care for her, her grandmother said. They would guard her if she respected them.

"Honey is the blood of our spirits, and the bees teach us the best way to live with each other," her grandmother told her. "You must dance, because they do. And you must sing to them, since their honey gives us our songs. So we give back what we receive, and are given more. Do you see?"

She did. It made sense to her that the world worked that way. Everything went in circles. What lived would die and what died would live. That's how it was.

But today, on Rasa, her grandmother sniffed, wiped back a strand of thin gray hair from her face. "Go outside," she said. "Your sister is making wreaths for the river."

"In a little while," she said. "I want to watch you first."

All the young people who lived in the cluster of wooden houses near the fields and farms would float wreaths on the river at dark, waiting for messages about love and marriage. She wanted to be with them, but that presented a problem she didn't know how to solve. Her sister, Daina, was getting older. She wore her hair up, fussing with it often, while Austeja still kept two braids hanging down her back. Daina had recently chosen a man she liked, a newcomer named Naktis, and he was with her now, making wreaths.

He showed up just as winter turned to spring, and he brought stories from Netimer's lands, about dangerous men with a new god who murdered trees. He said he'd killed them before they did harm, and that impressed the men. He was handsome and strong and had a serious face, so they trusted him. Besides, some had already heard such rumors and wanted to learn more, so they could protect their own sacred groves.

Naktis told all he knew, and made himself useful in other ways, living with her uncle, helping in the fields and tending the animals. Soon he was no longer a visitor, but part of their world. But he gave her an uncomfortable feeling. Naktis, he called himself. The night.

She didn't like the way he watched her. Everyone believed he had his heart set on Daina, but his eyes looked elsewhere. They looked at her.

"Senele," she asked now, "are you afraid of the new god?"

Her grandmother turned and looked at her, grunted. "No. Of course not."

"What's he like, that everyone worries about him?"

"He's like Dieve, living in the sky. Or Perkunas, because he has a temper, but he doesn't bring lightning."

"What does he bring?"

"I don't know, child. He's new. It's not him I worry about. The gods find their own way to get along. But the men who bring him fear snakes and toads, and have no understanding of the trees. They talk always about their own god, but know nothing of ours, so they disrespect them."

"Can't we teach them better?"

"They don't want to learn."

"Is it good that Naktis killed them?"

Her grandmother sighed. "Killing is hardly ever good. Sometimes it's necessary, but less often than men think. That's a secret only women seem to know."

"Then you don't like Naktis?"

The old lady scrunched her face up and thought. She always thought before answering, and Austeja liked that. Most adults gave her answers like good milk thinned with water.

"He's caught between gods, and they tear at him," she said. "It makes him smell dead. Like a vele or vaidila."

Austeja nodded. She knew these terms. A vele was a ghost. A vaidila was a ghost who served something evil, and had evil intent. That was exactly her impression, but her grandmother was much better at putting it into words. "Are we the only ones who know this?" she asked.

"It's something only the old and the young can smell."

"What can be done for someone like him?"

"He must find his heart and mend it. There's no help until then."

"Senele," Austeja said, speaking carefully, "he watches me."

"Hmmph," her grandmother said, as if she knew this already. "They say some women in our family – the ones with silver eyes - draw veles to us. And Vielnas, too."

Vielnas. Another word she knew. The one who ruled the underworld, and might trick you, for his own ends. "Why are we like that?"

A sly grin formed in her wrinkled face. "Well, they can be fun," she admitted.

"How?"

"You'll have to wait until you're older to understand that. And you must be careful. You have the old eyes. That's why he watches you, hoping you'll stop the gods from ripping him apart. But that isn't your job. You have trees to tend, and bees to mind. Now go outside. It's Rasa, and outside is where you belong."

Her grandmother lifted her large arms and shooed her toward the door, but she was laughing, and Austeja did the same.

She made her way toward the river, past the bonfires burning along the way. Young men would jump over them, seeing who could leap highest. There would be singing and dancing to honor the bees, and midus and honey bread well into the dark. Now she heard a familiar song, picking out Daina's sweet high voice among the others.

Ka tar teka per dvareli? Saula, ridolela. Who rises there upon the farm? The sun, the rolling sun. Sunlet, sunlet! What does its rising bring?

Ahead of her she saw the silver river, misty in the lingering evening. A group of young men and women sat on the bank, the girls in their best skirts, embroidered with designs of sun and tree, tied with their most colorful sashes. And there was Daina, with Naktis by her side. She wore a coronal wreath of flowers, small and white, over the braids carefully twisted around her head. Her face shone with happiness.

Austeja reached them as the song finished in laughter. Her sister saw her and called her over. "Austeja, come here! You haven't made your wreath yet."

"I don't have any rue. I have to go pick it," she said.

"I have plenty. Use this." She held up the sharply scented branches, with tiny round leaves and little white flowers.

Austeja took it, thanking her. Her sister petted her head. "You stay inside with Senele too much," she said softly. "It makes you quiet, and I think, a little sad."

"I'm not sad," she said, sitting and twining her wreath. "I like what she teaches me."

"Life is more than learning," Naktis said.

She didn't look at him. If she did, she'd see that following in his eyes.

"What else is it for, Naktis?" Daina asked playfully.

"Well, for love, of course. And children and good midus and laughter."

"If you like such things," Austeja said. "My sister does."

Daina laughed, kissed her lightly on the head. "And so will you, someday."

Austeja held up her finished wreath, a sorry, thin thing next to Daina's. Her sister took special care, hoping her wreath would touch Naktis's, signaling a wedding.

"I don't know if you'll catch a man with that," Naktis laughed.

She sniffed. "My mother has one already, and my grandmother. That's enough men in the house."

"I can't wait any longer," Daina said. "Let's toss them now."

Austeja looked around. The evening was still thin, silver as the river. "But it's too early," she complained. "The sky is still silver and the sun isn't down."

"It's almost blue over there in the east. And we'll make more if this proves untrue," Daina said.

She tossed her wreath in the water. Others quickly followed suit. Austeja closed her eyes and did the same. She heard a gasp, and opened her eyes. Her wreath landed on top of Naktis's. Under the shifting mist and silver light, they seemed to struggle with each other until his was taken by the whirlpool, and went under.

Austeja saw Daina's floating close to the wreath Giedrus had tossed, a boy who followed Daina with his eyes the way Naktis followed her. Everyone was silent, and a small frown made a crease on Daina's forehead.

"Well," Austeja said, "I told you it was too early. Now we'll have to get more."

At this, everyone began to move about, laughing again, as if a spell had been broken. They went down the riverbank, in search of more rue and flowers and ferns. Austeja walked away from them, toward the forest. She'd find ferns and rue enough near the beehives her grandmother tended.

೨

The woods were dimly shadowed, but she had nothing to fear from them. She knew every tree, and they knew her. She listened for the sound of buzzing, of singing bees within the rustling of the leaves and pine needles, and when she discerned it she found her way easily to the old oak, where the honeybees had built their largest hive. They would not settle down on the longest day. They, too, stayed awake to praise Saule.

She stood under the tree and sang back to them. "Little bees, will you dance dance dance from the sun to me? Can we dance together beneath the trees?"

Their soft humming called back to her, and she lifted a hand, laughing. She liked being in their presence, feeling herself among friends.

"You have a lovely voice, Austeja," someone said.

She turned. It was Naktis, and he was alone. "Where's my sister?" she asked.

"She's with the others. I told her I wanted to find a special flower." He licked his lips nervously. "Do you understand?"

She shook her head.

"It's you I wanted to find. To talk with you," he said.

She frowned. "About what?"

"About you, and me. It's been many years, but I have not forgotten. I've waited for you to return."

She didn't understand him. "You – you belong with my sister," she said, not knowing what else to say.

He waved that away. "Daina is beautiful, and perhaps I'll wed her. But you - you have the silver eyes. Only you can free me from Razak."

She took a step back from him. "I don't understand."

"I know what they say about you. What your grandmother says. You carry the soul of a woman from long ago. I knew her, you see. I – I knew her. I heard about you and your eyes, and came here to find you." He sighed. "You don't remember. Well, never mind. You can still free me. If you say it's so, it will be so."

"Say what is so?"

"Razak said I would be free if I repaired an error from my past, and so I have, by protecting the trees and killing the priest. If you agree it's so, I'll have my soul back."

She stood still, said nothing. His soul? She didn't have that.

He took a step closer. "You'll do that, won't you Austeja? Then I'll marry your sister, and I'll look after you both. There are lands promised to me for what I did."

He grasped her arms. Frightened, she tried to move away but he held on. "Don't worry," he said. "I won't try to – to have you. That's over for me. I ask nothing of you except your word. You must agree that I've done right by you. It's only fair."

"I - I can't help you," she said.

His grip on her tightened. "You must," he said. "I live and yet I don't. I pretend to be like you, but I am not and every day I feel less, taste less. Razak never told me that would be so, but it is. And it will only get worse, going on like this forever, unless you help me, as you should."

She remembered what her grandmother said. "You must mend your own heart. I cannot do that."

His face darkened and he shook her hard. "I served you. I slung the sword. That priest's head fell by my hand. I stepped in his blood, for your trees."

"You did it for yourself," she whispered, knowing somehow this was true. She squirmed against him, but it did no good. He put his hand to her throat.

"Be still," he said. "It was for you. All for you."

Her head swam with fear, but inside herself she heard a soothing voice, like one she'd heard in dreams. It belonged to a woman who sang to the trees and carried a small jar of sap and honey just like her grandmother's. When she was born, her grandmother smeared her lips with its contents, the spirit of the bees and their ancient goddess becoming part of her flesh. Now her mouth spoke as that woman would.

"How does killing undo murder?" she asked.

Fire blazed within the dark circle of his pupils. His hand tightened at her throat, but she heard a sound that drove her fear away. A woman's laughter, joined by the singing bees. She looked up and saw the swarm, circling high above. She sighed with relief. They would protect her.

When Naktis heard the swarm he gasped, released her and stepped away. The bees descended and enfolded her. He gaped at her through their thick blanket of motion.

"If you want her, go get her," the bees sang in whispers like grass, like fire.

"I cannot!" he cried out.

The swarm laughed. Austeja turned away and walked out of the woods, blanketed by their protective dance. She made her way back to her house, feeling the little bites of Saule as she walked. She didn't hold it against them. They always did what was right. She trusted them, knowing they gave their lives in this.

When she got to the house she heard screams, saw dimly through the bees that people were gathered, staring. Her grandmother pushed through them and went to her, talking quietly with the bees, thanking them and sending them on. "Leave her to me, now," she said courteously. "I'll take care of her."

They listened, and flew back to the woods. Austeja, dizzy from their fiery stings, fell to the ground. Her grandmother and sister knelt by her, and there was Naktis, staring down at her.

She let her eyes meet his, and he cringed. One bee flew out from her hair, landed on his hand and died in giving him the sting. He cried out as if a sword had pierced him, ran from there and did not return.

Her grandmother treated her with the midus she brewed only once every five years, made by fermenting the entire hive with all its bees, each one giving themselves to this drink. Her grandmother said it cured everything except old age, and she was right, because Austeja was soon well.

Her sister was very kind to her, and told her she was glad Naktis left. Now she spent her time with Giedrus, who would be good to her.

More priests would come, but the trees sheltered her family from them, and the bees continued their dances and their laughter and their song.

Chapter Five

Upstate New York, Early 21st Century

Tamsa took up a post at the front window at 8 pm on Saturday, a toy in her mouth, clearly anticipating some happy event. Chaos stalked her, occasionally licking one of her legs. All of this signaled to Stacey that her sister and family would return soon.

Soon she heard the car pull into the driveway, and Tamsa started her butt-wiggling tap dance, while Chaos stalked majestically toward the cellar. He was not yet prepared to forgive them for abandoning him.

Jim entered first, bearing luggage, and dealt with Tamsa's enthusiasm. He looked travel weary, but relaxed, happy.

"Hey," Stacey said, "You made it back."

"Yeah," he sighed, and pushed his way past the dog to go to her and give her a quick hug. "Martha's got Alicia. I'll just put this stuff away."

"I opened wine, if you need it," she said to his retreating back.

"Thanks. I will, once I'm settled," he called back. She knew from Martha that Jim took care of tasks before he took care of himself. Both women had long since given up trying to change that.

Martha entered, hanging on to a bag of road detritus, her daughter limp in her arms. She put her lips together and said 'sshhh,' to Stacey, picked her way through the house and disappeared to deposit her daughter on her bed.

Stacey waited, pouring three glasses of red wine for whoever came back to the kitchen. She sipped at one until her sister returned, looking tired and happy. She came over, grabbed the wine, hugged Stacey, and sat on a stool by the kitchen counter across from where Stacey perched on a similar stool. She raised her glass.

"Here's to good sisters, who take care of animals."

Stacey raised hers. "And here's to successful vacations. How'd it go?"

"It was great. No cooking, and lots of fairies. Alicia was in heaven, and we weren't far behind."

"Next year, leave Alicia with me and you and Jim can run away alone."

"Next year? How about this August – just for a weekend?"

"Absolutely," Stacey agreed, glad to encourage her sister's small debaucheries.

Martha glanced around. "How was everything here?"

"Fine. No fires or floods, and it was nice to be out in the country," Stacey said, thinking it was best not to mention the incident in the woods.

"Bring any guests up?"

Stacey raised her eyebrows. "Does it look it?"

"Not really. But maybe you cleaned up."

Stacey laughed. "Nobody."

"What? Grant can't drive up a hill?"

Martha knew all about Grant, of course. She didn't think much of him and sometimes said so, just to remind Stacey she could do better. Stacey, also aware of Grant's limitations, took it as a compliment. Martha wanted the best for her little sister.

"Actually, he can't," Stacey said. "Which is why he's just . . . .Grant."

"Yeah. You have to get him some competition," Martha said.

Stacey laughed a little nervously, and Martha caught it immediately. "What?" she asked. "Something? Or someone?"

Stacey hesitated. How to explain a guy who wanted to broker the sale of her soul? "No," she said.

"Oh, come on. It's all over your face. What is it?"

"Okay," Stacey admitted. "I met a man who isn't Grant."

"You mean, like a real man? Not just one of your friends with benefits?"

"A real man. But no benefits, and not really a friend. He's a little off my usual type."

"This is good," Martha noted judiciously. "How so?"

"For one thing, he's rich and powerful. And he's older."

"How much older?"

She considered, and realized she couldn't actually tell. "Maybe ten years?"

"That's nothing. But let's get back to the rich and powerful part. You say that like it's a bad thing."

"He's pretty eccentric," she said.

"Likes women's underwear? Has a lot of piercings and lives in an airplane?"

"None of that. At least, I don't think so. But he's . . . I can't tell if he's interested. Anyway, he was fun to talk to, and I might see him again."

"Good in bed?"

"I wouldn't know."

"Ah. I see."

She made a face. "Don't go all big sister on me. I've been watching your animals for a week, and you owe me."

Martha laughed, came over and hugged her quickly. "I do. I had a great time. So pour some more of that wine, and if we can't figure this guy out by the time we see the bottom of it, we'll just have to open another one."

Stacey was soon sorry she'd mentioned Nick to Martha, because she kept asking about him, and another week passed without any word from him. She told herself that was good. She didn't need a nutcase in her life, however rich and well-connected. She would chalk it up to experience and move on. She told Martha the same thing. Still, she noticed she was grumpy when the phone rang and it wasn't him. Noticed that she snapped at people who called that weren't him.

Then flowers arrived at her office - five sprays of delicate white and gold orchids nestled among ferns, bearing a small note. "I'm out of the country for a bit, but we'll continue negotiations on my return," it said.

Her heart beat a little faster when she saw his scrawling signature at the bottom, and she scolded herself for that, but she was still staring at it, smiling at his assumptions, when Grant knocked on her office door and walked in.

He looked at her, at the flowers, at the note in her hand. "I guess I have competition," he said.

"Get your A-game going," she said.

"That bad?"

"It's always that bad. If you're not using you're A-game, you're in the weeds. Didn't you know that?"

"And here I thought you were low maintenance," he muttered.

She put the note down. "What did you want?"

"The Christians are here."

"Radio Station? They're not scheduled for today."

"Not them. The Priest. St. Francis College account?"

"Oh. Don't scare me. Father Pete's not Christian. He's Catholic. It's different. And he's Franciscan, which is very different. Send him in."

Grant left, and Father Pete peeked his head in, came over and greeted her fondly, shaking her hand and then pulling her close for a quick embrace.

"Labas, biciule," he said, with a good Lithuanian accent, and she returned the greeting.

Like her own family, his was Lithuanian, and they often talked about the strange cultural accretions of that heritage which remained with them both. Though she'd been nervous about him when they first met, she'd grown to like him a great deal.

He was in his fifties, in good shape, and had a good head with thick silver hair. He was handsome for a priest, but not so handsome as to be worrisome. Martha met him when he did a guest sermon at the church she attended, there for the feast of St. Francis, which was traditionally the day they blessed the animals. She liked what he said about the divine in nature, the way he greeted children who brought their pets in for blessing, the solemnity with which he raised his hands over hamsters, goldfish, kittens, bunnies, and shaggy old dogs.

Talking to him afterward, Martha found him sympathetic, intelligent and funny. He even played the violin a little, sometimes using it at services. When he said he was looking for help putting together promotional material for the Franciscan college he worked at, Martha sent him to Stacey, who wasn't thrilled at the prospect.

She was, in general, wary of all religious types, figuring they had something to sell that she didn't want to buy. But when she told him bluntly she wasn't Catholic and didn't know what she believed, he didn't bat an eye.

"You okay with that?" he asked.

"For the most part, though sometimes I worry about being Alicia's godmother. Maybe I should've said no to that?"

"You love her?" he asked.

"Absolutely. Who wouldn't?"

"You'll look out for her well-being? Support her if she wants to be Catholic, or help her find what she needs if she doesn't? Teach her what's important – holy – to you?"

"I can teach her how to paint," Stacey said. "How to see what's beautiful and interesting in the world. Does that count?"

"It's a damn good start," Father Pete said.

They shook hands on it, and he beamed at her. "Y'know, a lot went wrong between Lithuanians and the Church. War, a determined destruction of indigenous culture – the usual. Maybe you and I are making some of that right. Reconciling various angels."

She wasn't sure about that, but she agreed with Martha that for a priest, he was okay.

Though his budget wasn't what she was used to, she'd helped design a website and some print material for the college. It was easy work, and he was easy to work with. Her boss didn't mind, saying it was good for community relations, and maybe they'd get some Diocesan accounts out of it. Never underestimate the power or deep pockets of the Catholic Church, he'd said. Stacey wondered if he had his eye on the Vatican, richest city in the world.

"We're going over the website today, right?" she asked Father Pete.

"We are," he agreed, and they got right to it.

They were well into the paragraph describing the overlap between Franciscan theology and environmental policy, which needed some tightening, when she realized she was staring at her flowers and hadn't heard a word he said.

"I'm sorry," she said. "Could you repeat that?"

He smiled up at her. "I already did, twice. I'll try it again if you want, but maybe you should clear the field first."

"Hmm?"

"What's on your mind? Tell me, and then it won't be distracting you."

His face was kind and patient, as a priest's should be, she thought, and so rarely was. She was going to brush him off with a story about working too hard, but instead found herself saying something else altogether.

"It's. . . well, I had this strange conversation with someone, about selling your soul. Does the Church still think that happens?"

"All the time," he said. "People sell out for power, money, security, success."

"So to keep your soul you have to be poor and a failure?" she asked, thinking of Vince.

"Not at all. Some people give it up for drugs or booze, or just to sit home nights watching Reality TV. There's nothing wrong with money and power, as long as you don't trade in your real self for it. What profits a man to own the whole world if he loses his soul, and so on. It depends on your intent in getting it, and what use you make of it."

Intent was all. But wasn't the road to hell paved with that? It all seemed a little amorphous to her. "Can you sell your soul to the devil for love?" she asked.

"Never. For desire, maybe, but not love. In fact, love's the prevention and the cure. You mind telling me what this is all about? I mean, do I have to worry about something here?"

She laughed. "No need to call the exorcist yet. It was just small talk, but it got me thinking. I mean, what you're saying, that's different. The church doesn't believe that actual devils still go around trying to buy souls, does it?"

He grinned. "Sure. Only now, they wear business suits."

She found that answer disconcerting, and wasn't sure what to say to it.

"Think of it as a metaphor, if you like," Father Pete said.

She shook her head. "I don't do metaphors."

"But you're an artist. You live by them."

"Not really," she said, "To both."

"Please. I have one of your paintings, remember?"

He'd made a special effort to go to Martha's house to bless Luna and Chaos when Alicia was too sick to bring them to church, and Stacey was touched by that. She gave him the present of a watercolor on the death of St. Francis, which he referred to as the

Transitus. Something about the word made images appear in her mind, and she'd come up with a man slowly morphing into a variety of animals, ending in a great blue heron rising toward the sky. She was almost happy with it, but since then, he insisted on calling her an artist, and she continued to deny the charge.

"Paintings aren't metaphors," she said now. "Not for me. They're real. Things I see."

He grinned at her. "You see what the angels see," he said. "I don't think you have to worry too much about devils, in that case. If you run into any, remember that tears drive them away."

"Tears?" she asked.

"That's from a lot of old stories. For instance, when the miller sells his daughter to the devil she weeps on her hands, and he can't touch her." He shrugged. "Maybe it's the salt. Like the thing about tossing salt over your shoulder to chase the devil away?"

"Okay. So if I meet a devil, I'll cry on him."

"That's the ticket. Tears and laughter, confidence and the truth, drive them away. And love, of course. That's the biggest safety net in the universe."

She was saved the need to respond to that more complicated notion, because her office door opened and Julie, a copywriter, stuck her head in.

"Hey," she said, "Anyone know what that noise is?"

"What noise?" Stacey asked.

Julie's glance flicked about the room and she twitched her nose. She was a nervous young woman. "I guess you can't hear it in here. Come to my office."

"We're kind of in the middle of something," Stacey pointed out.

"Yeah, but I think something's wrong. Really."

Father Pete stood up and shook his pant legs down. "I'm game," he said.

They followed Julie down the hall to her office, which looked out over the edge of the park. They stood inside it, and Stacey understood what Julie meant. She heard a persistent buzzing sound emanating from an undefinable source.

"What the hell is that?" Stacey asked.

"See? Sounds like – something electrical, you think?"

As they listened, Grant appeared at the door.

"What gives?" he asked.

"Shh," Julie said. He came and stood inside, never one to miss an event.

Stacey tilted her head this way, and that. The buzzing grew louder, but it wasn't actually in the room. She moved toward the window and looked outside.

"Holy shit," she murmured.

"What?" Father Pete asked, coming over. When he saw, he agreed. "Holy everything," he whispered.

Bees. Hundreds, maybe thousands of them. They flew in a thick cloud just outside the window, their low pitched buzzing loud and insistent. Individual bees broke away from the central mass and beat against the window, bouncing and pinging off of it, then rejoining the larger group.

"Get back," Julie warned.

"They can't get in, can they?" Grant asked nervously.

Stacey didn't move. She was mesmerized by the pattern of their flight, the sound of them. It was a golden cloud that floated and zipped and buzzed in a spiraling swirl. They were talking to each other, she thought. Telling each other things she could not understand, speaking in their own ancient and complex tongue.

Her grandmother told her bees were the best possible example for a human society, with everyone working together for the good of the hive, all supporting the queen who gave new life. Biciule, the word Father Pete used in greeting, meant both close friend and someone you share your beehive with. Her name, which had been her great-great grandmother's name, was also the name of the Lithuanian bee goddess. In spite of that, she was allergic to them, and the thought of a swarm just creeped her out.

"My ancestors," she muttered.

Father Pete stared at her.

"What?" Grant asked.

"Nothing," she said. "Just – I think they'll go away. It's a swarm, looking for a place to make a new hive. They aren't killer bees or anything. They'll find a tree and settle down."

"How do you know that?" Grant demanded

"My ancestors," she said, clearly this time. When Julie and Grant looked at her blankly, she elaborated. "My grandmother knew about bees."

"It's a Lithuanian thing," Father Pete confirmed. "They had a bee mythology. Bees were a kind of model society, and queen bees were representatives of the divine."

"Really? Your peasant background comes out, Stacey," Marcia commented.

"Right," Stacey said. "Anyway, it's good they're here. Honeybees are in trouble. We're killing them with neonicotinoids."

"Um - neo - what?" Marcia asked.

"Pesticides," Father Pete said. "It's a problem. Right, Stacey?"

"Yeah," she agreed vaguely, feeling a little queasy for reasons she couldn't explain. "Let's finish up."

She exited the room with Father Pete, hoping to get on with her day. But she found it difficult to concentrate. She stared at her flowers a lot, read the note quite a few times, and continued to hear the mild buzzing of bees as a background noise to all her thoughts. By 6:30 she decided it was time to go home, make it an early night for a change.

Chapter Six

As she drove home she was still mildly agitated, like the bees, though she couldn't pinpoint why. She didn't want to go home, and she didn't want to go out. Her gym things were in the back seat, but running on a treadmill didn't appeal to her, and neither did Chinese take-out and a Netflix movie.

She flicked through radio channels, looking for something that would engage her. When she hit the local classical music station, she got the Sibelius violin concerto, second movement, with all its sweet, sad yearning. She remembered her brother saying his music was infused with the natural world of his home country, Finland, but to him its intense yearning and defiance sounded Lithuanian, as if the composer knew both lands and could sing their souls. When he was a teenager he often said things like that, and believed them.

He'd spent countless hours practicing this concerto, one of the most difficult to play, working for the day when he could do it professionally, with full orchestra. Hearing it always brought a sharp memory of who he once was, and with that an even sharper pain, because of who he'd become and why. It also reminded her that she hadn't seen him in a few weeks. With a sigh, she turned right, heading to his place instead of home.

She pulled into the visitor's parking space at his apartment complex and turned her car off. It wasn't bad, as these places went. She'd helped him find it, looking for something close enough to the city to keep him from being isolated, but far enough removed that it would feel like a retreat. She paid for the place, sending out the monthly check. And she'd bought him the second-hand Toyota that was good enough to get him around when he smashed the one he'd bought with their parent's insurance money. Martha wasn't sure that was wise. "It'd do him more good to find his own way, learn to be responsible for himself," she said.

But the world had done him an ill turn, and showered her with all kinds of good luck. She was just trying to keep the universe in balance. In spite of that, Vince spent more time with Martha than with her, and was more cheerful in her presence. With

Stacey, he tended to get broody, defiant, more like their father. And for reasons she couldn't explain, she always felt guilty around him, relieved when he was gone. When she got out of her car and went to his building, part of her hoped he wouldn't be home.

But he was. His deep voice came over the intercom right after she pressed the bell. "Yeah?" it asked.

"Hey, Vince," she said cheerfully, realizing she always made her voice cheerful for him. "It's Stacey. Just dropping by to say hello."

A brief pause. Then, "I'll buzz you in."

He did so, and she went up the stairs, down the hall to his apartment. He was standing at the open door, his lanky form leaning against the frame.

"Hey," she said. She was struck, as always, by how much he physically resembled their father. Pictures of Vince at 17 and her father at the same age were virtually identical – light haired, sharp-nosed and heavy chinned, with slanted light brown eyes. Martha had the same eyes, but the more delicately carved features and high cheekbones of their mother. Stacey was the only one who got the slanted silver eyes. Her grandmother said they were a family legacy, appearing every few generations. She figured they were the combined work of Mongols and Teutons who ran roughshod over Lithuania, just as their father rode roughshod over Vince's life. Oppression breeds oppression, she thought. She'd lived that paradigm.

As her brother stood in the doorway he rested his left hand against the frame, its fingers clutched in an eternal fist, a different kind of family legacy, born of their father's drinking, and his rage. The thing she hadn't told Nick. The thing that ruined his life well before he lost the Amber.

"Hey yourself," he said to her. "C'mon in."

His apartment didn't look too bad, she thought, though she wasn't happy to see the open bottle of whiskey on the coffee table. She supposed he wasn't entirely sober, but he'd been working pretty steadily, a part-time job at a local nursery he said he liked. They left him alone and let him do his work was the way he put it.

"Can I get you something? Coffee, or a beer or something?" he asked

"I'm good. How's the job's going?"

"Checking up?"

"Of course not," she said, a little sharply.

"Sorry," he said, though clearly he wasn't. "Well, I'm gonna have a drink. You sure you don't want one?"

She shook her head, bit her lip to keep from saying anything critical. As he went into the kitchenette and got a glass, she continued talking, keeping it upbeat.

"Hey," she said, "I met this guy who asked about the Amber."

She heard his motions stop briefly, then continue. When he returned to the living room she saw a look of mingled hope and anger on his face, and immediately regretted what she'd said.

"Does he know where it is?" he asked.

"No. He's – well, he's kind of a powerful guy, and he made some talk about trying to find it. That'd be great, wouldn't it?"

"Sure," he said. "If you could come up with the money to buy it back. I can't."

"I think he'd trade it for my soul."

"What?"

"He's also eccentric," she said. Then, more thoughtfully, "Would you give your soul for it, Vince?"

"I don't think I have one," he said. "But I'd give yours." He laughed, making light of it, but she felt a small punch in the center of her chest.

"Gee, thanks," she said.

"C'mon, Stace. Your soul's worth a helluva lot more than mine. You think I'm not aware of what you've done for me?"

She heard the distant sound of Nick's laughter. Get him out of the gene pool before he breeds. It's survival of the fittest out there, and clearly he wasn't all that. Then, she saw him clumsily try to hold his drink with both hands. Success was contingent on many things, most of which were just the luck of the draw.

It was Vince's bad luck to have a drunk father, who came home particularly drunk a few days before his Julliard audition. She remembered it vividly, with full emotional impact each time it came up.

Vince was excited, practicing almost nonstop. He was in the living room, playing Sibelius. Her father came home from the job he hated making huge cement pipes at a factory. He'd stopped at the bar on the way and was already pretty well soused, but the first thing he did was pour a few fingers of whiskey in a glass and toss it back. Her mother said something softly about waiting until after dinner. She had his favorite pot roast. He glared at her, and poured another glass.

"Can't that damn kid stop playing?" he snapped.

"His audition – this week – " her mother muttered.

"He's not the only one who lives here," her father said, his voice getting louder. Vince, wrapped in music, didn't hear. Martha was out, at a friend's house, and Stacey stood in the kitchen, frozen, thinking she should go warn him, but she was too afraid to move. When her father got angry the tension in the house buzzed like live wires, and held her still as a deer in the headlights. Some part of her believed that if she stayed still, he wouldn't see her, and it seemed to work because he slammed down his glass and stormed right past her, into the living room.

The ensuing struggle was a quiet one, with soft cursing and breath caught in rasps. She couldn't see it, and Vince never told her details, but she could imagine it well enough. Vince protected the violin, their father grabbed for it, but neither would hurt the instrument itself, that beautiful amber wood, that glorious tone. Better to break Vince's fingers, tear the ligaments in his hand prying the violin loose from his hold.

Then her father's voice roaring, saying he'd stop that noise for good. A hideous cry of pain, followed by silence.

Her father left by the front door, while she and her mother took Vince to the hospital, where they did what they could for the breaks and the muscle tears. The audition was cancelled, pointless now. A year of physical therapy and a few operations did nothing to fix what was broken. Vince's hand was permanently maimed.

Their father never apologized. Nobody ever talked about it. Vince stayed at home, flunked out of community college, and was systematically fired from a variety of jobs while he gambled away any paycheck or unemployment check he had. A few years later their parents were killed in a car accident, driving home from a wedding. They never found out for certain if their father was drunk. They assumed he was.

She and Martha did what they could for Vince, each in their own way. But sometimes he seemed to hate her for helping him. She wanted to tell him he had a choice: He could feel guilt or gratitude. She didn't really care which one he picked, but she wished he'd stop bouncing back and forth between them. She had enough guilt of her own for not protecting him, for not somehow stopping the disaster that was his life. She also thought about grabbing the whiskey bottle and smashing it against the wall, shouting that he was being just like their father. She doubted that would help, either. She could think of only one thing that might.

"What if he could get it back? The Amber," she said. "I'm asking seriously, because I think maybe he could. So do you want me to try for it?"

He slugged down some whiskey, shifted his shoulders. "What good would it do me?" he said dully.

"It'd be money. Quite a bit."

"Then what?" he asked. He looked her full in the face, and deliberately made the clumsy transfer of the glass to his bad hand, pushing it into the clenched fist. He raised it to her. The pain in his face almost swallowed her whole.

"I can't play, and I never wanted anything else," he said, his tone staying neutral. "If I can't have that, I don't know what to do, Stace. I really don't."

This was simply truth. His truth. And another truth - what he wanted was the one thing she couldn't give him, not even by trading her soul. Not unless Nick really was a devil, capable of healing this wound. But somehow, she didn't think devils did that kind of work.

"I guess that's a no," she said.

He threw his good hand up, let it drop at his side. "That's the strange thing. I do want it back. More than almost anything. I just don't know what for."

They didn't have much to say after that, so she left, feeling worse than when she'd gotten there.

꙰

When she got home she microwaved a frozen dinner and ate it standing by the sink. She tossed the remains in the garbage and went to bed, still feeling like crap. When she finally fell into sleep, she dreamt she was driving along an endless highway in the rain, going way too fast and feeling out of control. Next to her, in the passenger seat, there was an angel, and it was beautiful. A visual rhapsody. A painting by O'Keeffe, a song that poured out from the charged mind of Sibelius.

Through the dull and rainy night, its wings, composed of light and shifting colors, rippled the way light ripples on water. Its eyes were just like those in a painting she'd done in college, of luminous eyes isolated from any face, open and exposed to a moon that poured white-gold waterfalls into them, bright water stabbing dark pupils. Its eyes were open. Very open.

"Who are you?" she asked.

"Who are you?" it replied.

"What do you want?" she asked.

"What do you want?" it replied.

She heard sirens and saw a state trooper in her rear view mirror. She pulled over and he came to get her license and registration. He wore a Roman Catholic collar, and she realized he was a priest. She leaned out her window, "Officer – um Father," she said tentatively, "I have an Angel in the car with me."

"Yes, ma'am," he said. "No law against it, if you stay under the speed limit."

As he walked away she glared at the angel. "He doesn't care," she growled. "He sees you, but he doesn't care."

"No," the angel agreed cheerfully. "They don't care. Not at all. "

Its detachment angered her. She reached over to touch its wings, to see if her hand would slide off it like water over the surface of an eye, or if she'd feel layers of feathery moving air, but it shrank away. It gazed at her from wherever it lived, and in a voice that tripped like a million tiny spheres of mercury tumbling down a flight of stairs, it asked, "What do you want?"

Why did it ask that? Was it possible to sell your soul to an angel? Did they do that?

"What do you want?" the angel asked again. Its eyes shimmered with silver, their light entering her like the glare of sun through a windshield. The kind of light that caused accidents, and pain.

"What are you?" she whispered hoarsely, reaching for it. It dodged her hand. "What *are* you? What? *What*?"

At the back of her eyes colors formed hollow spheres and shattered into fragments of razor light that took slices from her brain. She screamed in rage, lunging for it, getting closer, closer, until finally, she grasped the wrist.

It was cold hot soft hard strong malleable as death implacable as plums in her hand, like water over stones honey over bones all asking what do you want what do you want

"Will it hurt?" she asked.

The angel sighed. "You always ask that. Why?"

She woke from the dream with a start. She stared around, and realized she was home. Her alarm clock said 3:33.

She groaned. She had a busy day coming up and she needed to sleep, but she was wide awake, and she felt an old, familiar compulsion. It hadn't happened in a long time, but she recognized it, and knew she couldn't refuse it. She pulled herself out of bed, got drawing paper and pencils from her study and began sketching.

She'd given up art because it took over her life. Her hands were not her own. They belonged to the image until it was complete. She'd never been able to change that. Now they sketched a woman who held a bowl of flame in her hands, and behind her were the shadows of other women, all her. She stood in front of a thick forest, her aspect proud and unyielding, and at her side was a little girl who stared at the ground. At first Stacey didn't know why she was staring there, but then her hands began to sketch a ribcage, at the girl's feet. It sprouted wings like tree branches with leaves for feathers. And something lived inside those ribs, she thought. Something.

She thought of a Discovery channel show she'd seen, about bees making hives inside the ribcages of animal carcasses. She saw it in her mind, the tiny buzzing bees, the dripping honey inside the winged bones. Somehow, that was all connected with the woman who held a bowl of flame, and the shadow women behind her, and the little girl at her side, distant but directive, as if all this was theirs. They were familiar, these women and this child. She knew them, knew their lives and their hopes and their fears.

She worked at it until she could work no more. At six am she crawled back to bed to grab another hour of sleep, exhausted, emptied of guilt and compulsion. And in that hollow space, more dreams clamored for her attention, her ancestors pursuing her once again.

Birute

Palanga, Lithuania, circa 1345 AD

They walked for many days, and many of those days were hungry ones. When they passed through villages they traded embroidered cloth for food. On the farmlands they were given the hospitality of barns to sleep in, eggs for breakfast. But in between were miles of land where only trees whispered, providing solace but no food. Still, Austeja's grandmother wouldn't let her eat the honey or the honey cakes they'd brought along.

"That's for offering," her grandmother said when hunger gnawed her. "If it's accepted, you'll have all you want for as long as you live."

Her feet were sore, and her belly cramped with hunger and the onset of womanhood, but she did as her grandmother said. She knew what death they were escaping.

Not long ago the knights in metal armor with red crosses emblazoned on their chests rode through their village, killing as they rode, raping and burning as they left. They claimed they did so for their god, who was apparently hungry for human flesh. Her father said they did it for someone called the Pope, who ruled far away in Rome. Either way, those they killed remained dead. The land they scourged remained barren.

The Duke's army pushed them away, but when they were gone the plague came, and neither armies or Dukes could stop that invader. Many more died, including her parents. Many more would die before it was done.

"But not you, girl," her grandmother said. "I'm taking you away.

So they packed food and other necessities and walked to the shrine in Palanga, near where her mother's people lived long ago, a place between forest and sea.

Some of this history she knew. It went with her name. Long ago, her ancestor Austeja, for whom she was named, lived in the forests near the ocean. She was murdered, but her spirit, too strong for death, returned to live in her descendants. Those born with her silver eyes were named after her, and carried her songs and visions, a burden of light and pain they had to bear.

As they neared the coast and scented the sea, she drew close to her grandmother. Memories of storms and a man with a face made of night and fire flitted in and out of her thoughts. She shivered at his grim laughter.

"Senele, have I been here before?" she asked.

"Your blood has, long ago," her grandmother said. "Why do you ask?"

"I see a storm. I – I smell it. As if it's just passed."

"Hmmph," her grandmother said. "If it's passed, don't worry about it."

Finally they crested a tall hill between forests and walked down to its base on the other side. Austeja's grandmother took her hand and and they walked to a grotto built of stones where a flame burned brightly from a copper bowl. Next to it was a solitary rock as large as a bed, its surface carved like a bowl. A woman stood near the flame, watching their approach.

Austeja knew who she was. Along the way they'd learned her name – Birute the priestess, the Viadilute who guarded the flame and the trees. She was Samogitian, niece to Vidimantas, of noble blood, wise and beautiful, tall and strong, her eyes seeing far and clear. Her hair was dark and thick as sap, and her skirt and blouse were embroidered with birds and trees. Around her waist she wore a sash woven in many colors, and strings of amber adorned her throat.

"Say nothing," her grandmother counseled her. "Let me talk."

Austeja had no wish to speak. Her words were submerged under a great awe. Only war and death could give her or her grandmother the courage to be here.

"Well?" Birute asked as they stood in front of her. "What do you want?"

Her grandmother dropped her hand. "My granddaughter. She belongs here."

Birute looked at the old lady and the little girl in their poor homespun clothes, disheveled from travel and thin from hunger. "Take her home," she said.

"No. She stays," her grandmother insisted. She went closer. "The Knights came and slaughtered many. Then the plague. Her parents are dead. I'll die soon. She's reaching womanhood, and must stay here, if she's to have daughters someday."

"Is that important?" Birute asked.

Her grandmother nodded. "The soul of another returns through her, and her children and their children beyond. She is Austeja, and she must live."

Birute eyed the old lady and the child. Light flickered in her eyes, as if she read a story made of hardship and beauty. Finally, she sighed. "What did you bring?" she asked.

"Honey and honeycakes. Midus. And she has this." Her grandmother held out the small jar with its burden of honey and sap, the amber necklace with the bee in it.

Birute looked them over, stared at Austeja. "Leave her, then, but I make no promises."

The old woman grunted, bent down and put a gnarled hand on Austeja's cheek. She muttered a blessing, and left. Austeja was alone with the woman, the flame, the trees, and the ocean behind them singing its constant song. When she'd disappeared over the crest of the hill, Birute spoke.

"So. You are Austeja," she said. "You know the bees, then?"

She nodded, but said nothing.

"I'm called Birute."

"I know," she whispered.

"How do you know?"

"The people we met along the way told us about you."

"How do you know they spoke the truth?"

Austeja thought. "They said you were beautiful, and I can see that's true. They said you were noble, and your dress agrees with that. I don't know if you're wise, which they also said, but I know you're kind to take me, though they didn't mention your kindness."

A smile flashed across Birute's face. "Well, child. I know at least one of us is wise, and noble enough to speak the truth. Now tell me, what do you hope to do here?"

"I'll do as you tell me," she said, and offered a small curtsy, as she'd been taught.

"What if I tell you to go to the devil?" she asked.

"Then I suppose I'll go. But I won't stay, since you didn't command that."

Birute laughed long and hard. When she was done, she took Austeja's hand. "I like you already. But I must teach you to laugh more, if I teach you anything at all."

That night they went to the stone house where Birute lived. To Austeja it seemed enormous and important, with its many rooms, high ceilings and large fireplaces.

Certainly it was much greater than the small wood farmhouse she'd grown up in. An old woman cooked for them, good meat and bread that she hadn't had in many weeks, and when supper was done, she slept in a soft bed, with thick blankets. Now she understood her grandmother, why she'd saved the honeycakes in spite of their hunger.

The next day, they went back to the shrine. First they fed fat to the flame that had to stay alive at all times, and then they walked into the forest to sing to the trees. Austeja knew the songs already, and when Birute asked where she'd learned them, Austeja shrugged. "My grandmother says I was born singing."

Birute nodded. "So it seems. But here is one maybe you don't know, and it's a good one."

So Birute taught her new songs, and in return she taught Birute more about the bees and their dances, how to know which dance meant they'd found good flowers, what songs kept them at peace, or working. She showed her the best herbs to use for the smoke offered in return for their honey, and how to thank them.

The rest of their work wasn't hard. They made their offerings to the zaltys who slithered along the forest floor. They took offerings from the people and did ceremony for them. They sang and kept the seasons and danced for the bees. Sometimes Austeja cleaned and cooked, or embroidered Birute's blouses with delicate designs whose small white flowers called to mind the distant stars. On certain days they went to the broad and spacious bar of sand with its undulating dunes to bathe in the sea, or just sit and watch the sun course from horizon to horizon, listening for new songs. Sometimes they collected amber from the shore, which they brought back to the shrine to polish and drill for beads as they stood guard by the flame.

Austeja was happy, the terror of war and plague washed away. It was warmer here, the clouds fewer, and the sun itself brighter. The air here soothed body and mind. A nearby well had water good for curing ills, and all around were the trees she loved. She also enjoyed being with Birute, who laughed more than the people in her village.

"Laughing pleases the gods and the bees," she told Austeja. "They so often laugh at us."

After a time, Austeja noticed that Birute could do something else. She could look through time, backward and forward. She told stories about the woman everyone said was her ancestor, and of her struggles with the vele who pursued her.

"Why does he?" Austeja asked her.

"To get back his soul."

"Does she have it?"

"No. He sold it for a chance at her. But her spirit would not be caught."

"Then he should get it back from the one who has it," Austeja said, which seemed practical to her.

"You have a great deal to learn about men and women. Perhaps when you do, you'll laugh more."

"My Senele always said it was good to be *rimtas zmogus*." Serious. Trustworthy. Calm and in harmony with the world. The phrase had all that in it and more.

"Also good to laugh, child," Birute said. "A peaceful heart seeks joy."

But there came a day when Birute did not laugh. She stood by the flame staring out toward the sea. When Austeja asked her if she needed rue from the forest, she didn't answer. Her eyes looked far away, seeing through time. Austeja sat nearby, not wanting to disturb her, but not wanting to leave her alone. Birute stood until the sun was near setting, and then she blinked, and cried out.

A tall white horse bearing a grim-faced man in a rich blue cloak clattered through the woods to them. He wore a long sword in a sheath at his side, and Austeja, seeing him, was frightened. When he got off his horse, she ran to him and threw herself at him, screaming.

Birute came to her side and pulled her away. "Leave it, Austeja," she said quietly. "His business is with me. Stay and watch the flame."

The man brushed her aside as if he didn't see her. He went to Birute, and they walked off into the forest together. When they returned, he looked at Austeja, his dark eyes scornful. "Next time I come, greet me better," he said gruffly, and he got on his horse and rode away.

Birute went to Austeja and took her hand, leading her to the house. "Who is he?" Austeja asked.

Birute sighed. "He is a man," she said. "His name is Kestutis, a Duke."

"What does he want?"

"To marry me."

"But – do you want to?"

Her face grew grim. "No," she said. "I told him I am Viadilute. We do not marry. But what we want must sometimes give way to what is necessary."

The next day Birute sent Austeja to tend the flame and the trees alone. She felt ill, she said, but Austeja knew it was grief and fear that stalked her. Dukes didn't like to be refused. This Kestutis might return, and if he did, Birute might have no choice but to marry. Austeja went to the shrine with her hands full of prayer. She stayed until dark, asking Zemyne and Menulis to send help for Birute, to save her from sorrow.

As if in answer to her prayers, she heard a horse galloping toward her, and she whirled to the sound, almost expecting to see Menulis himself riding in. Instead she saw a man with dark hair and eyes like grass and amber and the night all at once. He was as richly attired as Kestutis, but younger and leaner, and he carried no sword.

He got off his horse and bowed. "Labas vakaras, Austeja," he said.

She was going to ask how he knew her name, but suddenly she didn't have to. Of course he knew her. She knew him, too. This was her vele, come for her at last.

"Labas vakaras, Naktis," she said.

He strode over to her. "This time you remember," he said.

She nodded. "Birute taught me how."

"Then I don't need to explain who I am. Let's sit down. We must talk."

He took her arm, and she was surprised by his courtesy, expecting something very different. They walked to a stone bench and sat. He closed his eyes, breathed in deeply.

"The air here is good," he said. "Even I can smell that. I expect you're happy."

"I am," she said. "I do not want to leave." She emphasized these words, in case he thought he could seduce her away, as the other man tried to seduce Birute.

"No. Of course not. And you don't have to. Neither does your lady, Birute."

At this, she turned and looked at his face. "You know about that?"

"Yes. Of course. I sent Kestutis here. My master wanted it, and I please him when I can. But there's also something I want, and that's why I'm here." He faced her. "I'll make it plain. I can't find a way to undo what I've done, so I seek a soul to trade, in order to regain my own. I'm here to get yours."

Austeja, suddenly understanding Birute's laughter at the ways of men and women, put her head back and laughed, a clear and silver sound in the darkness

Naktis waited until she stopped, then put a hand on her arm. "This amuses you, but maybe you won't laugh when you realize what you trade it for," Naktis said.

"And what's that?" she asked, still smiling.

"Birute."

At this, her laughter was swept away. This was why veles were to be feared.

"Kestutis will return for her soon," he said. "He's a very powerful man. A Duke, with a large army. He'll take her and marry her."

"She does not want to," Austeja said firmly.

"What does that matter? Besides, she has many reasons to change her mind. What do you think she dreams as she lays in her bed while you guard the flame?"

"She's sad and frightened. I do not think she dreams."

"Ah, but she does. She dreams what will be. Do you know what that is?"

Austeja shook her head. "I cannot dream as she does."

"Then I'll tell you, for I know it too. Do you know about the Knights who make war for the Pope and his god?"

"They came to my village," she said grimly. "I know them."

"Then let me show you what they'll do," he said, and his words painted a living picture of wars followed by more wars, and yet more again. Their little land, a crossroads between many places, would be overrun. And their own rulers would act in ways Austeja could not understand.

Kestutis would fight the Pope's Knights, then make alliances with them to fight the Mongols and Russians, for they also had armies and ambitions. Jogaila, nephew to Kestutis would seduce the knights to his side and send them to fight his own uncle, who would make other alliances and fight Jogaila, and so it would go on. One week Kestutis would speak with the Pope, and the next slaughter his men. One week he and Jogaila would think alike, and the next curse each other. And stretched between their battles would be the people and the forests, the farmlands and the houses, all burning as blood poured over this land, sorrowful and beautiful as a woman in prayer.

Austeja could see the swarming armies cutting down poor folk who had nothing to do with their argument, only to change sides the next day and kill some others they named enemy. She could see the price they would pay for the arrogance of others.

"Among men, nothing is true for very long, is it?" she asked. "But isn't it foolish to waste your life fighting when the bees continue to dance, and there are trees and farms to tend?"

Naktis laughed, but it was a bitter sound. "That's the way of the world, Austeja. You've avoided it all this time, while I could not. Now you must face it, because your lady's life is at stake."

"How so? She won't marry this Kestutis. She and I can stay here."

"But if she marries, perhaps the future will be different. Or perhaps she believes it will be."

"How so?"

"I will show you," he said.

As the stars bloomed in the sky, he laid a different future in front of her. In it, Birute would marry Kestutis, and live in his castle, tended by many servants, eating fine food and wearing silks. She would have a son who would be a great man, Grand Duke of their people, who would forge new alliances and best the Knights, best all those who warred against them.

Austeja felt herself grow pale. A hard choice might face Birute. "Their son will prevent these wars?"

He laughed. "No. Nothing can prevent them. But she *believes* he will. Like women everywhere, she believes her child is blessed, and can do great deeds, so she'll sacrifice herself and go with Kestutis." - unless you stop her."

"Her son, he cannot stop the wars?"

"That," he said, "remains to be seen. But will you take the chance? Or will you stop your lady from giving herself away for a fortune which might never occur?"

Austeja licked at her dry lips and felt her heart beating hard. This was tricky. Birute had told her that the future was always a mix of possibilities, and knowing which to choose was a talent only owned by a few. It was not her gift, and yet she would do anything to save Birute from pain.

"How?" she asked. "How can I stop her?"

Naktis smiled. "Give me your soul. I'll see to the rest."

The night swam around her as she tried to know what was right. "You said your master wants them to marry. He'll be angry with you if they do not."

"He'll have no claim on me if you give me your soul," Naktis replied. "Anyway, that's my business. Birute is yours. Wouldn't you give your life for her?"

She nodded. But was that the same as her soul?

"Come now," Naktis said, "Say yes, or no. We haven't much time."

"Please," she said, "I must think. Give me until morning."

She expected him to be angry, but he only laughed softly. "Then go and think. Think, and sleep. Perhaps your dreams will tell you what to do."

She was not so sure. Dreams came from many places – the gods, the ancestors, wind and water. But they also came from his master. She left him, but she thought she would not sleep.

She entered the house quietly, not wanting to wake Birute, but she was in the front room, seated by the fireplace, waiting for her. She was pale and drawn, but seemed at peace. She held a hand out, gesturing Austeja to her.

"Your vele came, didn't he?" she asked.

Austeja fell to her knees next to Birute and grabbed her hand. "Do not marry this Duke. I beg you."

Birute smoothed her hand. "I must," she said. "There will be a son. He cannot be born unless I marry."

"But he will change nothing. Naktis told me –"

"Naktis lied," Birute said. "That's the problem with veles. They lie, or tell only the truth that suits them."

Somehow, it hadn't occurred to her that he would simply lie. She thought his power was so great he didn't have to. "Then your son will stop the wars?"

"No," she said. "The Pope's knights will keep fighting. My son will do the same. But of course, he will be victorious. He will win against them as no other could, yet, in the end he'll accept their god."

"Then you must not marry!" Austeja cried.

"Hush," she said. "It's my decision, after all."

"But our gods will die."

"Not if I'm there," Birute said clearly. "My son will carry me in his heart as I carry him under mine. He'll let the people keep their own gods, as his mother does. The new god will come and perhaps he'll bring good in spite of greedy men. But the old gods will remain, through me. Through women like you and me. And that is why I must marry. Do you see?"

Austeja did. The blood of the mother would be shed in childbirth for her people, to help them keep what was rightfully theirs. To help them keep their souls. She pitied the choice and was in awe of the courage it took to make it. She laid her head on Birute's hand, her tears the only gift she had to give in return. They stayed there for a long time, and both slept, their hearts worn out. When Austeja opened her eyes again, a soft dawn showed through the window and Birute smiled down at her.

"When Kestutis returns, I'll send you home," she said.

"I do not want to leave you," Austeja said.

"You must. I'll find you a good man, so you can have your daughters, who will also have daughters. He won't be perfect – none are – but he'll be good." She smiled. "Naktis waits. Go and see him."

Austeja rose, but at the door she hesitated.

"Don't be afraid," Birute said. "The bees will always protect you, just as they protect houses from Perkunas in a temper. And you will know what to say."

&

Naktis waited for Austeja at the shrine. Before she spoke, she fed the flame and sang her morning song to the trees. He waited in patient silence.

"What did she say to you?" he asked when she finally turned to him.

"She told me the truth," Austeja said. "As you did not. As you *never* have."

His smile became a scowl, and she felt the quick sizzling of his anger. He strode to her, grabbed her wrist. "Do you think she knows any truth? What are her songs and little flames compared to swords and my master's strength?"

She looked him full in the eyes, neither angry or afraid. "They are everything."

To her surprise his anger dissolved, and his eyes showed a great hunger that could not be assuaged. Pity at his plight moved within her.

"I am sorry," she said gently. "I hope you find peace."

He tossed her wrist away, got on his horse and rode away at a gallop.

The next day Kestutis returned to take Birute away. She kissed Austeja, blessed her, and sent her home to the forests where she was born. She never saw Naktis again, but sometimes she thought she felt him near, watching and waiting.

Once she spoke to him, saying, "You want another chance at me, but you'll not get it until you take the right chance. Your power cannot raise flowers from the ground, or feed wheat in the fields as my songs do. It is a very different song, and as long as you sing it you'll have nothing at all."

She waited for his answer, but she heard only the soft sloughing winds, and the lazy bees in flight.

Chapter Seven

Upstate NY, early 21st Century

Stacey felt much better than she thought she would at work the next day. In fact, she had more energy than usual, and she was racing through her morning tasks, busy with the *I Love New York* Account, when she became aware of a strange sound in her office.

She picked her head up, looked around. Somewhere beyond the city traffic below her, beyond the radio she had playing as white noise in the background, she heard a new sound. It registered low on the Hertz scale, and seemed to emanate from the walls themselves. A buzzing.

She looked at her desk light. Was something wrong with it? She listened. No sound. She looked around. Was there a fly in her office? She saw nothing. It wasn't as loud as the bee swarm outside Julie's office, but she looked out the window anyway. Nothing. She stood in the middle of the room and closed her eyes, tried to locate the sound. A low, deep, and persistent buzzing. Keeping her eyes closed, she followed it to the source, which was low to the ground, near the electrical outlet next to her desk.

She pressed her ear against the wall there and heard it clearly. Something was buzzing inside the walls of her office. She opened her eyes, and looked at the outlet. A short in the wires? She got the pair of scissors from her desk drawer and worked at the screw on the outlet covering. When it was loose, she tugged at it, and immediately, many pairs of small wings and feet pressed out.

"Bees!" she exclaimed, and pushed the outlet cover down.

Her first thought was that last night's painting had come to life, and the bees were here to kill her and make their hive inside her ribs. When she calmed down, her mind worked on it more logically. The bees they'd seen swarming had apparently found a way in, and made their way through the walls to, of all places, her office.

"Shit," she said. "Double shit, and hell."

In spite of her ancestral prerogative, she was frightened. She'd had one bee sting that sent her to the hospital. Now she had what might be a small army of them behind her office walls.

She sat on the floor and thought. The logical thing to do was call maintenance, and vacate the premises. But her grandmother's voice plagued her, reminding her that these were holy creatures, like toads and snakes and trees.

She got up, went to her computer, and googled in 'honeybees.' That led her immediately to Wikipedia, which told her everything she ever wanted to know about honeybees, including their current plight. A weird fungus or microbe was attacking them, and the new pesticides, neonicotinoids, were killing them. They were in trouble. So was she. Nothing on Wikipedia told her how to get them out of her office wall without killing them.

She went back to google, and tried "bee removal." This turned up a lot of phone numbers of people who do such things, but when she called them they all told her the same thing. They'd shoot a lot of poison in the walls, then suck out the bodies.

She tried beekeepers next, and actually talked to a few. They said once they were in the walls it was impossible to remove them without ripping everything apart. It would be incredibly expensive and messy. Stacey doubted any of her bosses would go the distance for honeybees.

There was no appealing solution, and part of her was ready to give it up. Yet, she felt pity for them. After all, they were just trying to find a home, and they ended up in the wrong one. They were a little like her brother, she supposed. She decided she'd have to take matters into her own hands.

She went to the break room, dug through the cabinets and found duct tape, and a plastic container that looked about the right size. Back in her office, she got two pieces of card stock. She loosened the outlet cover, slapped the Tupperware container over it, then jiggled around inside with the scissors until the cover fell off completely.

The next part was the tricky bit. She had to slide the two pieces of cardstock under the container, and get one secured to the wall to hold back the bees that remained, then take the container to the window with the other piece over the top, get it all out the window and set them free, then get her hand back inside without getting stung.

She managed three trips that way, saving what looked like about a quart of bees, but the effort left her shaking with adrenalin and fear. She didn't dare do anymore, and she supposed the rest would survive until morning, so she duct taped the plastic container over the outlet and went back to work. She hoped nobody would notice.

For the next three days, she repeated her performance, waiting until near the end of the day when they grew less active. She'd get as many as she could outside before the creeps and adrenalin made it impossible for her to do more. In the meantime, she lived with their constant song as they sought release, circling the clear plastic, seeking light, certain that was the way out. Each morning she noticed that the clump of dead bees in the bottom of the container grew bigger, and that made her feel awful. She imagined being trapped in a clear bubble that looked like it offered release, only to find it was impenetrable. The glass ceiling, in living color, with the remains of the dead all around. At the end of each day, painstakingly, and with a lot of apology to those who remained behind, she did what she could.

At a certain point she grew angry at their frantic buzzing and scolded them. "Look, nobody said you have to come in here, did they? Unlike Congress and the EPA, I'm trying the best I can, and all you'll do for my trouble is kill me. So give me a break, would you? Okay?"

On the third day, she noticed that one of the bees in the container was larger than the others and had no markings on it. It was surrounded by smaller bees, who circled protectively. The queen bee, she thought, created by worker bees, raised on royal jelly to foster her sexual maturity and her size. She was the bee to save. She went through her now familiar ritual, but this time when she released the bees the queen lingered near the window.

Stacey saw the small eyes and thought of her dying grandmother, staring at her. You see, the bee seemed to say. You'll always know what to do. Intuitively, without rational explanation, you'll know. Only follow that call when it comes.

She did not want to be someone who heard bees talking or got lost in the woods with dogs. She was practical, realistic. Yet, her grandmother's insistent voice told her these creatures carried the true wisdom, the true power. They could not be shrugged off.

"Listen," she whispered, "I'm guessing this is a combination of adrenalin and family neuroses. But if I'm wrong, I want you to know, I appreciate the information."

The queen bee continued to linger at the window, and Stacey waved a hand at her. "Go on," she encouraged. "Get out of Dodge." And the queen flew off with the others.

On the fourth day there was no more buzzing, and only a cluster of bee bodies in the container. She removed the duct tape, put the outlet cover back on, and took the dead bees to her desk where she examined their small, shriveled remains. They were gold and brown, quiet in death. She wondered if she could grind them up and use the powder in her paintings. She wondered if they'd mind.

As she poked among the fallen, her phone rang. It was after hours, so she let voice mail take it while she attended to the fallen bees. She'd take them home, she decided. Use some for her painting, and scatter the rest in the woods around Martha's house.

Before she left her office, she listened to the message, in case it was anything urgent.

"Hello, Austeja," a familiar voice said. "It's Nick. I'm back in the US, and I hope to see you soon. I'll be in touch."

The sound of his voice caused warmth to spread through her skin, and an inexplicable fear. Maybe because of the timing, and the bees. A coincidence, really. Meaningless and unimportant.

In spite of that, somehow, she was not at all surprised.

Chapter Eight

Stacey's pencil moved over her notebook as she read material for Father Pete's campaign. She paused at the section about environmental policies of the college and instead of writing words, she began sketching out an image. A tree. A small, pre-renaissance tree. When it was done she stared at it, not completely satisfied.

She contemplated, trying to see what it needed, but instead her mind dredged up a story her grandmother used to tell her and Martha. Something about a man who wanted to cut down a tree in Vilnius, Lithuania, and a woman who tried to stop him. A woman who was one of their ancestors. His axe fell on her, and she died, defending the tree. Her ghost still haunted that place, haunted all who mistreated trees.

As little girls, they were thrilled at having their very own family ghost. Later, Martha found other Lithuanian folktales like it, but her grandmother's version was embedded in her mind as something uniquely personal. She'd wanted to draw it for many years, that murdered tree, that ancestral ghost. Of course, it wouldn't be appropriate for Father Pete's PR campaign, but her hands chose to start on it anyway.

She mumbled her irritation at them as she got a clean piece of paper and put the report aside. She'd give it five minutes. She couldn't concentrate until she did this.

A complex, gnarled stump took shape on the page, but something was missing. A honeybee, a tribute to all those she couldn't save from her office, a small gesture to mark their importance. She found gold paint, gilding for some graphics sample, and used her pinkie to dab it in the right place. It was just a thought, a placeholder, but she needed it there. She picked up the pencil again and to her surprise, no female ghost shaped itself. Instead, she drew the outline of a man emerging from the broken stump, trapped and trying to escape. He had tattered brown wings, with small dried leaves instead of feathers. He was reaching desperately, hopelessly, for the bee.

As she worked, she knew she'd need oils to do this justice, and a really large canvas. This was just the merest outline, but she was totally absorbed when Grant knocked on her door and stuck his head inside.

His beach boy face showed excitement.

"What?" she asked.

"Someone here to see you," he said, his voice raised a notch in pitch. Something big was going on. Normally she'd be interested, but right now she was irritated at the interruption, which reminded her how bad art was for her life.

"Well? Who?" she demanded.

He made complicated gestures with his hands. "Nick Vecchio."

Unaccountably, her heart started beating faster. She scolded it, and kept her face neutral. "Oh," she said. "Him."

"Well, yeah. Him. You could've mentioned."

"Mentioned what?"

"That you know him. I mean, I thought we had each other's backs. I help you, you help me?"

She was going to ask if that wasn't Erin's job now, but decided against it. None of her business, really. "Is he a big deal?"

"Are you playing dumb, or do you really not know? The joke is what he's got more of in his pockets – money or politicians."

Okay, she thought. That was at least confirmation of his status. But how the hell did Grant know about him before she did? "If he's so important, why didn't you tell me to look out for him?" she demanded.

"Because nobody can get to him. He's a name. Like trying to send Jesus an email, okay?" Grant narrowed his eyes at her. "Hey – he's not the flower man, is he?"

She smiled, and said nothing.

"Hell," he said. "Are you . . . you know, with him?"

"Actually, not. We're negotiating a deal," she said.

"For what?"

"My soul. Show him in, would you?"

Grant opened his mouth to say more, but she waved at the door. "Now, please." He clamped his mouth shut and left.

She counted to ten, breathing slowly to calm herself. She saw, in her peripheral vision, that her pinkie was covered in gold paint. She wiped it on the inside of her jacket, hoping it wouldn't show. The suit was Armani, her one and only, and it looked damn good on her. By the time she was done the door opened and Nick entered, closing it behind him. He was carrying a garment bag, slung over one shoulder.

He stood with his back against the door, looking at her, head tilted to one side. The equivalent, she thought, of the dog sniff. She let him.

"Hello, Austeja," he said. "How are you?"

"Good," she said. "You?"

"Better, now that I see you," he said.

She twisted her lips into a grimace. "If I want that, I can go to Janus," she said.

He laughed, and they both relaxed, became themselves. He dropped the garment bag on her desk, pulled a chair up and turned it to sit with his chin resting on his hands against the back. In this position, he looked around. Still sniffing, she thought.

His gaze went from her diploma to her awards, to the framed pictures of her sister and family, to her brother as a teenager holding the Amber. He stayed with both these for some time, then moved to the top of her desk, where she'd managed to cover her sketch with the radio account report. A corner of the tree stump peeked out of the bottom. When he saw it, a smile twitched across his face.

"I see you're working," he said. "Which account is that for?"

She slid the sketch off the desk and into a drawer. "A new one. Not nailed down yet," she said.

"Can I help? I have all kinds of connections, if you remember."

"No," she said curtly. Then she remembered who he was and put her bright face on. "So. You've been traveling. Anywhere good?"

A sound of small laughter, held in the throat. "A few countries I have business in. Some of it you might find interesting and perhaps I'll tell you about it, by and by. I came to see if you're free for dinner. Are you?"

She debated playing hard to get, saying she was booked, but his eyes glittered with mischief. He anticipated that, probably looked forward to the ensuing joust. She would forestall it.

"I'm free," she said. "Where and what time?"

His face showed approval. "My place, at seven," he said.

"Okay," she said, deliberately casual. She grabbed a pencil. "How do I get there?"

"Go downstairs at six-thirty."

She stared at him.

"My car will be waiting for you," he said. He stood, touched the garment bag on her desk. "Occasionally I dress for dinner, and I didn't know if you had anything handy, so I took the liberty. Do you mind?"

She raised an eyebrow. "What if I do?"

He shrugged. "Then I'll meet you at Ichiban's and we'll have Sushi."

So. She could dress for dinner at his place, or banter over Sushi in her Armani. That was his version of negotiation. His face said she should get used to it. Being a realist, she did. But the deciding factor would be the dress. She'd go far to make connections, but not so far as to wear something hideous.

She pulled the bag to her, unzipped it and saw blood red silk layered with gold, richly beaded. Sue Wong, she guessed. And she loved Sue Wong. "Red's never been good for me," she noted.

"This red will be," he said confidently. "The gold will ameliorate any glare."

"You sure you know my size?

"Of course."

Yes, she thought. Of course. She was drooling to try it on, and he knew that, but she'd reserve her right of choice.

"I'll let your driver know," she said.

"Certainly," he said. "I'd love to stay and chat, but I have a few things to go over with your boss. I'm sure you understand."

"Actually," she said, "you're sure I don't, and you enjoy that."

He grinned. "See you at seven, one way or another," he said, and made his exit.

When he was gone, she let herself lean back and smile. He entered a room like lightning, putting everything in sharp relief. She was glad he was back.

⌀

He was right about the dress. The combination of gold and red cast just the right light on her face, her hair, and it made her eyes glitter silver as a sunlit ocean. It also happened to go perfectly with the old amber necklace she was wearing, once her grandmother's. She wished she'd had time to get her hair cut, though. It was getting long and more than a little wild. In spite of that, when she left the building she felt confident that she looked good. Nick's car – a black Mercedes – was waiting out front.

She got in. The driver turned to her. "Where to, Miss?" he asked.

She stopped herself from giggling, wondered what Martha would think about all this, and said, "Mr. Vecchio's residence."

He rolled up a dividing glass between them and moved out into traffic. She saw a bottle of champagne chilling in an ice bucket in a compartment in front of her, a fluted glass next to it. One glass, she thought, but no more. She wanted her wits about her. Wanted to keep track of where she was going, in case she had to call 911.

The car moved east, exiting the highway about 20 miles past the city, then turned south, over the river and through the woods. She followed signs as she could, and realized they were heading into money property – Columbia County, where people from both New York City and Boston were buying land, setting up their country homes.

They turned onto a dirt road and traveled along it until they arrived at a wrought iron gate that stood between two stone pillars topped by gargoyles, flanked by more wrought iron fence. The driver rolled down his window, pressed a button on one of the pillars, and was buzzed through.

The gate closed behind them and they drove on, up a steep and winding hill hedged in by pine trees. As they crested the top, the road opened up to a wide lawn, and they moved toward a house that reminded Stacey of every fairy tale she'd ever read.

She stared ahead at what looked like a small castle, cast in red and light brown brick arranged to create a mosaic of patterns perfectly placed. Broad steps fronted double doors painted blue, and one side of the house had a balcony, while the other had rounded turrets topped by golden minarets. All around was a meticulously groomed landscape, with perennial gardens in full bloom to the right of the house, and a soft, broad meadow fronting woods to the left. Near the door of the house silky white moonflowers bloomed, gaping slothfully at the onset of evening.

"This is so not Kansas," she murmured.

"What, miss?" the driver asked.

"Um - nothing," she said. The driver stopped, opened her door.

She exited the car and moved up broad stone steps to the front door, which opened before she touched it. She found herself smiling at a tall and broad man in evening wear. He was as bald as Kojak, as pale as a vampire, and had absolutely no expression on his face.

"Hi there," she said. "I'm Stacey. Here to see Nick."

"Yes, Ms. Vitautis. Come right in," he said blandly, and led the way.

She followed, then stopped in the spacious foyer and stared around. A curved staircase on the right led to long hallways. On her left, a door was partly open to reveal what looked like a ballroom. In front of her was a long, wide hall. She recognized a desk along a wall as a kidney shaped Edwardian, rare and terribly expensive.

"Big place," she noted. "Did he build or buy?"

"Bought, Ms. Vitautis. It was designed by one of the River School artists, for a friend named Van Schaank."

"It must've cost a pretty penny."

"Yes, Ms. Vitautis," he said, still neutral. "The dining room is this way."

He relieved her of her purse and the Armani jacket she'd kept on her arm in case it got cold on the way home, then walked forward. At a set of massive oak double doors, he put his hand on a handle. When she turned to thank him, he was already gone.

She entered the dining room, glanced at the long, narrow windows along the eastern wall, took in the table, set with crystal and fine china. The room was big, and she imagined the table could expand to seat more than two dozen. She saw Nick, in evening dress, standing by a fireplace on the western wall. He had one hand on the marble mantle, a glass of wine in the other, and was staring at the contents of his glass.

"Your butler is archetypal," she said.

He lifted his head, looked to her. "Henry? I know. That's why I chose him. His resume said he was an actor who played a butler on Broadway for many years. He told me he wanted to leave the bright lights for a more dignified life." He gestured to the table, where ruby liquid in a thin crystal carafe waited near an equally thin crystal wineglass. "The wine has been breathing, anticipating your arrival."

She moved toward it and he joined her. He poured her a glass, handed it to her. As he did so, he ran his glance up and down her, stopping at her necklace. "The dress goes well with amber," he said. "Where did you get it?"

"Like the violin. Passed down from my grandmother," she said.

He studied it more closely. "The tears of Birute," he murmured. He touched the stone lightly, and she twitched back, surprised.

He raised a courteous face to her. "That's what amber is called in Lithuania," he said. "It's a fine piece, and I was admiring the bee in it. I see you found my choice of dress satisfactory."

"It'll do," she admitted. "But I didn't bring anything to change into, so you'll have to wait to get it back."

He waved a long, fine hand, brushing that aside. "It's yours, Austeja. I had it made for you."

"You - what?"

"Before I left the country I stopped in New York, gave Ms. Wong some specs, and asked her to make it. Your online photo helped with coloring and so on."

Suddenly, she understood how Vince felt. Obligation and gratitude struggled within her. A number of sentences formed in her mind. You shouldn't have. Thank you. What do I owe you? I always wanted a dress like this. None of them seemed quite up to the occasion.

She took a sip of wine, looked the room over. "You bounce around all alone in this big house?" she asked.

His mouth turned up in a half grin. "Very good," he said. "You stifled your best and worst impulses and moved on, choosing to seek rather than give information."

"Maybe," she said, "but you haven't answered my question. There's no Mrs. Vecchio, off on a cruise or something?"

"Nothing of the kind. But I'm not entirely alone. There's Henry, and the rest of the staff. And I sometimes entertain people who like a lot of room for their money to bounce around in."

"In Upstate New York? Not the Big Apple, or Paris or something."

"I have places in both cities. And Prague, and – well, a few others."

"Of course." She walked around the room, doing her own sniffing. Then she looked up at a wall and stopped cold. She saw an oil painting, an original, of what might be a tree, or a neural ganglion, or twisted bones rising through mist. It was all browns and oranges, with shadows of black, disappearing into forever. The title was Memory.

"Is that – O'Keeffe? An original?" she asked, stunned.

"Yes. I admire her work. You?"

She reached up, wishing she could run her fingers ever so lightly over the air just above the surface of it, wanting to know how the paint was laid on, how choices were made for shadow and light. "I might be convinced to trade my soul for this one," she admitted. Her arm stayed reaching, and she couldn't seem to pull it back.

"I can ask Henry to bring a ladder," Nick said.

She lowered her arm. "Sorry. She's one of the holy of holies for me. I don't know what I like more – her trees, bones, or flowers. What else do you have?"

"A small Monet. Some contemporary American artists I expect to do well, for investment purposes. Also a Mikalojus Ciurlionis, because I like his style."

She turned to him abruptly. Another holy of holies. A Lithuanian musical composer and a brilliant painter. He'd said he perceived vision as music, and music as vision. She'd seen his work online, but to see it in the original was something else altogether.

"Which one? Where?" she asked.

"I'll show you."

He led her down the hall, up the curving staircase and past a number of doors until they reached a double oak door carved with leaves and trees. She wanted to stop and admire it, but he opened it to what was apparently his bedroom.

She noted that none of it was flamboyant, as she thought it would be. It was, in fact, rather austere, with a white and green leaf printed bedspread and soft blue curtains, the furniture all simple mission style. She would have worried that this was the equivalent of an invitation to see his etchings, but she raised her eyes to the wall facing the bed and saw the painting, at which point she no longer cared.

An authentic, original Ciurlionis. The Angel, with its lush red and orange wings that managed somehow to be almost translucent. It was folded in on itself at the top of a butte as if it grew from the earth, overlooking water crossed by bridges, and stairs traversed by ancient robed figures. Memory and possibility mingled here, an invisible world existing simultaneously with everyday reality.

"The emotional landscape of your people, Austeja," Nick said.

"Maybe," she replied, as she continued to stare at it. "My grandmother had an Estonian friend, who told me Lithuanians weren't good for anything except making art. She advised me to marry an Estonian man, and then I could do as I pleased."

"But you haven't taken her advice," he said, a statement rather than a question.

She shook her head. "I've had enough of Baltic men."

She approached the painting, which was perfectly placed to be viewed while lying in bed, low enough on the wall for her to reach it. She didn't touch, but ran her fingers in the air just above its surface, tracking brushstrokes, discerning the melding of colors that created depth.

"You always look with your skin?" he asked.

She shrugged. It hadn't occurred to her that this was worth remarking on. And right now, she cared more about the painting than herself.

"I like his angel," she said. "It's more sensual than most. More earthbound."

"Like you, draped in red and gold. Do you think that's a Lithuanian sensibility?"

"Could be," she said, thinking of her sketches, of bones and trees and bees. "My angels are heavier. Maybe because I grew up with strange photos of funerals, and groups of grim faced people posed in forests or cemeteries for no apparent reason."

"Your relatives?"

"I suppose. My mother didn't know, and my grandmother died before I was old enough to ask her."

"Do you still have people in the old country?"

She smiled at this term. Her grandmother always referred to Lithuania that way, and in her mind it had become a fantastic place of castles, demons and fairies. This painting, in sepia tones.

"I don't have a clue," she said. "My grandmother used to get letters from people, but she didn't write back. She was afraid. I think the Soviets did something to her when she was young, and she never got over it."

"She didn't talk about it?"

"No. Even my mother didn't know."

"Ah. A family trait. Not talking about things. Well, they're free of the Soviets now. The first country to make the move, in fact. You know how they did it?"

She smiled. "They sang," she said.

She'd watched coverage of the event on the news. First there was the Baltic Way, where two million Estonians, Latvians and Lithuanians made a 370 mile human chain across the Baltic states. Then came the people gathering in the squares of cities and towns to sing their ancient folk tunes, their forbidden Catholic hymns and national songs. The Soviets attacked the peaceful protestors who gathered in Vilnius, at the TV tower, killing fourteen people, wounding many others. But the rest kept singing, and on March 11, 1990, they were the first Baltic state to declare their independence.

"That's right," Nick said. "The Singing Revolution. Your ancestors were a people insane enough to try and change the world through song. And now, after centuries of fighting off Teutonic Knights and Russians and Poles and Mongolian hordes, they belong only to themselves."

"They've had other times when that was true. They were independent from 1918 to 1940. And they creamed the Teutonic Knights under Vytautus, who had the Kahn brothers golden horde in his service, and who also beat the tar out of the Brits."

"Austeja, you know your history. I'm impressed. Have you been to the ancestral homeland?"

"No. Not yet."

"You'd like to go?"

"Someday. It's not first on my list."

"What is?"

"Italy, I think. The Etruscan tombs."

"Any artist would," he granted.

"I'm not an artist," she pointed out. "I'm in marketing."

"According to your Estonian friend, you have no choice. It's genetic."

She opened her mouth to protest, but a small tone, emanating from an unknown source, interrupted. Nick gestured at a red light above the door. "That's Henry, giving fair warning. Dinner is served. Let's proceed in stately argument to the dining room."

❧

Whether through research or paying attention or good guesswork, he served all the food she loved best. A truffled foie gras, germiny l'oseiol, duck in port wine cherry sauce, sweet young peas. She had a high metabolism and a healthy appetite, and she ate it all. He watched her, seeming to enjoy her pleasure more than his own plate.

"You like the duck? My cook is archetypal as well."

"It's wonderful," she admitted.

"Good. If you can slow down long enough, tell me what you've been doing with yourself."

"Working," she said.

"Working at tree paintings? Angel paintings?"

She looked up at him, startled. "How do you know that?"

"There's the drawing you tried to hide in your office, and your comment about your angels compared to Ciurlionis. And it's under your nails. Browns and greens, white and grey. I'm not sure why the gold stain on the pinkie, though."

He pointed at her fingers as he spoke. She looked at them. "Oh," she said.

"I told you, I pay attention," he said. "And I'd guess it's going well, since you're too distracted to clean them. Do you talk about it, or does that interfere with the process?"

"It's nothing. Just a dead tree sketch, and - and a ribcage with a bee hive in it."

His fork clattered against his plate. Unlike him to be clumsy. He lifted a cool face and smiled at her. "Honeybees?"

"Actually, yes," she said. "I've been having these dreams, and then we had a bee invasion at my office. So it all kind of mixed in together." She gestured helplessly, suddenly finding that she was, in fact, inarticulate about it. She'd never been asked to talk about painting before. Her parents saw it as a hobby to be indulged, and Martha admired, but didn't ask about process. The one time she tried telling Grant about it he said she was too interior, and she should get out more.

Nick scanned her and didn't press for information, for which she was grateful. Instead, he went back to history. "Your Lithuanian ancestors stayed pagan longer than any other country in Europe, and they worshipped bees," he noted. "Did you know that? Your name . . ."

"I know," she said. "The bee goddess. It was my – let's see - my great great grandmother's name. Supposedly, I also have her eyes. And her attraction to devils."

"Pardon me?"

Stacey shrugged. "Something my grandmother said, when she was dying."

He lifted a hand. "More, please," he requested.

"She said to be careful. That the devil would find me, but I'd know what to do."

"Oh, really?"

"She warned my mother, too. Something about the women in my family liking devils. I guess she thought it explained why mom married my father."

Nick continued to regard her with his smoothest deadpan, and she took it as in invitation to continue. She found herself telling him about her grandmother's love of toads and snakes, and moved from there to telling him about the angel dream she'd had, how different her angel was from Ciurlionis's. He listened attentively, courteously, seeming truly interested, and she let herself ramble on for quite some time.

Finally, she grew uncomfortable with the one-sided nature of the conversation and stopped. "Is this all terribly boring to you?" she asked.

"No," he said, though he offered no enthusiasm either.

"Do venture capitalists have odd dreams?" she asked, hoping he'd take the conversational ball and run with it for a while."

"I don't dream at all," he said, and again was quiet, watching her. He seemed a different person here in his own home – less flashy, more brooding and watchful.

She paid attention to her food, found that her plate couldn't tell her what she needed to know, and raised her face to his. "Why am I here?" she asked.

This earned her a grin. "Is that an existential question?"

"I told you. I'm a realist. And realistically, you aren't someone who just invites a person over for dinner, however nicely you dress them, unless you have an agenda."

"Is that what you think?" he asked.

"I think," she said, "you're goal oriented. So just tell me your goal, and we'll see if it'll work out."

He put his fork down, leaned back in his chair. "If my interest was romantic, you've successfully squashed it. You realize that, don't you?"

"It's not romantic," she said. "If it was, you'd have done something about it in your bedroom."

"Not if I'm courting you," he said.

"Are you?" she asked.

He smiled. "In a sense. I'm considering taking you on as a kind of project, to see if it's possible to tempt a 21st century woman away from the fast track. All to serve the purpose of determining if your soul is worth brokering, of course."

Back to that again. She shook her head. "I wish I knew if you meant that, or if it's just an elaborate pick-up line."

For the first time since she'd met him, she saw him scowl. He rose from his chair, moved to where she sat, slipped his hand behind her neck and tilted her face up to his.

His hand was cool and smooth against her skin, large enough to easily cup the back of her head. It held her firmly, with confidence in his right to do so. From this perspective he looked less like an angel, more like a degenerate rock star. His dark eye flashed, and his light one stayed cool green. The aspect was confusing, daunting. She closed her eyes, not sure if she anticipated a kiss, or just wanted to avoid looking at him.

"What makes you think I'd need a line?" he murmured.

She felt his hand slip away, and she jerked herself upright. When she opened her eyes, he was seated again, good duck on his fork, on the way to his mouth.

There was no reasonable answer, so she attempted none. Instead, she picked up her own fork and ate in silence. Let him come up with something to say.

Soon enough, he did. "I'm not in this for cheap thrills," he said. "But I do want to corrupt you, in ways you can't yet imagine. And in service of my mission, I'm taking you away for a small vacation."

"Are you, now? I think my boss might have something to say about that."

"I cleared it with him."

"You what?"

"That's what I had to talk with him about."

"He agreed?"

"I know him. More importantly, he knows me. And you won't be gone long. He seemed to think it was worth it."

"Well, jesus almighty. What if I don't want to go?"

"I think you will." He reached under the table and pressed something. The archetypal butler appeared silently at his side. "Bring the catalog, would you, Henry?"

"Certainly, sir," Henry said. He slid out of the room and returned quickly, laid a full color catalog at the side of Nick's plate. He gave a discreet bow and slid away again.

Nick pushed the catalog at Stacey. "See if you like it," he said.

She leafed through it, more to give herself time for a polite no than anything else. But then, something caught her eye. Delicate colors on stone, ephemeral, but detailed and intricate in their complexity. She stared at it, then read the copy.

This was no travel agent's catalog. It was from an auction house, selling certain antiquities that happened to be located on private property, also for sale. A villa in Italy, outside of Rome. A villa that happened to have two Etruscan tombs on its property.

She couldn't help herself. She whistled low and soft.

"Roberto was a very nice man, but a very old one when I met him. He died recently, and the estate's up for grabs. I'm considering a purchase. I don't currently have a place in Italy and I'd like one. I want you to go see it with me."

"I – I don't have a passport," she said.

"I've got one for you," he said.

She blinked up at him. She could have asked how he managed that, but she didn't really care. There was only one pertinent question in her mind. "Why me?" she asked.

"Haven't I stated it clearly enough, or do you just refuse to believe me? I'm trying to lead you astray of the American dream, seduce you with higher things. Art, vision, and long withheld aspirations."

"I wouldn't sell my soul for that."

He leaned close, tapped the back of her hand with his fork. "Before you even consider selling it, you have to find it," he said. "I take these things one step at a time."

She pulled back from his touch, toyed with her food. He waited it out. In not too much time, she grinned up at him.

"When do we leave?" she asked.

The rest of the evening was composed of deciding the logistics of their trip, with Nick at his most dry and practical. His car returned her to her own, and from there she drove home, smiling and still unkissed.

When she crawled into bed and fell asleep, she dreamt not of Italy, but of trees, and their burnished pain, caught between two worlds.

The Tree

Kaunus Lithuania, Circa 1415 AD

"Well?" the Bishop demanded. "Who will do this thing?"

The crowd shuffled and murmured, but no one answered. The Bishop raised his eyebrows and struck his staff against the ancient oak tree he stood under, near the great stone church where he said mass. Someone in the crowd gasped. He cast a steely glance that way.

"Idolatry," he declared. "You worship the tree, bring offerings, pray to it for blessings that come only from God. The old temptations must die. It must be cut down."

Audra stood with the Bishop's servants, just behind him. It was her day to work at his house, a way of paying rent for the land they farmed, which church and lords laid claim to. Though she didn't understand how the land could belong to anyone who didn't work it, she knew the Bishops and Dukes were powerful and wealthy, living in fine houses, always eating well while many others went hungry. They could do as they pleased, setting rules for all no matter if they made sense or not.

But she was surprised she'd heard no murmurs of his plan to cut down the tree. She usually learned all the Bishop's plans, either by listening carefully as she worked, when no one thought she understood their talk, or from gossiping with his other servants. She knew when Gintaras got in trouble with the priest for keeping a zaltys in his house and feeding it. She knew when Gabija would be scolded from the pulpit for keeping the ceremonies of hearth and fire. But none had mentioned killing this ancient tree, which the people still honored with gifts and prayers.

Of course they did, because trees gave a home to the honeybees, to the spirits of the ancestors and to their ancient gods. They were kind enough to offer them shelter, and kind enough to let you speak with those who lived within them, gathering their wisdom, learning your own destiny. But these men who worked for the Pope didn't understand this. They hated the trees, as if they were enemies, though she didn't know why.

She searched the crowd and caught sight of her mother, whose face questioned her. Why hadn't she told them of this? She shrugged. If she'd known, she would have, her look said, and her mother accepted that with a small nod. Then she set her face tight and spoke loud enough to be heard.

"Why can't you have your churches, and leave our trees in peace?" she demanded. She shook her head, her silver eyes flashing.

Audra thought her mother beautiful, her hair like honey and amber, her eyes like the sparkling silver waters of the river. Though the nobility in the cities had taken on this new god, those in the countryside continued in the old ways, and their farmlands prospered because of her mother's songs. Even her name, Austeja, was that of their ancient bee goddess, and she knew the bees and all their ways.

The Bishop moved his glance toward her. "What are you saying? You there!" he called out, pointing at Austeja.

She lifted her proud chin. "I said our trees have done you no wrong."

"What is your name?" The Bishop asked.

"Austeja," she said. "I'm mother to Audra."

"Who?"

She turned a smile to those nearby. "Audra, who stands behind you. She works for you two days a week, because you claim our land. Don't you know her?"

The Bishop was abashed, but turned that quickly to indignation. He looked down at the crowd, disgusted. "I know you all," he said. You practice secretly in your pagan ways, adoring sun, moon and trees. You hold snakes and toads as gods, feeding and housing the evils things, treating them better than priests, though your own rulers teach you better." He pointed a long finger at Austeja. "Your ways are over," he declared. "You live in sin, but your daughter will not."

There was murmuring, some of it from those who disagreed, and some from those who agreed. The Bishop turned his attention to the crowd. "Well? Who will cut this tree, ending your sin?"

Nobody moved.

Austeja laughed. "No one will do this evil, Velnias."

Audra was frightened, hearing her mother call this powerful man Velnias, a name the priests said belonged to devils, to the most profane of creatures. The Bishop served the god of the wealthy and the learned. Surely he would not let a peasant call him such names. Yet, what he wanted was wrong. Audra knew that as well.

How could he kill the tree? Why would he do so? Its branches and thick trunk were home to so many. Honeybees lived there, in a hive high up, near where lightning had sheared off its back, leaving an open hole. Perkunas came to scorch it, but the bees protected it from his wrath. And birds nested in it, singing morning and night, bringing messages her mother was teaching her to understand. Somehow, those who worked for the Pope didn't understand any of that.

The Bishop, seeing the crowd divided, turned back to Austeja, who held the old world in her hands. "You risk damnation, but your daughter will learn God's word."

Austeja drew herself up tall and eyed him hard. "You cannot take her from me."

The Bishop hesitated. The crowd stared at him, their eyes watchful and impenetrable. He'd spent many years here, and had learned the stubborness of this stiff-necked people. He held a hand out, offering rather than demanding. "She works here. And here, she learns to read and write. Would you deny her that?"

Austeja frowned. Learning was not something to be turned away. Not ever. And she trusted her daughter to know what was true, disregarding what was not. "Then teach her. But she is still my daughter. She comes home to me."

Quick whispers moved through the crowd, confirming that Austeja, protector of the old ways, had done well. Her daughter would learn the new ways, but she would remain one of the people. The Bishop, hearing none of it, grasped Audra firmly by the arm.

"She will choose," he said. "The old ways, or the good way."

The crowd murmured, shifted, knowing a challenge had been laid before them, and it all rested on the daughter of Austeja. She looked back at her mother, and saw her reassuring face. It said she would know what to do, when the time came.

æ

The tree remained standing, and Audra continued to cook and clean for the Bishop as she'd always done, sleeping in the good beds he provided at the back of the house.

In between these days she'd go back to the farm and her family, where life remained unchanged. Though the farm house was small and poor, events were rich with interest. Girantas wanted to marry her older sister. The hay was growing high in the fields, and the bees were making honey. Her mother taught her the songs to sing to Alkos and the trees, and her grandmother went to the hives, singing in thanks for their honey.

The only change was that now she went into the Bishop's study, where he taught her to read from a book he called the Bible, and then asked her questions about what she'd read. Some parts of it were like stories her mother told, about how things began. Others weren't as interesting, but she learned to pay attention because if she didn't, he'd crack a stick across her back. Fortunately, her mind took in stories easily and held them close once they were in. Only twice had she gotten the stick. After that, he sometimes even praised her, saying, "You learn well. You'll be a good Christian, in spite of your upbringing, and that will be an example to your people."

One day, while he was reading to her, they were interrupted by one of his servants bringing in a young man. He was dark-haired, and had strange amber and night eyes. He said his name was Naktis, and he'd heard the Bishop needed help.

"You have a tree that needs cutting," he said. "I can do that."

The Bishop looked him up and down. "Where are you from?" he asked.

"I was born in Nida," he said, "But I travel, doing work where it's needed."

The Bishop nodded. He turned to Audra. "You see. There are men who do God's will everywhere, in spite of your people's wickedness."

When Audra went home she told her mother, who listened carefully and seemed unworried until Audra said the man's name. At that she grew determined.

"Leave it to me," she said. "I'll take care of this. But listen. If I fail and the tree is cut, take the sap and put it in this." She handed her the small jar she wore around her neck when she went into the forest to sing or find honey.

"What do I do with it?" Audra asked.

"Keep it. You'll know how to use it, when the time comes," her mother said.

When Audra returned to the Bishop's house Naktis found her as she was cleaning the kitchen. He stood in the doorway, eyeing her as he often did. She ignored him.

"You told your mother, didn't you?" he said at last. "What is she planning?"

Audra said nothing. She got a broom and began to sweep. He put a hand on it, stopping her. "Tell your mother I must do this, to redeem my soul."

She shuffled from one foot to the other, looking down, saying nothing.

"She'll understand," he continued. "I lost my soul, long ago. Now, I cannot feel, except for an old hunger, a burning that won't cease. Everything else is dim, as if someone else felt it. Sometimes I almost grasp it, but it slips away and that is even worse torture." He bent to her, spoke quietly. "I tried serving your gods. I killed the priests and protected the trees, and still I suffer. But they say the bishop's god has power over any demon, and forgives all wrongs."

"The tree is innocent," Audra noted. "Should it die to save you?"

"Yes," he hissed. "Am I not more than a tree?"

She looked at him and wondered what the right answer was. He was a man, and that was a splendid thing. But no birds nested on him. No bees made their home inside him. No spirits crowded around him. He offered sustenance to nothing. And he would kill for an idea, which no bee or bird would ever do.

"I think," she said, "the tree has some things to teach you."

He scowled, raised his hand and slapped her with the back of it. "Little girl. What do you know?" Then, he stalked away.

The next week the people gathered by the tree at the Bishop's command, but they were a sullen, silent crowd.

"God always provides for his will, and he wills this idolatry to end," the Bishop said. He nodded at Naktis, who stood nearby with an ax. "This man will cut the tree, and then all will attend mass."

Naktis moved to the tree. Audra, standing near the bishop, was startled to see her mother move out from the crowd. She went to the tree and stood in front of it, her strong back pressed against it, her arms stretched out as if she was crucified here.

"Blasphemy," the Bishop gasped, furious. "Get her away," he commanded his men.

They dragged her off, but she began a great wailing, and the crowd stirred. The Bishop pointed at Naktis. "Cut it now," he called out, and Naktis raised his axe.

Just as he did, Austeja slipped away from those who held her, ran to the tree and pressed her back against it. Whether Naktis could not or would not stop his axe nobody knew, but it fell just as she arrived, catching her at her belly.

For a moment, all was still. Naktis stared at her, and she at him. His eyes grew wide with disbelief, and hers grew large with what looked like triumph.

"Their god cannot save you from yourself," she said. Then, as the blood poured out of her, she closed her eyes and slumped over.

Somebody screamed. Someone else began to wail. Naktis dropped his axe and pointed at the Bishop, crying out, "I was doing your work. *Your* work!"

Audra, frozen in horror, thought she heard someone answer him, saying, "No, my friend, you were doing mine."

She blinked, and saw a man standing near the Bishop, a tall shadow surrounded by fire. She felt the world going dim, and slid to the ground.

Audra woke in a soft bed, with the Bishop looking down at her. When he spoke, his voice held sorrow, and kindness. "I would not have had that happen, child," he said gently. "I meant no harm to your mother. I've sent what I could to your family, to make amends, and I'll continue to do so. You can live and work here for pay as long as you want, and all the girls in your family after can do the same."

Blood money, she thought. Well, maybe it would help. Her mother had done a lot of work, and who would replace that? Still, it wasn't enough.

He patted her hand. "You must rest," he said. "One of the monks will bring herbs that are soothing."

"Where is he?" she whispered.

"Who?" he asked.

"Naktis. Stribas."

He winced. Destroyer, she called him. "It wasn't his fault. He had no time to stop his ax. You must forgive him."

"I know," she said. "I want to tell him that."

He looked at her solemnly. "You are a true Christian. But I sent Naktis away. The people were angry, and I didn't want them to do him a harm."

She sighed. She had also hoped to do him a harm, after she forgave him.

The Bishop touched her head, blessed her. "Sleep, child. God watches you."

But she did not sleep. When he was well gone, she rose and dressed, let herself out of the house. She carried the small jar her mother gave her, which held the sap of many trees and the honey of ancient hives, and drops of the special midus they still knew how to make. She moved quietly through the dark until she came to the place where the tree was fallen, its branches still scattered on the ground.

She saw the dark patch that was her mother's blood, but she had no time to grieve that now. She must do as her mother asked.

She put a hand on the stump, feeling its sorrow. "I will care for you," she whispered to her mother, to the tree. "You'll live on in many ways."

She scouted among the fallen branches and picked a good one. She looked among the rest of the branches and gathered sap with her fingers and put it in the jar. Last, she wet her fingers and wiped them in her mother's dried blood. That, too, she put into the jar. Then she returned to her bed in the Bishop's house.

Someday she would have daughters. Perhaps one of them would have her mother's eyes. If not, then some granddaughter. Either way, she would tell them all that had happened, so they could protect themselves against evil when it found them, as it surely would.

Chapter Nine

Upstate New York, early 21st Century

Nick's driver picked Stacey up in the morning and brought her to the airport, led her to a back gate through security, and from there to a runway where a small jet waited.

She eyed it. "This?" she asked. She was a nervous flyer at best, and avoided small airborne vehicles.

"It's Mr. Vecchio's private jet," the driver said. He saw the look on her face. "Don't worry. It's fully stocked, and his pilot's the best. I've been in it myself."

He gestured to her to go up the steps, and she did so. Inside, she saw Nick, seated in a swiveling leather chair, talking on his cell phone.

"No," he said. "They'll merge. I'm telling you, not asking you. Get the stock." He smiled tightly, closed the phone, and swiveled to her, looking her up and down.

"Oh," he said. "You don't like flying."

"It shows?" she asked.

He pointed at her hands. "Fists. Not a good sign. Have a glass of champagne. It soothes all ills, for most people."

She drank two glasses, which got her through take-off. Then she had another, and was convinced to look out the window at the tiny cities below. She saw them through her fingers pressed against the glass. At her back, Nick chatted about points of interest. She had a sudden impression of being hovered over by a winged creature, as in her dreams, but she wasn't sure if the wings were feathered and white, translucent red and gold, or made of darkly drying leaves.

Her other hand stayed in a fist, and after a while, he stopped talking. "Well, I was going to give this to you once we arrived, but maybe it will help now." He handed her a sketchbook and a pack of good pencils.

She stared at them. "I can't," she said.

He didn't bother to argue. He unwrapped the pencils, took out a red one and put it in her hand, opened the sketchbook and put it on her lap. "Let's see what your hands say about it," he said. "There's plenty of champagne, if you want more." Then he left her alone.

He went back to his cell phone, talking commerce to a variety of people in different languages. The feel of a pencil in her grasp sparked the right neurons, and she started to move it across the paper. She sensed Nick watching her, but she ignored him. Her random lines were becoming something. Working out the perspective of a hand on a window that looked down over tiny cities, with dark wings hovering somewhere behind got her through most of the flight. More champagne took care of the rest.

❧

They landed in a gust of wind, to find heat and a setting sun. Nick took her arm and led her through Rome's airport toward a car that brought them into the city and their hotel. To her surprise, they had separate rooms. She didn't comment on it, but he saw her face, which was incapable of hiding anything after the champagne.

"It's an old world courtesy," he noted. "You'll be glad of it, as we go on. For instance, you'll want to shower in decent privacy and get your head back on straight. By the way, we have two days before the villa viewing. What would you like to see?"

"Everything," she sighed happily.

"Well, let's start with dinner. I'll knock on your door in an hour, and we'll go find something interesting to eat. That's impossibly easy around here. Tomorrow, the Vatican. Do you want an audience with Il Papa?"

"Can you get one?"

"If he's in town."

She considered, then shook her head. "I'm afraid of what I'd say to him."

"A good Catholic like you? Rude to his Holiness?"

"I'm not a good Catholic, and he's not holy to me," she said.

"What is, besides O'Keeffe and Ciurlionis?"

His tone had changed, and she saw that brooding expression he'd had at his house. He was serious. He really wanted to know.

"Lots of things," she said. "Certain slants of light. Certain feelings or experiences. Incredible acts of courage or love. Trees and stones. Snakes and birds and toads and whatever gives them life."

"You mean that, don't you?"

She nodded. "I decided some time ago to only tell you the truth. You expect lies, and it's more fun to see your shock when you don't get them."

He laughed. "You're still drunk, or you wouldn't be confessing all that. Fortunately, I'm in no position to absolve you. Go shower, and I'll see you soon."

☙

They found a trattoria near the hotel and had some of the best pasta she'd ever eaten, rich with olives and artichokes. Puttanesca, it was called. Nick said that meant whore's pasta.

"It's what working women made, between customers. Or to draw customers."

She raised her wine. "Then here's to working women," she said. But she noticed he paid more attention to her pleasure than his own "Don't you like it?" she asked.

"I recognize that it's good, but I have the same problem with food that I have with alcohol."

She raised an eyebrow at him, fork poised in front of her mouth.

"I don't taste food the way you do. Flavors are muted."

"Is that a neurological thing?"

"Don't worry about it, Austeja. It's not your problem."

She realized he knew a great deal more about her than she did about him, and she thought it was time to correct the balance.

"Yes, but I'm curious. Was it genetic, maybe a Y chromosome thing?"

"No," he said shortly.

"Oh. Well, what was he like – your father? Italian, right? Vecchio."

"No. That's not his name. I told you, I chose the name for myself."

"Vecchio. That means old, doesn't it? Are you?"

"I'm like the song. Stardust, golden, and billion year old carbon. So are you."

"Maybe, but I'm not caught in the devil's bargain. Not yet, anyway. So tell me about your father. What was he like?"

"You might say he's pure evil."

She was shocked, and her face showed it. His deadpan dissolved, and he laughed.

"Or you might say he's pure good. Or a mixture of the two. You might say anything you want about him, and I wouldn't contradict you, because I left him when I was too young to judge. Let's leave it at that. Are you sure you want to see the Vatican?"

She considered wrangling more about it, but saw it was useless, so she moved on. "Sure," she said. "They had the most money and got a lot of the best art." She tilted her head, determined to get at least one piece of solid information about him before the night was through. "Are you Catholic or - or anything?"

"You can call me a freelance pagan," he said. "Though I do admire the church."

"For what?"

"For their attachment to power, and their ability to maintain it. During the AIDS epidemic, their infallible leader went to Africa and advised its citizens not to use condoms. And he got away with it. Amazing. I'm surprised you don't want to meet a man like that, but I'll let it pass. I can arrange private tours of other parts, if you like."

"No," she said. "Let's be peasants, and join with the madding crowd."

"*Kaip norite, valstiete.*"

"What?"

"As you wish, peasant. Finish your pasta. No desert tonight. In about five minutes the time change and the carbs will catch up and you'll drop off in your tira misu."

He was right. She was stumbling and bleary eyed as they made their way back to their hotel. And he was also right that she was glad to have her own room. She didn't want any gropings in the night, though she wondered if and when he'd make a move.

In the morning he knocked on her door and they moved through heat and teeming tourists to the Vatican, where she admired the art, and the general air of ancient power.

As they stood staring up at the Dome of St. Peter's Basilica, Nick raised his head and breathed in gustily. "You can smell the sanctity and the blood, can't you? I suppose there's actually more of the latter here than in the coliseum."

A few tourists turned his way and looked shocked. He showed them a wicked grin. "Diabalo," a middle-aged woman in black dress and headscarf said. He bowed to her and moved Stacey forward.

"You trying to get us killed, or arrested for heresy?" she hissed at him.

"Neither is possible," he said. "They know me here."

He remained bright and cynical as they made their way through various chapels, whispering brittle words in her ear as the tour guide spoke, or saying them loudly when he was quiet.

"The Vatican's a very homoerotic institution, isn't it?" he asked her in the Sistine chapel as everyone stared up at God's hand reaching toward Adam's. "Big man touches little man and gives him life. But it's not all male. You see, Michelangelo painted Despair as a woman."

His knifelike wit stayed busy, and she wasn't sure if it amused or disturbed her. She'd said this wasn't holy to her, and being inside hadn't changed that, except for the art. To do this kind of work, on this scale, would be divine. Also, she supposed, tedious and difficult.

"What are your thoughts, Austeja?" he asked as she stared up.

"I'm wondering what I'd paint if someone gave me a ceiling this size."

"Nothing, if you're not an artist," he said. "A big if, I think."

She unbent her neck, raised an eyebrow at him.

He turned his face up to stare at the ceiling. "Michelangelo resented this commission," he said. "And the Pope was pretty upset that he didn't clothe his figures decently. Naked people prancing about the holy city wasn't what he had in mind."

Nick kept up his patter until they reached Botticelli's Temptation of Christ, when suddenly he grew silent. She'd gotten so used to his whisper in her ear that its absence disturbed her more than the biting commentary. She turned to him, saw him staring at Botticelli's Satan. His expression was neither mischievous nor acerbic. Instead it was grim, his pupils dilated.

"Are you okay?" she whispered.

He stayed silent, and she grew truly frightened. Was he having a seizure? A heart attack? She touched his arm, and he jerked into awareness, flicked a glance at her, then returned to the painting.

"It doesn't work that way," he said, his voice cold and grim as his face.

"Um – what?"

He pointed at the painting. "The story of Jesus and the Devil. Satan doesn't work that way. Laying the world at your feet and saying it's yours if you worship him is far too obvious. Makes it too easy to say no."

"Then what does he do?" she asked, keeping her tone light, not sure if this was more of his banter. But Nick's answer had nothing of fun in it.

"He sells you happy meals, and doesn't mention obesity," he said, his voice thick with bitterness. "He suggests war is sacred, if you'll gather souls to God or democracy or communism with it. He finds your need to belong, and whispers that strapping a bomb to yourself and blowing up children will get you virgins and admirers. He finds your greed and tells you the current economy is more important than the planet. He finds your fear of women and says you can control them, but doesn't mention that the only control is death. That's what he does. That's what he did."

His expression shifted, all feeling washed from it like an unpainted death mask. She thought if she peeled away the skin, she'd see a portrait of torture in a very deep hell. She blinked at him, trying to come up with something appropriate to say.

She thought of Father Pete. "I know a priest who says the devil wears business suits these days," she said. "I'd imagine they're good ones."

"Yes," he said dully. "The very best. Though sometimes they also wear mitres. Like the bishops in Lithuania, when Catholicism was accepted. They went through Vilnius and cut down the ancient oaks, the sacred trees."

"Huh," she said. "I didn't know that. Why would they?"

"They believed it was God's will, but I know who was behind it." He nodded at Satan. "But they couldn't tell the difference. How do you tell, when the time comes?"

Words fell out of her mouth, though she wasn't sure where they came from. "You feel it," she said. "In your heart."

He whipped around, stared at her hard. One hand clenched into a fist. He stared at it, deliberately relaxed. Then he turned and walked away, exiting the chapel.

Stacey stood still, chewing thoughtfully on her lower lip. She didn't think she'd said anything offensive. Nor did she believe he'd abandon her in Italy. He was strange, but she trusted his courtesy if nothing else. Finally, she decided that whatever just happened was between him and him, part of his past she knew nothing about. She thought it best to give him a little time to work it out.

She turned back to Botticelli, stared blankly at the devil being tossed off a cliff.

"Well," she said. "I suppose that's one way of doing it, if you're out of tears and love."

She spent another ten minutes staring at great art, then made her way outside.

In the bright Italian sun, she found Nick conversing, in fluent Italian, with an old lady who was putting down food for a milling group of feral cats. He was laughing, petting the cats. When he saw her, he showed her a bright smile.

"Ready for the coliseum?" he asked.

"Sure," she said. They moved on.

❧

Nick's good mood stayed with him throughout their Coliseum visit, but by the time they finished Stacey felt overwhelmed with antiquity and great deeds. She was glad to walk the streets and see bland people interacting in bland ways, sitting at cafes and rubbing weary feet, arguing in Italian or English or French or Russian about where to eat while Nick went back to amusing her with Vatican trivia.

"Did you know there was once a female pope? She passed herself off as male, but then she got pregnant. After that, when a pope was elected he had to sit in a chair with a hole at the bottom. The cardinals would pass beneath him and say, in Latin, 'he has balls. They hang well."

"You're making that up," she said.

"I don't think I am," he said. "I believe it's actually true. Gelato?"

"Of course."

They stopped at a stand and got two. He put his money back in his pocket, but when he pulled his hand out, a bill - an American fifty – came with it. It fluttered to the ground behind them as they walked.

Stacey moved to retrieve it. He grabbed her arm, kept walking forward.

"Let it go," he said. "Someone will pick it up. I'm not littering."

"But – that's fifty dollars," she said, looking back through the crowd.

"Austeja, your peasant roots are showing."

"What? Were you born rich? Family money?"

"I obtained wealth early. On my own. I have no family."

"You were born," she noted. "You didn't spring full grown from Athena's head or anything."

"I was very young when they died," he said flatly, and she detected no emotion in the statement.

"Oh. I'm sorry. How'd it happen?"

"An accident at sea. Don't sentimentalize. It was a long time ago. And I prefer staying in the present. For instance, I'd rather imagine who found that money, and what they'll do with it."

Part of her was irritated. She considered insisting he tell her more, insisting at least that he explain his behavior in the Vatican. But the sun was shining, and she was in Italy, and Nick was smiling mischievously. The day could be full of information, or fun. She chose fun.

"A little girl finds it, and she'll get all her friends together and they'll buy things their parents won't let them have," she said.

"Or," he suggested, "a drunk grabs it. He buys whisky and gets sloshed. Then he goes home and beats his wife to a pulp."

"Then you should go back and find it before that happens."

"Much too late for that. Your turn."

She saw what he was doing, putting her in the positive position while he stayed firmly in the negative. She wouldn't let him. "Hmm. Well, then maybe a sociopath, who'll buy a gun and kill a bunch of people in a church," she suggested.

He laughed. "Or a woman, out of work. She's got an interview coming up, but nothing to wear. She'll buy good clothes, get the job and live happily ever after."

"Ha," she said. "On fifty dollars? In Rome? Now who's dreaming?"

They walked the streets until dinner, found a place for another great meal, went from café to café trying local wines for a few hours, and returned to the Hotel, tired and satisfied with the day.

At least, Stacey was tired. Nick seemed as bright as when they started, and said he was going back to one of the cafés to get some wine shipped home. She was glad to let him do so on his own.

"What's on the agenda for tomorrow?" she asked as he saw her to her room.

"I thought the violin museum in Cremona," he said.

She made a face. "Staring at violins in cases?"

"Actually, they have to be played regularly, or they fall apart. And I happen to know the old man who has that job, so you could hear a Guarneri, a Strad, and an Amati."

"An old man plays them? Is he any good?"

"Quite good. And he takes the job seriously. He compares it to Michael Schumacher driving an F1 car. And the museum is full of information about how they're made, with the old forms and patterns to look at."

"Oh. Well, that sounds fine," she said.

He eyed her. "What's the problem?"

"You don't want to go to Mantua, and show me Pietro's house?"

A small smile came and went. "Austeja, I'm always surprised at what you know. You're aware of Pietro's history? How he left his family for Mantua and so on?"

"You bet. I know where and when the Amber was made."

"Then, if you'd prefer, we can go there. I thought that might be too much for you. Too emotional a journey."

His point. He was right, but she didn't know why. Something inside her hands twitched. Something in her soul stiffened at the thought. But she wouldn't admit it to him for any price.

"Not at all. Let's do that," she said.

"Are you sure? You look nervous."

"No. Of course not. I'm just tired."

His eyes glinted with either triumph, or amusement. "Then get some rest," he said, and took her key, opened her door, and waved her inside.

When the door closed behind her, she scanned her room and saw a package on the desk with her name on it. She opened it, and found a pack of oil pastels with Aquarelle paper, which she preferred for this medium, along with the right blending tools. Apparently, he knew how to shop for art as well as wine. A note was attached.

"This is not the last temptation," it read. "Not even close."

She toyed with them, then began to draw. Small sketches, just the outline of intent in colors and shapes. She hadn't worked with these in a while, and her hands needed to remember their limits and possibilities. She played with a fountain. A cat. The old lady who fed the cats. Then she stopped. That wasn't what she wanted to draw.

She got another piece of paper and sketched money falling onto a crowded street. A hand reached for it – a thin hand, pale white with bones showing through transparent skin. Another one – plump, rosy, with rings. A dirty bare foot trod on it, moving on.

She got that far, and suddenly felt exhausted, drained of all will to continue. But her own peculiar angel wouldn't release her yet, and so her hand kept going.

"This is why I don't want to be an artist," she grumbled. "It *owns* you."

Her hand insisted on a bench in the upper corner, some distance away from the fallen money. A creature sat on the bench – devil or angel or both, laughing or crying or both. Next to him sat a satisfied pope, female and pregnant. Underneath she wrote, 21st Century Temptation.

"Arrogant little bitch, aren't you?" she chided herself.

But none of that was what she really wanted to draw. Inside her mind, she saw a violin, glowing gold, a living creature filled with the blood of trees and the sting of ancient bees in human flesh. Something about going to Mantua, to the house of Pietro Guarneri. Something of memory, and frustrated desire.

She shook it off. "No," she told herself. "That's not what this trip is about."

Having decided not to give in to errant obsessions, she moved to her bed and fell quickly into determined sleep.

She slept for a few hours soundly, without dreams. But in the middle of the night she woke, or dreamt she woke, and saw that she stood near a grassy field, contemplating a golden violin she held loosely in one hand. Nearby, a man stared at her with dark hunger. An angel, the same she'd seen in her other dream, approached her, touched her arm, and led her to a mirror in the middle of the field. Only her image was reflected, though the angel stood behind her.

"Look in the mirror," it said, its voice containing and releasing all voices.

She did so, and saw her long legs as they were stripped of skin, flesh peeled away like masking tape, and underneath were silver flowing rivers. Her slim hips and torso became loamy earth, her breasts and shoulders grew into rounded hills with trees spreading and blossoming from them. Her eyes darkened like the sea at midnight, fringed with the pointed hair of stars.

All of this was poured into the violin she held, which glowed with the incandescence of moonlight poured over a grassy field. Her blood, her flesh, her voice, all became part of its wood and string. She carried it, and it carried her into the future, into days that were yet to be. And somehow, here she was made safe. Made secure against the incursions of all worlds.

But the transformation made her blood moan. Her burdened bones bent and swayed and she felt she would break, become brittle, thin and unimportant as dust dancing in the streams of light that pass through panes of glass in empty houses.

The Amber

Kaunus, Lithuania, circa 1665

Austeja was sweeping the steps to the Bishop's house when his guest first arrived. He stopped, stared at her, then moved on, disappearing inside. She didn't think about him again.

Many people came and went here, and it wasn't her job to think about them. Her job was to clean and cook, and learn her letters and Catechism as the Bishop insisted. This had been the job of girls in her family for generations. They received good pay, working here until they married, and then returning to their farms. They did this because long ago a Bishop had hurt one of their women. Caring for those who followed remained a debt of honor for all who came after him.

Her grandmother said she would work here longer than usual, because she was built lean as a boy, and might not round out for some time. Nobody would want her for marriage until then. But she didn't mind. She liked living here, where the beds were soft and the food was rich. She liked the learning and she especially liked the music. At home she sang the old songs. Here, she sang the new. It didn't matter, as long as she could sing.

She finished her sweeping, and brushed her short hair off her forehead. It still showed marks from where she'd been stung by bees on her last visit home. That was her own fault. She'd gone to the hives on a windy, cloudy day, and she brought no smoke. Naturally, they were angry at her discourtesy. She apologized to them and walked slowly back to her grandmother, who scolded her for her forgetfulness, blamed the Bishop for taking her away from her natural learning, then smoked her hair and cut it to release the now peaceful bees.

With short hair she looked even more like a boy. Her grandmother said the bees intended that, though she didn't know why.

"They'll tell you when they're ready," she said. "You just make sure you listen."

Her Senele was strange that way, following the old practices. When she made bread, she gave a piece to Zemyne. She used water from the Alkos, and dropped honey or pollen into a tree stump near the church whenever she passed, to feed the ancestors and gods who lived there.

Austeja was confused by this. She thought Senele should follow the Bishop's church, since so many others did. On the other hand, she felt a peace in the forest and with the bees that she didn't feel in the Bishop's house. She had to hide this part of her life with the Bishop, for he was vigilant against the old ways. When he asked what happened to her hair she said she'd got it full of sap climbing a tree for fruit.

He only sighed. "You're more like a boy than a girl, but I suppose that will change soon enough."

Once she finished sweeping the porch she went inside, expecting she'd have to wash the floor in the big dining room, but Marija, a kitchen servant, told her otherwise.

"Petre is sick," she said. "You'll wait on the Bishop's guests tonight."

"Who are they?" she asked.

"Some friends – and a visitor. Naktis. Take care with him. He's important."

She remembered seeing the man who stopped and looked at her. That must be Naktis. A name that meant night. "Why?" she asked.

"The Bishop wants a violin," she said.

"A what?"

"It's a musical instrument. They make them in Italy. The Bishop wants a good one, from the best violin maker, but they cost dear and are hard to come by. Naktis knows the violin maker, so the Bishop will go far to please him."

"What does he want with a violin? Does he know how to make music?"

"No, but his sister's son does. The Bishop wants to raise him up to play music for the church and the Dukes. No more questions. Get dressed – quickly!"

Marija gave her clothes. They were Petre's, but they fit, though they made her look even more like a boy. The Bishop's guests were a very beautiful woman, a priest, and Naktis. The talk was lively and filled with laughter, the Bishop less serious than usual. When Austeja carefully placed the wine on the table, Naktis turned to look at her.

"I saw you on the porch, sweeping. What's your name?" he asked.

She looked to the Bishop for permission to answer. He nodded kindly. He was a kind man. "Austeja," she said.

"That's a girl's name. Are you a girl child?"

She nodded.

"You look like a boy," he said, amused.

"It's the hair," the Bishop said. "Her grandmother cut it, after she got it full of tree sap. These people are both stubborn and stupid. In spite of all we teach them, the farmers still keep snakes and toads in their houses, letting them drink from the cows. They won't give them up, saying it's how they speak with their ancestors. If a priest tries to take one away, they fight like the devil."

Everyone laughed, but Austeja blushed from both shame and anger. Naktis saw it, and looked at her with something like sympathy.

"But I'm instructed to return with a servant for Pietro, and this specimen might do," he said. "Someone who listens well. She is obedient, isn't she?"

"Quiet and obedient," he said. "She knows her letters and her Catechism. She'd be a good member of the church, if her grandmother left her alone."

"She'll have to, if I take her. And I'd like to do that."

The Bishop seemed uncertain, but Naktis said, "sir, it's a good deal all around. Pietro will be pleased to have a servant you pay for. You'll be pleased at getting your violin, and the child will profit from learning better than what her grandmother teaches. Also, God will be pleased to claim yet another soul."

The Bishop considered, but then he shook his head. "I would not put her in harm's way," he said. "We owe her family a debt that should not be repaid with ill treatment."

"Nor will it be. She'll be well treated. None will trouble her innocence."

At that he assented. So the arrangement was made, without consent of her or her family. But two days later, her mother and grandmother came to tell her goodbye.

"You're going to another land, child," her mother said. "A place full of good chances."

"Maybe," she said, "I don't want to go."

"If you don't go," her grandmother said, "we'll all suffer for it."

Austeja sighed. "Then I'll go," she said.

Her grandmother grunted, satisfied. "I may be dead before you come back," she said. "Take this with you." She gave her the small jar of sap and honey she wore on a cord around her neck, a short oak stick, and a chain with a piece of amber, along with a pair of amber earrings.

"Will I come back?" Austeja asked, already homesick for the bees and the forest.

"You must," her mother said. "The women in our family always find their way home."

⮞

Naktis brought her to a boat whose motion made her stomach turn. "Don't get sick on yourself," he said. "You won't meet your new master green and stinking."

Austeja worked hard to hang on to her breakfast, and Naktis kept talking. "By the way, since you look like a little boy, you're going to be one. I didn't tell the Bishop, but Pietro would never let a girl see his craft. Girls can't be trusted with secrets. So your name is Razak now, and you'll dress as a boy, keep your hair short."

She frowned. "Why did you take me, if he wants a boy?"

Naktis stared out at the water. "Because I want you there. That's all you need know."

She accepted that, but had another problem. "I don't like that name. Razak."

"What's wrong with it? It belongs to a friend of mine from long ago."

She couldn't answer, but knew her own mind. "I don't like it. I won't take it on."

"Then choose one of your own."

"I'll be Azuolas," she said. That meant oak tree. It would remind her of home.

Naktis brought her to a city called Mantua, a dusty, noisy place compared to her home. But there was a great deal of music in it, and she liked that. Someone was always singing, or playing an instrument, and usually they did it well. For the most part, she did her work as she'd done for the Bishop, sweeping or cleaning without complaint or comment.

Her new master was often away playing music, for he was a fine musician as well as a violin maker. That meant the boys could joke more, and there was often laughter in the shop, which she liked even if she didn't understand what they said. The language here was slippery on her tongue. Little by little, she was learning it, but the way she pronounced it made the boys laugh even more. She called her master Signor Pietro, because her mouth wouldn't make his last name at all.

When he was present, the work was still easy. She swept the sawdust and wood curls from the floor and put them in the firebin. She cleaned his varnish pots and kept his tools in order, mysterious and beautiful things, cool and weighty in the hand. She liked the smells, the fresh wood, the varnish mixtures, the bee glue that sealed the wood. Between gestures and the new words she was beginning to learn, she managed to ask where the bees lived, and was told they stayed in hives at the Signor's house.

"Can I tend them?" she asked.

"*Non e tua laborio,*" she was told. It wasn't her work.

That made her sad, but at night she sang to the bees she knew were nearby, and thanked them for helping with the violins.

The Signor was neither cruel nor kind. In fact, he paid no attention to her, except to tell her what to do. His eyes were always on his work, which he did perfectly. She admired his hands as they cut and planed the pieces of spruce, glued them, prepared and bent the ribs that were so important, used the small plane on his thumb to complete the arching. He stroked the varnish on his violins as if it was a woman's flesh.

In her first year, she learned a great deal just from watching. After everyone left the shop she would linger to clean, and then she'd pick up the tools, practice using them on discarded pieces of wood. Her hands liked to do this. Soon she knew the names of all the tools, and how to make them move just as she wanted.

At the end of her first year, when she was cleaning brushes and Signor Pietro mixing varnish, she saw him grab the oil pot when he'd already added oil. She rushed over and put her hand on it to stop him. "Signor, the wrong pot," she said in stumbling Italian.

His face darkened and she flinched. Then he saw the pot and knew she was right. He relaxed, and smiled, spoke to her, and she understood both what he said, and his good humor in saying it. "Well, that's the first mistake I've made in two years. It would have been a waste. Thank you."

After that, he sometimes spoke to her. On a day when he called to one of the boys to bring the palm gouge for scroll carving and she brought it, he eyed her.

"You know the tools?" he asked.

She nodded.

"Show me your hands," he said. She did so and he examined them closely. "Name the tools, and what each is for."

She made no mistake. He handed her wood and a plane. "Use it," he said.

"For what, sir?"

"Because I tell you to," he said.

"I meant, for what violin part." She named them all.

He frowned, and then said, "the ribs."

He peered closely at her every move but she hardly noticed him. She liked the feel of wood in her hand, the rhythm of planing. She sang softly, a tune her grandmother taught her. "See the poplar by the roadside, the kankles at the root, the bees buzzing in the center, the falcon's children at the top."

"That's enough, boy," he said after a while.

She shook her head. "A little more." She continued until her song was done.

Her master took the piece from her, flicked his finger against it and listened. He grunted, and put it aside.

"What's your name?" he asked.

"Azuolas," she told him.

He struggled to say it.

"It means oak in our language," she said.

"That's not a good wood for violins," he said. "It will eat your hands, besides."

"Perhaps for the neck and scroll," she said.

"I'll teach you how to make them, and you can decide for yourself."

So she learned to carve necks and scrolls, and when she was alone, she took out the oak her grandmother gave her and began carving it just for herself. Signor Pietro was right that it hurt the hand, but she was satisfied when it was done. That night she dreamt she poured the contents of the jar she carried close to her chest, under her shirt, onto wood. As she did so, the wood began to sing in the voice of a thousand honeybees, in the voice of a woman whose blood ran within hers.

"Do not be afraid," the woman said. "The devil may find you, but the bees will protect you. And you'll know what to do when the time comes."

She woke with a start, at the edge of time between dark and light. And she knew it was time to make her own violin, pouring all into the task.

She didn't start right away, but in her mind she was choosing her wood and shaping it. She was no further than this when Naktis returned, coming to the shop to talk with Signor Pietro about a commission. His presence disturbed her, maybe because he kept eyeing her as she worked. She was glad when he left. Then she was frightened when he showed up again that night, while she was in the shop alone, cleaning up.

He came in without knocking as if that was his right, and stood leaning against a table. "Labas, Azuolas," he said. "How are you?"

"I'm well," she said, but didn't return the greeting.

He grinned as if he understood the deliberate discourtesy. "Your master says you have some talent. Good hands, he says. But I wonder how much longer you can play the little boy. When he learns the truth, he'll be angry."

She knew Naktis was right. She had to bind her breasts now, and she was in her womanhood and had to tend herself every month in private. The boys whispered that she was odd, and wouldn't go to the brothels with them. She had to wear high necked shirts to hide her throat, and keep her voice low when she spoke.

"Maybe I can help you," Naktis said. "I'll be very nice to you, if you'll do the same for me."

The way he said it made her shiver. When he was gone, she decided she must go faster to finish her violin before Signor Pietro threw her out. She chose her wood and began that night, working late every night after that and hiding her work before morning. She was surprised at how easy it seemed, the wood doing exactly as she asked. Sometimes she stared at her hands, wondering that they knew how to do this, as if they belonged to someone else.

Only when it was done did she realize she had a problem. It now had to sit in the air and sun to darken. Saule must sing to it. She couldn't hide it any longer. Fortunately, Signor Pietro was called away to play for a duke, so she took a chance and put it on a table with two others. If the boys noticed, they wouldn't give her away. By now, she held some secrets of theirs as well.

But Signor Pietro came home a day early, and her violin still sat out. He spotted it quickly. "What's this?" he demanded. Everyone turned to him. He held her violin.

"A violin, sir," one of the boys said.

"I can see that. Who made it?"

The other boys stirred, but didn't speak. She drew in breath and then spoke. "I did, sir."

He looked at her, then at the violin. He held it close to his face, ran his hand along the back and the front, the neck and scroll. "Come here," he said.

She went to him and stood with her head down.

"You used the oak," he said.

She nodded.

"You liked it?"

"No, sir," she admitted. "But for this violin, it seemed right."

He raised an eyebrow, hefted the instrument under his chin. He hummed quietly, listening to the echo in the wood. Then he put it down, got one of the small paper labels he put in his violins. He wrote his name on it, handed pen and paper to her.

"Put your name under mine," he said.

She hesitated. She didn't want to put her boy's name, and could not put her real one. Instead, she put the letter A, with a large flourish. Signor Pietro glued the back of the paper and pressed it inside the violin. Then he went back to work.

❧

That night, she stayed long in the shop. It was Rasa, the longest day. If she was home, she'd wake at dawn to wash her face with dew. Instead, she spent this night sealing and varnishing her violin.

She mixed the bee glue with the Signor's mineral powders, but she also took her amber earrings and ground them in the mortar, adding some of this. She stirred the remaining amber, along with sap and honey from her jar, into the varnish, cooking it and straining it, letting it cool. This violin would hold all the songs of her land, carried in the sap of the trees, the amber washed by the shore, and the honey made by the bees she'd known as protectors and friends.

As she brushed it on the wood she sang songs she'd heard since before she was born.

They held whispering grass, storming ocean, dancing bees and sighing trees. Tiny frogs, birds on the wing, lightning sizzling, and the joy of her people moved into the wood as she stroked the varnish over it, and the sun lingered in the western sky. Then, from somewhere far away, the sound of a woman singing, a voice like her own, but older and holding more sorrow, more wisdom. It was a voice she wanted to hear more of, and she knew she would, every time this violin was played. When she was done, she hung it on a hook, and went to sleep.

The next day, Signor Pietro narrowed his eyes at it, grunted. "It's too light."

"It's as it should be," she replied, and felt her face flush deep red. She'd never spoken that way to him. He put his head back and laughed, long and loud. He walked out of the workroom still laughing, and she let out a long breath of relief.

The following week Naktis returned. He spent some time talking to Signor Pietro, a thin smile on his face, but he didn't speak to her at all.

She stayed in the shop until well after dark that night, not to work but to guard her violin. She expected him this time, and wasn't surprised when the door opened and he stepped inside. He regarded her silently, sensed the absence of fear in her. She said nothing.

"You're here very late, Austeja," he said. "Keeping watch over your handiwork?" He gestured at the violin on its hook.

She nodded, remained silent.

"It looks well made, though its color is strange. Still, I'd like to buy it."

"No," she said quietly, her first word to him.

His eyes flashed anger. "No? What makes you think you can say that word to me? Signor Pietro tells me I can buy it."

She met his fierce glance. "I want to keep this one," she said.

"Do you? And what can you offer me in its place?"

Her face flushed, thinking of what he might want, not sure she was willing to give it.

He laughed. "No, Austeja," he said. "I don't want that."

"Then what?" she asked.

"You carry a small jar," he said. "I saw it on the ship. And I've seen it here. I've thought about it for a long time, and I want it even more than the violin."

"Why?" she asked, surprised.

"Because I knew a woman who carried the same thing. One of your relatives. She stole something from me, and I've been trying to repair her wrong ever since. I think what she carried in that jar will compensate me for my loss. It holds some power belonging to the women of your family, doesn't it?"

"It held everything," she said. It held the blood of the trees, the blood of the women who made her, the song of the bees. Everything.

"That's what she said," he whispered, his face taut. "So give it to me, and keep your violin. All the wrong she did will be healed."

Austeja shook her head. "I can't," she said.

"Of course you can," he said. "Why not?"

"It's - it's not yours," she said.

He moved closer, grabbed her chin, forced her to lift her eyes to his. "Stubborn girl, born of stubborn women. I should have known you'd be as foolish as the others. You have her eyes, her voice, her soul. And what do I have? Nothing. That's her fault. But now you'll give me what should have been mine long ago, if you want to live."

"It's gone," she choked out.

At this he released her. "Gone? Where?"

She stepped away and kept her eyes averted. "I emptied it," she said. "Used it up."

"Aah, you're a wicked girl, and untrue to the mothers who came before you."

"No," she whispered. "Their word asked it of me. Put it in the wood, they said."

He stared first at her, and then at her violin. "You put it - there?"

"It is *her* song, and it will sing. It will always sing. You cannot have it."

For a moment he stood very still. Then his face twisted into rage, and he turned his hand into a fist. "Neither you nor she can stop me," he hissed. "Not this time." And he reached up for the violin.

She cried out, put a hand up to stop him, then was stopped herself by a sound she never expected to hear in this place.

The room was full of it. Not music, but the tense buzzing of hundreds of bees. When Naktis touched the violin they flew out from its center as if from the hollow trunk of a tree, and covered his hand. He stared in horror at the crawling mass, then turned a burning gaze to Austeja.

She closed her eyes, anticipating attack, but it never came. After a while, she heard only her own breathing, and she opened her eyes and peered about. He was gone. The bees were gone. The violin hung from its hook, unchanged.

She took it down. She had to leave. Now. The bees said so. She had money in her pocket, and would find her way.

Slowly, inexorably, she would make her way back to the forests, lakes, and rivers, the peaceful bees, the rolling sun and the singing honey. She would play the violin for the trees, for the bees and the earth itself. She would marry someday, and have a daughter. If her daughter didn't want to play it, perhaps some granddaughter would.

The Amber would be kept among her people, safe in the trees from which it was born.

Chapter Ten

Rome, Italy, early 21st century

When Stacey got out of the shower in the morning Nick was in her suite room, looking over her work from the day before.

She tightened the belt on her robe. "Did I say you could?" she asked, gesturing at the door, then at her sketches.

"You didn't say I couldn't," he pointed out.

"What happened to a decent privacy?"

He looked her up and down. "You're more than decent, Austeja. Sleek and lovely as a siren. And some of these sketches are quite good. I like the fishbowl perspective here, in spite of the arrogant title," he said, pointing to her Temptation. "And this sketch approaches brilliance. I wonder what it will look like when you paint it, on a very large canvas."

He held up a drawing of a woman standing in front of a mirror in tall grass. She was being slowly transformed into a river, the earth, a tree. She was seen only in reflection, but an angel or devil stood at her back, a golden violin in one hand. Its wings were leafy, and its face was Nick's. His image didn't appear in the mirror.

She went over to it, frowned. Her heart beat hard. Was she going mad? That was a dream, not an action. Wasn't it? Why couldn't she tell?

"Austeja, sit down," he said sharply. He took her arm, and placed her on the couch. The room spun around her. He was gone, and then he was back, a glass of something in his hand. "Drink this," he said, and she did.

Wine. Way too early for it, but she didn't care. It did something good for her.

"I – I don't remember drawing that," she said. "I dreamt it. I didn't do it."

He frowned at her. "Are you sure?"

"I – maybe?" she tried.

He pointed to the lower left hand corner. "It's your signature."

She peered down at it. He was right. The large A and V with smaller letters in between, because she signed her work Austeja rather than Stacey. It was titled Lady of the Grasses.

"Am I cracking up?" she whispered to him.

"No," he mused. "I'm afraid not. You're remembering."

"I'm *forgetting*," she said, and fear made her voice strident. "I don't remember doing this. Dammit, that's why I stopped painting. Because it – it *takes* me. I can't – it uses me, *takes* me."

"Cara," he said calmly. "Artists often work in an altered state of consciousness. There's nothing wrong with that."

She groaned, and he patted her shoulder. "Or it's fatigue, induced by jet lag and an overload of antiquity. Don't worry about it. Not at all."

She took in a ragged breath, shuddered, forced herself to relax. "You're sure?"

"Yes," he said with comforting certainty. "Of course. We'll go slowly today. We can skip Mantua and stay in Rome. Shop a little, eat a little, rest. Tomorrow we'll go see the villa, and you'll relax even more."

They did just that, and the normalcy of trying on shoes and feeling the good leather of many purses helped her reground. Nick was remarkably patient with her, commenting on the quality of the goods she purveyed, which shoe looked best on her, which scarf went well with her eyes. His cynicism was buried somewhere for the day, and instead he trotted out his best courtesies, which she found singularly comforting.

By evening, she felt like herself again, and they sat at an outdoor café sipping espresso, watching people and imagining their lives while Nick periodically pretended to teach her Italian. That night she left her art supplies alone, and slept well.

The next day he got a car and driver, and they drove to Roberto's Villa, leaving Rome behind and climbing up into hills where small villas nestled in a richly flowered countryside. Their destination was only an hour away, but it might have been a different planet. When they exited the car, the world was quiet except for the lazy buzzing of bees in the many gardens surrounding the main building. It was all stucco and stone and light and the saturated colors of unfamiliar flowers. As they approached the front door, Nick cast a glance into her new bag.

"I see you brought your sketch book and so on," he noted.

"I didn't know if you'd need to spend time alone with the lawyer," she said. "Sketching's a good excuse to temporarily go away."

"That's considerate of you. You're not afraid?" he asked.

She looked around. "Here? No. All the angels here are restful and content."

"Fat cherubim," he agreed, "and lazy seraphim."

Roberto's lawyer, John Wilkins, was British, middle aged, and anxious to please. As soon as they arrived, he took them to see the tombs, which were under a mound at the back part of the land, and had only recently been excavated. They walked the rolling land, small birdsong the only sound except for John's continual chatter about the value, the importance of such art, and the need to find the right owner to preserve it. Nick let him go on and said little. Stacey simply looked around and enjoyed the sun, and when they took careful steps into the tomb itself, even John hushed his mouth.

Exquisite was the word that came to her mind first. And then, surprisingly, joy. The scenes painted on the walls were festive, lively. Men and women embracing. A reclining woman with a bunch of grapes lifted eternally to touch her smiling lips. Flowers and trees and birds, goblets of wine and tables laden with food.

"The Etruscans didn't fear death," John noted. "They saw it as a transition rather than an end point. The party, apparently, went on."

She reached up to put her hand closer to the woman and the grapes, and John made a fussy sound. "Now, really, you can't –"

"Leave her alone," Nick cut in sharply. "She doesn't touch. She just sees with her fingers."

She did so, to her heart's content.

&

As they made their way back toward the main house, Nick invited John to sit on a garden bench with him and discuss business. She politely excused herself to go make a few sketches, and gave them enough distance for their own decent privacy. In the time it took for her to sketch a flower and a bee, Nick was back.

"Keeping to the safer subjects, I see," he noted, peering at her sketch.

"You bet. Did you buy it?"

"Not yet. It's never good to appear too eager. We're invited in to lunch."

The food was as good as everything else she'd eaten in Italy - quail eggs on an artichoke bruschetta, home made pasta with a ragu of duck, truffles and rosemary, fruit and cheese to end the meal. When it was gone John left, but encouraged them to spend the day getting acquainted with this house and the smaller ones on the premises. They did, roaming the rooms, looking at everything from arches to plumbing problems. It was late evening when their driver took them back to their hotel in Rome. They were flying back first thing in the morning.

"Well? Should I?" Nick asked as the countryside merged with the city.

"Buy it? Up to you," she said.

"If you had the money, would you?"

"In a silly little minute."

"Then consider it done," he replied.

She had a moment of retrenchment, wanting to take back her words. She'd never had the kind of power that would influence someone to buy what was probably a very expensive villa. She was still getting over the Sue Wong dress. She thought maybe they should talk about it, discuss it like two adults who were not really in a relationship unless you counted one of the adults wanting to buy the other one's soul.

When she turned to him to say something about it, he smiled. "What would you like for dinner?" he asked. "More pasta, or maybe seafood?"

She sighed, and let it go.

Instead of pasta or seafood they had bracciole and good bread for their supper, and then Nick sent her back to her hotel room, insisting she get more rest before they traveled again. She took a glass of wine to the bathtub and lay back to relax. It seemed strange to travel so quickly and casually to Europe, but she supposed that was his life. She thought about coming back here on her own, but she found herself hoping he'd bring her again. It was more fun with him.

That thought frightened her enough that she got out of the bath quickly. No more daydreaming, she told herself. She focused on packing and realized she had more to take home than she'd come with, which presented logistical problems. She solved most of them by punching down clothes and smashing in shoes, but when she got to the sketchbook, she found she was reluctant to pack it just yet. She felt a familiar itch in her fingers. Her mind moved to thoughts about the shape and weight of things she'd seen, and their motion. The way a woman's face looked chiseled from heavy gray stone, or the detailed way wind carved out space for its passage down a crowded street.

"No," she scolded herself. "No painting or daydreaming. Go to sleep."

And she did, falling into rest like a rock into a pond.

Her next awareness was of struggling against something that held her, or wanted to take something from her, she couldn't tell which. She fought it silently and ferociously until it held her so close she had no more room to fight.

"Wrestling with angels, Austeja?" A familiar voice asked.

She gasped and looked up. Nick was holding her in a tight embrace, and she had one of her hands dug hard into his shoulder.

"Jesus Christ," she said.

"Hardly," he replied mildly. He released her, and she pulled back, looked down to make sure she wasn't naked. She saw a long t-shirt, and felt immense relief.

"You were having a dream," Nick said. "A very loud dream. I thought it best to come in before someone called security. Do you remember any of it?"

She frowned. "There was a violin, and it was full of bees. An angel was trying to take it. Or maybe a devil. Or a ghost. I couldn't tell. I - that's all I know."

"Did you draw tonight?" he asked.

"Absolutely not," she said. "I resisted the urge."

He sighed. "Did it ever occur to you that you should simply give yourself to it, say yes to it, and then maybe it won't ride roughshod over you this way?"

"Is that what you'd do?" she demanded. "Let something else control you? Give your life to it, no matter what it asked of you?"

He was silent for a long moment. "No," he said at last. "Of course not. Well, it's over now. Get some sleep." He stood and moved toward the door.

"Wait," she said. "Just – wait a minute."

He stopped and turned to her. "Como?" he asked.

There was something on her mind. It was a question, and she might as well ask it. "Tell me why you don't want to – to – have sex with me," she said.

"Oh," he said. "Really?"

"Well, yes. I mean, here you are, and here I am, and it's Italy. Am I not the kind of thing you like, as a rule?"

"You mean, am I gay? No, Austeja. It's not that."

"Then what? I mean, just tell me the truth. I probably won't be too insulted."

He ran his hand over his face, through his hair. "It's late. You know that, right?"

She shrugged. "It's the kind of conversation you should have late at night. Makes it easier to forget it in the morning."

At this he smiled. He turned a hand palm up. "Would I sleep with someone who finds me attractive in a mildly repulsive sort of way?"

"Oh," she said. "That. Well, maybe you're growing on me."

"Hmmph. That's not quite enough to make it worthwhile. Not when the stakes are so high."

"What the hell does that mean?"

"I've told you repeatedly what it means. You just refuse to believe me. Besides, I'm not like other men. The same way I can't get drunk, and can't taste what you taste, feelings are also muted. My pleasure is dependent on the pleasure of my partner."

For the first time, she felt something like compassion for him. "You can't feel on your own?" she asked.

"I can't," he acknowledged.

"Physically?" she asked. "Emotionally?"

He went to the water pitcher on her nightstand, poured a glass and took a drink. "All of the above," he said.

"Maybe you need –"

" - The right woman?"

"I was going to say a shrink."

"I do not need a shrink. I just need to follow my own peculiar course in the world, as do you. For now, those courses join here in Italy, where we've both had a fine time so far, in spite of the occasional devils and angels."

"But – "

"Leave it alone," he said, his voice low and quiet.

Part of her was disappointed. A romance in Italy would be a fine thing. And she'd wondered, as she watched his fine hands touch silk and leather in the shops, what they'd feel like against her skin. She was a healthy woman, with healthy urges that she liked to explore.

"Is it like that movie about the angels?" she heard herself asking.

He looked to her, utterly dumbfounded. "What?"

"You know. They say angels can't feel anything. That's why they envy humans. Pretty pitiful, if you ask me. What kind of god makes helpers who can't feel anything? The same one that created Popes with well hanging balls?"

"You realize you're making no sense?"

"I'm making perfect sense," she said. "I just can't explain how."

He stared at her, then stared down at his hands. "I'm not an angel. There's many ways to lose feeling. You can, for instance, make a bad bargain, relinquishing feeling for - for control. If I told you that happened to me, what would you say?"

"I'd probably say cut the bullshit," she answered.

He sighed. "Go to sleep, Austeja. Tomorrow we'll pretend we never said any of this."

"Okay," she agreed. "Listen - I'm sorry I woke you."

"I wasn't sleeping," he said. "I need very little sleep. In fact, now I'll go walk the streets of Rome, contemplating various other temptations."

He turned away from her. The conversation was over. He left the room.

When he left the hotel he had no direction or destination in mind, but his feet moved him toward the Vatican and he followed, brooding over his day, his traveling companion, his choices. He paid no attention to what was around him and had no fear of meeting any trouble he couldn't manage easily. Still, he had a good instinct for danger, its muted signals unlike any other, and as he rounded the corner to the Vatican, he felt it distinctly, and stopped in his tracks.

Leaning against a low stone wall was a tall, dark eyed man, relaxed and grinning. "Fine night for a walk in the old town, isn't it?" he said.

Nick stood very still. Of course, he thought. Of course. "Hello, Razak," he said, and then was silent.

"That's all? Just hello? Not what are you doing here?"

"I assume you have a great deal of business to conduct here," Nick noted. "I wouldn't imagine all of it has to do with me."

Razak kicked at a stone on the street. "Well, you're right in that. But as it happens, my business tonight is with you. Would you like to go to a trattoria and have some espresso or wine, while we conduct it?"

"No," Nick said. "I'd rather get it over with here."

Razak's eyes blazed, then subsided into darkness. "Someday you'll learn courtesy for your betters, my friend."

"There's a difference between a better and a boss."

Razak inclined his head. "Learn to think of me as both. But if you're in a hurry, as you seem to be, let's talk business. What are you doing with that woman?"

Nick smiled. "I'm amusing myself," he said.

"Are you? But you know we've worked hard for many generations to make sure she doesn't utilize her own peculiar gifts, and we won't have that work squandered for your amusement. Do you understand me?"

He did. With each return, they'd made sure she remembered less and less of her own life, her own soul, reducing her power to a thin longing for career success and good shoes. And what he was doing now was, in fact, making her remember. But he'd started the game and he'd finish it his way. This time, he'd see it complete. "I know what I'm doing," he told Razak.

"Then tell me what you're doing. It seems you have plans for her, but those plans are primarily to serve your own interests. Is that correct?"

Nick nodded, but stayed silent.

"We have nothing against self interest. You might say we're the experts in that realm. But we draw the line when it interferes with our agenda. Your obsession with her blinds you to the reality of your situation, my friend. Knowing all you do about her, do you really think you can get her soul for us?"

His hand went tight. He didn't want Razak's interference right now. He had a delicate and complicated situation in hand, and he wanted time to manage it. "If I did,

I'd be free of you, wouldn't I?" he asked.

"You'd have gained a great deal of ground," Razak admitted. "But you'd gain just as much if you got the brother, and let us deal with her. He's much easier to get than she is. Have you thought of that?"

He hadn't. So far, he'd only thought of what he might make of her. But he didn't trust Razak, who had him gather souls then told him those souls weren't recompense for his own. He might just say the same about the brother.

"What would I get for the brother?" he asked.

"Power, my friend. Power and control. A great deal of it. If you could get hold of that blasted violin you'd get even more. Do you happen to know where it is?"

Nick eyed Razak. Though he spoke casually, there was a spark in his eyes. Razak and company wanted the violin badly, even more than they wanted the brother. Perhaps even more than they wanted her, because the instrument carried her ancestral song, which did so much damage to their work. But what did he mean by power? Razak's words rarely meant exactly what they said. In fact, most of his offers produced nothing of what Nick anticipated.

"I might be able to put my hands on it, if I thought the reward was worthwhile," he said. "But I want details. This time, I want details."

"You'll get them in good time. First, make sure you've got your head on straight about the woman. You've done well for us in many ways, but she is a continuing disaster for you."

He grunted. Much as he hated to admit it, Razak was right. All his past attempts with her had gone wrong somehow.

"Of course, we'd love to have her on our table," Razak continued. "She's a constant irritation, with her songs and her persistent bees. But you've failed at every possibility of bringing her to us. Quite frankly, our master's tired of it, so this time choose wisely or you'll have no choices left. And be careful, my friend. She's a tricky one."

"I know that better than you," he said under his breath.

"Yet you return to her, though she'll always slip your grasp. You realize that, don't you?"

"Again, better than you," he said.

"Well, keep it in mind. I'll be in touch soon, with details about the brother and the violin."

"Are we finished, then?" Nick asked.

"We are," Razak said.

Nick turned on his heel and walked back toward the hotel. He took no note of what he'd left behind, or the fine curl of smoke that drifted over the cobbled streets in its wake.

Chapter Eleven

Upstate New York, early 21st Century

"So?" Martha said. "Dish, already. How was it?"

Stacey opened the wine, poured two glasses. She'd come over to fill Martha in on her trip, and hoped to get a little advice as well.

"It was incredible," she said. "The light there is totally different. You see things in a whole new way."

"Great," Martha said "Now cut to the chase. Is he good in bed?"

"Oh," she said. "That."

Martha sighed, took a healthy sip of her wine. "Damn. I knew it. Too good to be true. Rich, good looking, smart, takes you to Italy on a whim. What? He's got a teeny tiny thing?"

"No! I mean, I wouldn't know."

"He's gay?"

"He says not."

"Then what?"

"He – he says he can't feel anything," Stacey admitted.

"Now that's a new one," Martha mused. "Is it physical?"

"Got me beat all to hell. He also can't get drunk, or taste food the way I do. And he doesn't sleep much. So he says."

Martha, ever hopeful, said, "Maybe it's a psychological thing. Bad love in the past, something like that?"

"I suggested a shrink. It didn't go over too well."

"It wouldn't. Do you really want to sleep with him?"

"Sure, but I don't want to *work* for it."

"Well, throw him back in the pond," Martha suggested.

"Maybe," she said. "On the other hand . . . ."

"Careful, Stacey," Martha said. "I've seen you through a few frogs that stayed frogs. Anyway, you remember how Grandma used to tell that story."

Stacey smiled. She did. In her version the young woman didn't kiss the frog. She slammed him into a wall.

"I meant to tell you," Martha continued, "we're doing a unit on folktales in my tenth grade class, so I researched that, and grandma was right. That's the original version. It got changed later."

"Really?"

"Really. The girl's pissed off at the frog, because it's rude and demanding. So she slams it into the wall. Then it turns into a prince. After that, she kisses him."

Stacey thought about it. "Wow," she said.

Martha nodded. "Changes everything, doesn't it? So don't kiss him. Find a wall to slam him against, just for ha-ha's. If that doesn't work, you can move on."

Stacey touched her glass lightly to Martha's. "Sounds good to me. How?"

Martha chewed her lip, thinking about it. "How about this - bring him here on Saturday, to Alicia's birthday party. We'll see how he manages that. And I'll get a good look at him. Scope him out for you."

Stacey tried to imagine it. Then, she grinned. "I'll do what I can," she said.

She brought it up with Nick when they were having sushi the next evening. "I have an invitation for you," she said.

He stopped toying with a piece of ginger and looked at her. "To what?"

"To meet my sister. This Saturday."

He put his chopsticks down. "Dinner at your place?"

"Actually, a birthday party, at hers. For her daughter's seventh birthday."

Nick opened his mouth, closed it, opened it again. "Will we be the only guests?"

"The only adult guests," she said. "Most grown ups are too chicken shit."

He raised an eyebrow. "I'd like to," he said coolly. "What time?"

She told him, and gave him Martha's address. She felt triumphant. He didn't even pause long enough to check his calendar.

೨

Stacey and Martha had managed to herd a gaggle of giggling girls to the back yard and the first amusement – a water balloon toss - when Nick arrived. Later they'd have Twister, and the sprinkler to cool them on a day that was overcast and breezy but warm. Stacey had already filled and tied about a million balloons for them, and she was helping her sister drag the picnic table to a shady spot under a large maple tree when she looked up to see him walking toward them, watching her with grave amusement.

He wore a t-shirt and jeans, perfectly appropriate, and he held a large, elaborately beribboned box. In spite of that, she thought he looked like a hothouse flower thrust into a rambling pea patch. She put the table down, put on her smile, and waved to him.

"Martha," she hissed, "He's here."

Her sister released her end of the picnic table and looked up. "Mother of God," she murmured. "That's him?"

"I told you," Stacey said. There was no time for more, because he was next to them, his eyebrows high and his face full of mischief.

"Hello," he said cheerfully, addressing Martha. "You've got your work cut out for you."

Martha held out her hand. "If you're not Nick, you're probably at the wrong party."

He took her hand. "And if you're not Martha, I'll eat grass and roll in mud."

"We look alike?" Stacey asked.

"I see the family lines in both faces. Strong bones, fine features. This is for the birthday girl." He held the box out to her.

Martha, torn between being flattered and suspicious, took what he offered. "She's over there, somewhere." She gestured toward the back of the yard, where girls tossed water balloons and screamed periodically for no apparent reason, while Tamsa pranced ecstatically among them. "You didn't have to, you know."

"Of course I did. It's a birthday party."

She looked at the box, shook it lightly.

"Careful," he warned, and then laughed. "Just joking. It's not explosive. Or live. Well, not yet. It's a butterfly habitat. So she can raise her own."

"Thank you," Martha said, now both suspicious and impressed. "She'll love that."

"Stacey told me she likes fairies," he noted.

Stacey cast him a glance. It was the first time he'd ever called her that. He gave her a look that said if she meant to test him, he intended to pass with flying colors. "Now," he said. "How can I make myself useful?"

As it turned out, there was quite a lot he could and did do. He and Jim brought out chairs and successfully transferred the cake to the picnic table. While Stacey and Martha got Twister going, Nick and Jim set up stereo speakers outside so the girls could listen to music later. When that was done Jim slapped him on the shoulder and invited him inside to watch what they could of the baseball game.

"You're coming back out for presents and cake," Martha reminded her husband.

"Of course we are," Nick replied, his eyes dancing with mischief.

True to their word, the two men reappeared when the girls were all settled at the picnic table, Nick taking his place demurely by Stacey's side. As they stood and watched the proceedings, Chaos came out from his hiding place and strolled over to Nick, curling a tail around his leg, while Tamsa trotted over and nuzzled his hand.

He looked down, patted her absentmindedly. "Black dog, black Cat?" he asked.

"Tamsa and Chaos," she affirmed.

"Of course. Your sister is also *Ragana*," he noted, using the Lithuanian word for witch. "Is this the dog that led you to me?"

"That's her," she confirmed.

He looked out over the land. "And those are the woods. You still don't want to say more about that?"

She shook her head.

"Hmmph. Someday you'll have to take me back there and show me. Are there pines? Oak trees?"

"A stand of old trees, like towers all around," she said. "A couple of really nice old oaks, too. I'm still trying to figure out where the music was coming from, though."

"Music?"

She caught herself, gave a quick smile. "Nothing. Just – nothing. It's kind of a whole different world back there."

"So it seems," he murmured.

He stayed by Stacey as the girls oohed and aahed over the gifts, which piled up in an abundance of pink plastic, with fairies of all kinds. When Alicia opened the butterfly habitat, she let out a screech of joy that made the adults wince. "Mommy, butterflies!" she screeched again. "Will they really grow? Where'd you get them?"

"They're from Stacey's friend," Martha said. "Mr. Vecchio."

Alicia turned solemn eyes to him. "You're the one mommy talks about? Grant?"

Stacey, sipping spiked fruit punch, almost spit it out. Nick cleared his throat, she was sure to check his laughter. "That's a different friend," he said. "I'm Nick."

Alicia let out a gusty sigh. "Oh, good. I don't think mommy likes Grant much, but he never gave me butterflies, so *that's* okay."

Martha bit her lip and tried for courtesy. "Thank Mr. Vecchio, Alicia."

"I think she already has," Nick said.

"Will they really grow?" Alicia asked.

"They should, if you take care of them. But let's ask them, shall we? Why don't you all call for them, and we'll see what they say."

Alicia's face lit up and she started calling out, "Butterflies, Butterflies!"

The other girls joined in, and the chorus grew in volume until Nick held a hand up, at which they were all simultaneously and miraculously quiet.

He walked to where Alicia sat, lifted a hand and cupped it near her ear. He pulled it away, opened it, and out flew a butterfly, all pinks and golds. The girls opened their mouths and forgot to scream as it fluttered over them, then disappeared in a puff of sparkles. Thirteen pairs of wide eyes turned to him.

"Do it again," a little girl at the end of the table demanded.

"I can't," he said. "They've already spoken. The butterflies will grow."

"You're a magic man," Alicia said. "I hope mommy likes you a *lot*."

The cake followed, and Nick remained by Stacey's side, stalwart throughout. Though he produced no more magic, he showed Alicia how to teach Tamsa to beg, which she did admirably, and which the girls practiced with glee as they ate cake and ice cream.

"Just one more piece of ritual," Martha said. "Stacey? You ready?"

Stacey turned to Nick. "If you're not up to it, you can collapse in a lawn chair."

"I wouldn't miss it for the world," he said.

She put a small slice of cake on a plate and poured fruit punch into a cup as Martha and Jim led the girls to a sapling oak at the back of the yard.

"We planted an oak tree when Alicia was born," Stacey said. "A Lithuanian custom."

"When a child is born, plant a tree. When someone weds, plant a tree," he chanted. "When a house is built, plant a tree. When someone dies, plant a tree. I know."

"I should've figured that. Anyway, on her birthday we sing to the tree, too."

They went and stood under the slim young oak and Stacey gave the cake to Alicia, who solemnly placed it under the tree, then poured fruit punch on its roots. Martha, Stacey, and Alicia put their hands on the silvery bark and sang, in Lithuanian, the song that honored the Life Tree.

It was a simple song about a tree by a roadside, the lyre at its roots, the buzzing bees at its center, the falcon's children at its top. Please stop, young brothers, it exhorted. Behold the falcon's children, the buzzing bees, the ringing lyre. Martha sang alto and Stacey soprano, their voices floating out to be absorbed by the leaves of the tree. The melody was sweet and pure, a breath of ocean and tall grass that quieted their souls.

When it was done, there was an extended silence that felt good after all the gleeful noise. Then, one of Alicia's friends started applauding.

"Yay!" she shouted. "Yay for the tree!" The girls went into motion, dancing and calling out in their high, shrill voices, yay for the tree.

"The sugar's kicked in. Head for the hills," Martha said urgently, and the adults moved back to the house.

Soon after, parental units started arriving to retrieve offspring, and Jim and Martha started clearing the detritus from the yard. Nick and Stacey offered to help, but Martha sent them inside to deal with clean up there. They gathered, sorted, rinsed and dried dishes in blessed silence, focused only on the task. When they got to wiping counters, Nick finally spoke.

"You lied to me, Austeja," he said. "You told me you have no music. But your voice is lovely."

"It's my mother's. She liked to sing. In fact, we always sang, like the Von Trapps or the Jacksons or something. At least, when my father was sober."

"That was the good side of him, then?"

"The very good side," she agreed. But she didn't want to talk about her father or her brother. Not today. She changed the subject. "How'd you do that butterfly thing?"

"Didn't you hear them? I'm the magic man. *Much* better than Grant."

"Ha," she said.

He gave a wicked grin. "You invited me because you thought I'd show gross incompetence in an uncomfortable and distasteful social situation. Isn't that so?"

"Maybe a little," she admitted. "But you did okay."

"Of course I did. I understand family."

She was still surprised by it, though. It seemed such a strange setting for him. She gazed around the kitchen, at the little girl drawings on the refrigerator, the muddy shoes near the coat rack, the dog and cat bowls, the family photos on the wall. One was a photo of her grandmother, taken shortly before she died.

He saw where she was looking, nodded in that direction. "Your grandmother?" he asked. "Giedre?"

She tilted her head at him, about to ask how he knew her name, then shook her head. He knew things. That's what he did. "That's right," she said.

"She was beautiful when she was young," he said quietly. Then, seeing her frown, he added quickly, "I can see the marks of it in her face. Yet, she came to that. And is that what you want? Marriage? Family? A brood of kids, a dog and cat and growing old with some man?"

"The human journey," she said.

"Yes. The human journey. Becoming that old lady on the wall."

"I don't think we have a choice about that, single or married. Unless you die young. Maybe I'll be a kick ass old lady, though. Full of fire and fun."

"I'm sure," he said "And the rest? Kinder, Kuchen, and so on?"

She considered, and answered as she always did, with an honesty she hoped would disconcert him. "I think it just plain scares me. There's nothing can hurt you if you let nothing in, right?"

He looked to her. "Maybe," he said, "you're more like me than you know."

⁊

When clean up was done they went back outside, where the grill was set up to make hamburgers for the tired grown ups. Jim went to the store to get more beer and Martha went inside to get plates and utensils, while Nick and Stacey watched Alicia play with her Magic Pony and a troop of plastic fairies in the grass by the side of the house.

"Almost over, and you survived," she said.

"So far," he agreed.

As if to contradict them, a high pitched scream tore the air, the unmistakable sound of a terrified little girl. They turned to it and saw Alicia standing, staring ahead, her back to them. Stacey heard a sound like an engine humming, a whirring machine. She knew what it was. She sought the source, and saw a thick swarm of honeybees swirling the air, moving toward Alicia as she stood frozen in fear.

Martha appeared on the deck, scanning the yard. "What is it?" she called out.

Stacey gauged the situation. For Lithuanians, swarms were a sign of honor, a way of saying the bees would stay your friend. And in scientific terms she knew swarms were usually placid, but on an overcast, windy day less so. But Alicia knew none of this. She might swat at them in panic, her excited gestures generating fear in the swarm, causing them to bite her. Stacey stepped forward.

Nick grabbed her arm. "You're allergic," he said.

She didn't ask how he knew. "So is Alicia," she said. She jerked free and moved, charging toward Alicia, picking her up and running back to Nick. The droning of the swarm grew louder, closer.

He met her as she ran and she pushed Alicia into his arms. "Get her inside!" she commanded. Nick moved to the house with Alicia sheltered against his chest. Stacey saw the swarm turn to them, as if they would follow. Did they track motion? She wasn't sure, but she wouldn't risk it.

She waved her arms at them, shouted, "Hey! Hey! Follow me!" And she ran away from the house, away from Alicia, toward the sapling oak. She heard the bees behind her and gaining. "Stay with me," she implored them. And they did, moving to her directive.

When she thought Alicia was safely inside she turned back to the shelter of the house, running as the swarm sang behind her. She glanced over her shoulder and saw them, like burnished raindrops gathering force. They swirled into a more coherent whole, moving with intent, as if they sought only her, only her.

"Jesus," she whispered reverently, picking up speed. But an old tree root caught her foot and she stumbled, fell, rolled over onto her back.

The swarm found her, hovered over her like an ancient cloud. She stared at them, and within their constant song she heard voices, speaking gently.

Don't be afraid, they said. *You'll know what to do when the time comes.* Then they began to descend.

She watched as if she occupied a nightmare. She put her hands to her face. She had to protect her face, she thought. It seemed important.

The bees covered her in a blanket of small motion, followed by sharp stings on her hands and throat. She didn't swat at them. What good would that do? Pain pierced her, and she knew she could die from this, but the thought of the swarm was worse, and she wished only to pass out, to leave this horror.

"Please," she whispered, and the world went dim, went away.

~

Martha met Nick as he was running toward the house with Alicia. "Take her in," he said, handing her over.

She did so, and came right back out to see Nick moving as if in a dream toward the back of the yard, near the young oak. Not too far from it was Stacey's prone figure, outlined in crawling bees. Martha gasped and ran past him, but he grabbed her arm.

She whirled to him. "Let me go! I'll get her."

"No," he said. His face was blanched, all blood drained from it. He stared at her with an intensity she'd never seen in any human face. "Go in the house. I'll do this."

"I have to help her," she insisted.

"*Goddammit, go!*" he roared. "This is mine."

Distant bird call lent a false calm to the scene. Nick's eyes were filled with darkness and light in equal measure. Something in them convinced Martha. He could do this better than she could. "Magic man," she mouthed. "Do it right." Then she ran for the house.

He strode over to where Stacey lay, the bees a golden net of motion around and on her. He looked at her, at the bees, and spoke quietly.

"No, Austeja," he said. "Not this way. It's cowardly of you to run away. To try and escape your human journey. See it through to the end this time, would you?"

The buzzing of a thousand bees replied, forming itself into words, the layered voices of many women speaking to him.

If you want her, go get her, they taunted.

He lifted a hand, let it fall. A moment of breath, of waiting. Then, a decision. He would not let this happen. Not this time. He laughed lightly, and moved into the swarm.

Small laughter answered his. The bees buzzed around him, whispering things in his ear, then rose and dispersed into the air. He dropped to his knees and moved Stacey's hands away from her face, placid and unstung. From the house, he heard Martha yelling at him.

"What are you doing?" she screamed from an open window.

"Stay inside," he snapped, more irritated than angry. "Let me work."

She receded from the window, and he turned back to Stacey. The poison coursing through her belonged to him, not her. He would take it back.

"Austeja," he whispered. "Stay with me."

He put his mouth to her throat, bit until he drew blood, and then he drank. He drank deeply, tasting venom, tasting the origin of stars, the iron of mountains, the ocean's home, and honey in her heart. As he drank he prayed, without naming any deity, angel or demon.

"Mine," he whispered, between tastes of her. "She's mine. You know she's mine. She will not slip away."

And whether from his unspoken intent or the venom he'd swallowed, as he drank, he felt pain, sharp and bright. It coursed through his muscles, snapped against his skin. Pain, which he hadn't felt in this flesh for so long, the gift of her blood and the bees.

"Aah, my queen," he murmured gratefully, sensation spreading through him, fiery and good.

He saw that the small wounds he'd made were closed, the swelling gone, and she breathed normally. He picked up her sting-pocked hand, pressed it to his mouth, bit and drank. With each drink he felt the same pain and rejoiced in it. He touched her face, feeling her life in his fingertips, feeling everything he hadn't felt in so long. He shivered with pleasure. Then he stood, wiped the blood from his mouth and walked away, moving toward his car.

Martha appeared in the yard, running after him. "Wait!" she called. "Wait!"

He turned briefly, looked at her as if seeing her for the first time. "She's fine," he said. "Give her a glass of wine when she wakes up." He strode away.

Martha changed directions and ran to Stacey, knelt beside her and put a hand on her arm. Stacey opened her eyes, blinked once, twice.

"Is Alicia okay?" she asked.

Martha grasped her hand. "Yes. Yes. She's inside."

Stacey lifted herself up on her elbows. "She didn't get stung?"

"No. Not at all."

She ran her hand through her hair and sat up. "Where's Nick?"

"I think he left. Stace, he – he did something. It was really strange. He made me go inside. He – I don't know what he did, but you're okay now. Look."

She pointed to Stacey's hands, and Stacey looked down at them. The remnants of small stings were there, but no other damage showed. "I got stung?" she asked.

"A lot," Martha said.

"Then . . . why?"

"That's what I'm saying. I don't know. He wouldn't let me watch."

She made a face that signified irritation. "You didn't even peek?"

"I was too scared. And I – I trusted him," she said, sounding surprised.

Stacey's hand went to her throat. She felt the memory of venom, and of his breath. Whatever just happened was important. She pushed herself to her feet and stood.

Martha grabbed at her arm. "What're you doing?"

"I have to go see him," she said, as if that was the only possible thing to do.

"But you almost died."

"I'm fine," she said, and in fact, she was. "Really I am. I just – I have to understand this, okay? Okay?"

Martha slowly released her. "Yeah. Okay," she said.

Stacey gave her a look of gratitude, and moved toward her car.

࿇

She drove in a state of grace, elevated beyond concerns of traffic or getting lost. When she got to Nick's gate she stopped her car and pressed the intercom button.

"Ms. Vitautis," a voice said. Henry.

"Here to see your boss," she replied curtly.

A brief pause. "Mr. Vecchio is resting," he said.

"I'm not surprised. But I want to see him anyway."

Another pause. Then, "Mr. Vecchio said you might come by, worried for him. I'm to tell you it isn't necessary. He's well."

"That's not why I'm here. You know that. So does he."

A quick sigh. "In that case, I'm to let you in."

"Good. That saves me the trouble of climbing over," she said.

When the gate opened, she rolled through, pulled up to the house, parked and got out of her car. As she ascended the front steps Henry stood at the front door, holding it open for her.

"Hey, Henry," she said, stepping inside. "Thanks."

He nodded acknowledgement. "Mr. Vecchio is in his sitting room. Down the hall, second door on the left."

She felt the urge to ask him how it was hanging, just to see what kind of answer she'd get, but he disappeared, swallowed by darkness. She walked toward the light that flickered from the sitting room, holding a million questions in her hand. What did he do? How did he do it, and why? Who was he? *What* was he?

She reached the room and stood in the doorway. She saw him sitting with a drink in his hand, staring at a brightly blazing fireplace, the only light in the room. His face showed wonder, as if some inexpressible miracle had occurred. She opened her hand and all her questions flew away, seeking light in some place safer than this fiery room.

"I thought you said alcohol didn't do anything for you," she said quietly.

He stiffened, but didn't turn to her. She stayed where she was. He began to sing softly. "My wild love went riding. She rode all the day. She rode to the devil, and asked him to pay."

She knew the song. The Doors. She walked to where he sat. He stood, put his drink down, and touched her face.

"The devil was wiser," he sang. "It's time to repent. He asked her to give back the money she'd spent."

She put her hand on his. He drew in sharp breath. His eyes searched her, as if she had all answers and he read them hungrily.

"Austeja. My wild love," he murmured. Then he pulled her close and kissed her.

His kiss was like whiskey in her throat, warming and burning, making the room spin. Her eyes closed, she saw images of ancient trees, wispy spirits dancing around them. She felt Nick's hands on her, tugging at her shirt as she tugged at his. They didn't try to move beyond this room. They weren't capable of it. When his clothes were off and hers were scattered on the floor he pulled her down to the soft rug by the hearth, his flesh familiar and strange, the scent of him full of pine and open air.

She felt outside herself, as if many people who were all her participated in this act, and approved. She belonged here, though she did not know why. Her body, outside her command, wanted only him, only him, while a part of her asked if this was truly her, someone who would give herself so completely to bliss. In this moment, she was no longer a realist. She was every painting she'd ever made, every vision she'd ever seen that needed painting. It was all perfect, and if it was meaningless that didn't matter because it was also beautiful.

"You are mine," he whispered defiantly. "Forever mine, Austeja."

Around her she heard the buzzing of a thousand honey bees, their frantic flight nothing in comparison to hers.

Chapter Twelve

She woke up next to him at three in the morning, still on the soft rug by the dying embers of the hearth. He slept, his face placid and content. She touched his lips. A smile formed, but he didn't wake.

"That's nice," she said softly. "And I'd rather leave it that way. God only knows what you'll think when you wake up."

She left, creeping out while he slept, driving home to lie in her own bed for a while. She slept dreamless, but was woken too early by her phone ringing. When she answered it, she heard his voice on the other end.

Why didn't you stay?" he asked peremptorily.

"Most men," she said, "like their space."

"When will you realize I'm not most men?" he asked. Then, "Never mind. Let's try another question. How soon can you pack?"

"Depends," she said. "What for?"

"I have a few more places to take you."

"Work day tomorrow," she commented.

"Your boss," he said dryly, "appreciates my attempts to cultivate the aspirations of his employees."

She couldn't help herself. She smiled broadly, glad he couldn't see it. "Where are we going?" she asked.

"New York City first. The rest is a surprise."

This time she wasn't afraid of his plane. She expected it to behave itself and get her where they were going. She relaxed and drank champagne, gazing at clouds and tiny buildings far below.

He stayed next to her, kept touching her hair, her hands, as if feeling them for the first time. Maybe it was the right woman he needed after all, she thought. Or maybe she'd slammed him into the right wall.

"Listen," she said, "there's a few things I want to know."

"Like what?" he asked, kissing the back of her neck.

"Like, what did you do? When the bees stung me."

"I removed the venom," he said.

"How?"

"With my mouth," he said.

"I didn't know that was possible," she said, trying to stay focused.

"It is, if you know how."

She pulled away from him, and asked the real question. "What are you?"

He regarded her with his strange eyes. "That you already know, Austeja, even if the realist in you fights the notion."

There were many ways to interpret that. He was the answer to her dreams, her only love, a handsome and wealthy man who was besotted with her. She believed in none of those things. Neither did she believe in the devil trying to buy her soul, using mysterious powers to keep her alive long enough to do so. She tried to formulate a response that expressed some of this, but it was complicated, and he was touching her lightly, then kissing the base of her throat, his breath warm on her skin. All of that seemed more pertinent, more present than unanswerable questions.

"Are you still nervous about flying?" he asked.

"No. Not now," she said.

"Then you're ready for a new experience," he noted, pulling her onto his lap.

As they passed over the earth, two unfettered angels with the grace of feeling, she decided he was right.

∽

"One room?" she asked when they got to the hotel where he had a suite. "What happened to a decent privacy and all that?"

"We're not in Europe anymore," he said. "New World rules are in order."

They did nothing more that day but go to the Museum of Modern Art, get some dinner, and go to sleep, both of them rising late. They ordered breakfast in bed and ate it leisurely, reading the paper and doing the crossword puzzle like an old married couple. Nick took a few phone calls out of the room, talking for some time with each, and returning with a look of satisfaction.

"Business going well?" she asked.

"Just as I want it to," he said. "And it's time to get up. I've got someone to see."

"More business," she sighed.

"Yes. Important business. Wear a nice dress."

He went so far as to put on a suitjacket. She expected to end up in Donald Trump's office. Instead, he sent their cab to a small gallery in Soho, where he'd bought a conceptual art piece, a collage of subway advertisements arranged to portray a Madonna and Child. Stacey wasn't fond of it, or the other paintings in the room. A small but insistent part of her ego said she could do better.

Nick introduced her to the gallery owner as an artist, and said he hoped they'd be amenable to a show when she was ready. The thought made her want to pass out, but she said nothing, and kept smiling while the owner gushed and she and Nick made their inexorable way toward the door and escape.

"Well," he said when they were outside. "What do you think of my purchase?"

"Good technique," she said.

"But you could do better," he said. "That's what you're thinking, isn't it?"

"Maybe. What are you grinning at?"

"I'm making great strides in my mission," he said. "I always enjoy success."

He said something else, but a siren tooled down the street toward them, drowning him out. Stacey pressed her hands over her ears until it passed.

"Let's keep walking. This is why City people stay inside."

They picked up their pace and he took her arm. "There were times when I liked noise better than music," he noted. "It could find me, where music couldn't."

She was surprised at the comment, and his tone. "What changed?" she asked.

He grunted, hunched into himself. "Possibly everything," he said, and moved forward. "I'll have to wait and see."

He didn't seem inclined to talk more, so she let herself ramble. "I think someone once said that heaven is either music or silence, and hell is all noise," she noted.

"What?" he shouted over a jackhammer.

"Hell. Evil. It's all noise. War, torture, my father's rage - all that. It's noise, made to keep us from hearing the music. Because if we hear the music, then we'll feel what we feel, and that's frightening."

She raised a hand, lowered it. She wasn't exactly sure what she was talking about, where these thoughts were coming from. It felt almost like painting. She sincerely hoped she wasn't going insane now, just when things were getting good. "It's a negative energy, and it sucks up positive energy, feeds off it to make more noise. We get addicted to it after awhile, feel like we need it. It kept my father angry, kept my brother gambling. Kept you from feeling. All noise."

He paused, then shook his head. "You're waxing philosophical," he said. "We'd better get you something to eat."

They found an Italian restaurant where the waiter laughed when she dipped her bread in her wine. "Only at home, they do that," he said, delighted.

"You see," Nick said. "You're a true peasant, of any nation."

"Best way to live," she agreed.

"Sometimes," he said. "Other times, it's good to be royalty."

She eyed him suspiciously. "What are you up to?"

"Something that will appeal to your patrician side. But first I have to see a man."

"About a dog?"

"Violin," he said.

"Not . . . ."

"Not the Amber. Just a violin he wants to sell. It's German. Maybe an early Klotz. I'm looking at it for him, to tell him what I think it's worth."

"You know about violins? You never said."

"You have a great deal to learn about me, Austeja."

He hailed a cab and put her in the back seat. The driver moved them through traffic to Lincoln Center.

"Um - we're at the Met," Stacey noted as they walked up the steps to the fountain.

"Yes. The orchestra's rehearsing here, while the opera's dark."

A security guard admitted them at the door, and Nick let her stop to admire the Chagall, one of her favorites. Then he touched her elbow and moved her into the theater, where musicians were setting up stands, tuning, checking reeds and other instruments in the orchestra pit. When they were near the front row, one of the violinists spotted Nick and waved a hand at him.

"There you are," he called out. "Stay. I'll come to you."

He was young, had violently short hair and thick-rimmed black glasses. His clothes were expensive casual, and he carried a violin case that he laid on an aisle seat. Nick introduced him as Frank, and her as Austeja, and they got right down to business.

"Not too much time for pleasantries right now," Frank apologized. "After, if you like, we'll chat. Meantime, there it is. Tell me what you think."

Nick opened the case, lifted the violin and looked it over, peering inside and at the purfling along the sides. "May I?" he asked, lifting the bow from the case.

"Oh, by all means," Frank said.

To Stacey's surprise, he hefted the thing under his chin and drew the bow across the strings. He stopped, adjusted the tuning to his satisfaction, and began to play. Of all things, Stacey thought. Paganini, La Campanella. Not an easy piece, and he played it well, his technique fine enough to make Vince writhe with jealousy.

When he was done, Frank pattered his hands in applause. "Nick, you're wasted on business. Come to New York and make music. Move away from the dark side."

Nick laughed. "All I have is technique. Besides, the dark side has better hotel accommodations. Speaking of which, are our accommodations here ready?"

"Oh yes. All set. So what do you think of my fiddle?"

"Five grand," he said. "It's an early one, not one of his best."

"Well, that's better than I expected," Frank said, not at all disappointed. "Since I only paid two, I'm the winner. Do you know anyone who could manage it?"

"Of course," Nick said, and gave him some names, which Frank wrote down on a small pad that he put inside the violin case.

"While I have you here," Nick said, "I've heard some rumors about a certain violin reappearing in the world, and I'm wondering if you know anything about it."

"Tell," Frank said.

"The Amber," Nick said.

Stacey tensed, unprepared for this, and equally unprepared for Frank's reaction. "Show me the devil who has it," he said. "I've got a soul I'll trade."

Nick grinned and turned to her. "You see? I told you it was worth it."

Frank turned to her as well. "Absolutely. You know about it?"

"A little," she said, unsure what her role was. "It's - got a good tone."

"Good? My dear, it's heaven. The color, and that strange oak scroll obscured its value and its origin. It's Pietro Guarneri, at his best."

"Oh. I thought it was Lithuanian."

"Well, that's the legend. That old Pietro had a little Lithuanian boy working for him – some trade with a Bishop in Lithuania - except he turned out to be a she, and she ran away with it. That's supposed to explain the big A written on the label under his name. I don't know why it's a different color, though. Do you, Nick?"

"The little Lithuanian varnished it," he said.

"I can't see Pietro letting that happen. But all kinds of stories have grown up around it. One says she sang to it while she made it, and put her mother's blood in it, so it's her voice you hear when you play it. Another says the devil made it, and she stole it from him."

"Legend aside, do you have any idea where it is?" Nick asked.

"I wish. About two years ago someone told me it was on the market. I followed a couple of leads, but they were dead ends. Sometimes I wonder if it even exists."

"It exists," Nick said. "If you hear anything, let me know first."

"Absolutely. Of course. Glad to be of service."

৯

"And glad to take the commission he knows I'll give," Nick muttered as they walked away. "Well, what do you think of that?"

"Not much," she said. "For instance, we were told the big A on the label meant it was a fake. The rest – it's rumors and myths. Like looking for Atlantis. Maybe what we had was just an old violin, and everything else is a story people like to tell. Then again, people are willing to pay a lot for a story, if it suits their illusions."

He laughed. "I so appreciate you," he said.

He led her through the theater, but not out. Instead, he took her up the red carpeted stairs and down a hall to a door.

"What's this?"

"I told you. Rehearsal for a performance in a few days, at Avery Fisher. I like the acoustics here better, so I convinced them to move it."

She wondered how much he'd paid for that, then decided she'd enjoy herself more if she didn't know. "What's the program?"

"You'll see."

He opened the door to a box seat, high above the orchestra pit. There were two large upholstered chairs, a table with an open bottle of champagne in an ice bucket, fresh strawberries and a bowl of dark honey. The box itself was surrounded by sheer curtains. She moved to them and touched them lightly.

"Won't they block the sound?" she asked.

"Of course not. I had them made not to."

She turned, and stared at him. He shrugged, then spoke.

"Sometimes I bring people here who need to discuss delicate issues. Privacy is important."

She touched the curtains again. "They're sheer."

"Only from this side. You can't see in from below."

"So, this is, like, yours?"

"Not like mine. It is mine."

"Right," she said. "Of course it is."

She turned away from the curtains, moved to a chair, sank into it and stretched out her legs. She might as well enjoy the perks while they remained available.

They drank champagne as the orchestra tuned and the conductor went over a few random parts. Oboes and horns, and then strings. They played a phrase and Stacey lifted her head. They played it again, and she knew what the performance was.

"Sibelius," she said. "Violin Concerto."

"And you said you had no music," he said, his face serious but his eyes lively. "I like it very much. He was a Finn, but I always think there's something Lithuanian, or at least Eastern European, in it. I've read that Slavic music was influenced by Nordic traditions during the Corded Ware era, so maybe that explains it. Or maybe it's because he admired Tchaikovsky, and was a nature lover, like your people. Of course, you know how hard it is to play."

"I know," she whispered. "My brother played it."

"Then it brings back memories for you?"

"Yes."

"Happy, or painful?"

"Both," she said. She would have changed the subject, gone back to discussing the double stops, the passages where the violinist maintained a trill with two fingers while playing a second moving line with two others on the lower string. She would have said anything to make the aching sorrow in her go away, but she couldn't speak.

"More pain than pleasure, I see," he said, regarding her solemnly. "We'll restore the balance, then. For every pain, an even greater pleasure."

She had no time to ask what he meant because someone called up from below.

"Nick? We're going through the whole thing now."

"Thank you, Frank," he called back.

She looked to him questioningly.

"Let's call it a commissioned rehearsal," he said.

"How rich are you, anyway?" she asked.

"Filthy," he said, taking his suit jacket off and dropping it on the floor. "Infinitely dripping with money. Quiet, now. We'll see if the soloist is up to her task, and if we can mark this music with pleasure on a new day."

The sweet, slow tremor of the opening phrase, pure and perfect in its yearning, reached them. The sorrow in her ran to meet it, but Nick lifted a strawberry, dipped it in honey, put it to her lips. She took a bite, and he watched her taste it.

"The food of your people, Austeja. Music and honey," he said. He dipped his finger in the honey, smoothed it against her lips and kissed her as the strings rose from yearning to a brooding anger that always reminded her of her father's smoldering rage, coupled with his sorrow. That brooding, which seemed so Lithuanian.

Nick leaned toward her as the tension built and the cadenza began. "You love this piece because it contains all emotions," he said. "The longing of that opening, and this angry, wild cadenza, and then, a celebration, a triumph. I will have her, an ancient man declares. She will be mine, if I have to search the entire earth for all of time."

His hand stroked her arm, feeling like thin, soft grass. "Aah – now that sweet innocence. Hear it? But it rushes headlong to its destiny, as we do. Can you see the man who yearns so?"

Flitting images of a man with strange eyes, fierce in his passion, flashed through her mind. He was swinging an axe against a tree. Slinging a sword against a priest's neck. Falling to his knees in tall grass and crying out in agony. Nick's finger, honey coated, ran up and down her neck, tracing the lines of the music as they rose and fell. His mouth followed, taking what was sweet and sticky from her flesh. She felt the back of her dress unzip, honey trailed down her spine, and his mouth moving over it lightly, delicately tasting.

"The violin argues with itself," he crooned, "as you have through the ages. What do I give? What do I hold back and at what cost? There is no answer. Only feeling."

One hand moved slowly down her spine, sounding each vertebrate for pitch and timbre. His other hand held her wrist, his fingers moving as if he played the score on her veins. The strings moved into their impossible trills, madness held in tight control.

"You hear the shift, my queen?" he asked. "Like you, changing. Once upon a time, your own song was enough, and you wouldn't share it. Now you scent something different in the air. You seek someone to sing with. Yet you still fight it. Listen."

The music took its wild flight toward the end of the movement. She thought of storming oceans, waves crashing. A group of people at the wild shore, and among them a man with a face of fire and darkness. She wanted to run, get away before she was sucked into that infinite water, but Nick's mouth was at her ear.

"Stay," he said. "Stay with me. For every pain, even greater pleasure."

He turned her to him as the violin raged, pressed his honey dipped finger to her face, anointing her and licking her clean. He smoothed honey on her lips, and then his mouth was on hers. She wrapped her arms around him, felt his muscles moving in tremors under her hands as the strings reached their climax and were silent.

"The slow movement," he whispered into her hair. "*Adagio di molto*. If it wasn't so sad, it would be too sweet. Instead it's like honey dripping from the bones of a murdered man. It has an edge."

He pulled back from her, holding her gaze with his, and touched her chest, ran a finger up to the base of her neck, pulled down the straps of her dress. She moved a hand to cover herself, but he stopped it. "I told you, no one can see us," he said. "Would I share this view with anyone?"

No, she thought. He was not a man who shared. The music returned to yearning as Nick got on his knees in front of her and reached under her dress. She put her hands in his hair, felt it thick and smooth in her fingers.

"Nick," she whispered, but it wasn't a protest. It was a welcome. Yes. She wanted this, here, with this music, pain transformed to infinite pleasure. Wanted the feel of his hair in her hands, the touch of his mouth on her skin to take the venom from her flesh.

His mouth moved along the inside of her thigh, its warmth and motion part of the sound that swallowed them both. The violin sang of loss, all that was unrecoverable in the human journey, and yet it rose and rose toward light, a fluttering of wings around and through her as his hands and mouth moved expertly to draw pleasure from her. She was lifted with the music, arched like a bow within it, as the adagio stretched home, and she bit her lip to keep from crying out.

Only a breath for the *allegro ma non tanto* to begin with its galloping joy. He got to his feet and stood over her, his eyes sparking with anticipated pleasure.

"My turn," he said. "For every pain, unabated pleasure."

He leaned over her and grasped her wrists, lifting her arms over her head, kissing his way down one of them, his mouth warm and soft against her flesh. She felt herself poured into pleasure, complex and complete. She was music, and all she had to say he already heard. He moved his mouth slowly over her flesh, lifting the phrases from her one by one with his lips. Slowly, carefully, as if she was a precious violin, he brought her to her feet, slipped her dress down to the floor, then kissed his way back up. His hands on her shoulders, he faced her, joyous in victory and surrender.

"Yes, Austeja?" he asked.

"Yes," she whispered, and the violin grew wild below them, within them.

Between his hands and hers, all final impediments to contact were removed, and he found his way in to her, crooning mine, mine, mine, but she understood who contained whom in this fiery dance. She put her hands on his face, made him look at her, his gaze and hers passing fire across oceans of time in hope and despair, joy and rage. Now he was instrument and she conductor, leading him into bliss.

This was hers to give. All hers and only hers. The music surged and receded, and she moved with it. This ocean would not drown her, would not drown him. This wave was theirs, and they would ride it to shore.

"You feel it," she said, triumphant. "Now you hear the song."

She had the sense that this moment had taken centuries to arrive. At last, she thought. At last, he hears the song. His only response was a cry of ecstasy, drowned by the rising strings. The music led them on, past and present joining in their flesh, and when it was complete, they sank to the floor, twined in each other's embrace.

An enthusiastic round of applause rose from the orchestra, and for a moment Stacey thought it was for them. Nick laughed softly, as if he heard her thoughts. "No, my queen. Not for us, though we deserve it. It's for the violinist."

Distantly, she heard people talking, congratulating each other.

"My God, I hope you play like that for the performance," the conductor said.

A murmur of reply, and she ceased attending to it, looked instead to Nick. His eyes were closed, and he looked perfectly victorious and subdued at the same time.

"You alive?" she whispered in his ear.

"Very," he murmured back.

"Can you move?"

"Not quite yet."

She smiled, glad to know that. "Okay. But does someone come and kick us out or anything? Because the music's stopped."

"Impossible. I still hear it."

She laughed, ran a finger down his cheek, then made an executive decision. She extricated herself from his arms, grabbed her dress, and assembled herself more artfully.

From the floor he groaned, "La donna e mobile."

"You better *mobile*, too, because there's footsteps heading our way.

He cursed vigorously, stood and rearranged himself as they heard a soft knock on the door at the back of their box.

"Nick?" a voice asked. Frank's voice. "How was that?"

Nick grinned at Stacey, held a hand out to her. She went to him. "Perfect," he said. "Beyond perfect. Brilliant."

"She was in good form, wasn't she? Inspired, you might say."

So you might," Nick agreed.

৵

Going outside to the lights and noise of the city was a strange transition. Neon ads and cabs honking were surreal in the context of her emotions. Stacey blinked hard.

"I know what you're thinking," he said.

"That's good," she said. "Because I don't have a damn clue."

"You're wondering if it's possible to paint what you feel right now, this transition between Sibelius and the City."

She sighed. He was right. "I'm seeing a furtive angel, pressed against a store window, staring at expensive shoes. It's distressed that it wants only shoes. I'm not sure what the rest of it is, though."

"You can work it out while we pack," he suggested.

"Are we going somewhere?"

"Home," he said.

She was disappointed. "I thought – didn't you say there was somewhere else?"

"Yes," he said. "Home."

She stopped, shook her head. "Nick, I'm not thinking too clearly, so you'll have to –"

" – Home," he cut in, speaking more vehemently. "The old country."

She tapped an impatient foot. "Spell it out, would you?"

His face was cool, neutral. He took her hand and traced letters in the palm as he spoke. "Home. V-I-L-N-I-U-S."

She pulled her hand away and stared at him hard. "Lithuania?"

"That's what the flight plan says. Are you ready?"

"No. Never. Yes. Always," she said. She grabbed his hand. "Let's go."

Chapter Thirteen

Lithuania, early 21st Century

They left around midnight for the airport. She slept restlessly on the plane, waking frequently to look down, waiting to sight land, wanting to see everything from the air, as her ancestors never did. Every cell in her body reacted to this, as if there would be some answers for her embedded in the land itself.

"We'll land in Vilnius by late afternoon, their time," Nick told her. "The pilot can do some maintenance and refuel while we walk around for a few hours, then we'll fly to Palanga, take the ferry to my house in Nida, near the coast. From there, we can do whatever you want."

"Okay," she said, staring down.

"You should tell me what you want," he suggested. "Basanavičiaus Gatvė, in Palanga, where the crowds go?"

"Okay," she said again.

"Hmmph. You're sure you wouldn't prefer Birute Hill. The Botanical Gardens?"

"Okay," she repeated.

"Right. Do you know about Birute? She was a priestess in the 1300s. Pagan, not Catholic. Viadilute, guarding the forest and the sacred flame. But the Duke Kestutis wanted to marry her, so he took her by force and they were wed. That's why amber is called the tears of Birute. But it paid off for the people, if not for her. Her son was the great duke Vytautus."

"I know," she said dreamily, staring below. "A little girl tried to stop the marriage because a vele told her lies, but Birute set her straight. Hey – what's that for?" She felt a pinch at her arm, and saw his hand, holding it hard.

He looked at it, too. "Sorry," he said, and released her.

"Did I say something wrong?"

"No. Except that's not in the history books. I wonder where you got it."

"I'm not sure. My grandmother?"

"You mention her a lot, but you never say anything about a grandfather. Parthenogenesis?"

She smiled. "I didn't know my grandfathers. Well, my mother's father, but just barely. He died before I went to school, though I have this vague memory of my grandmother throwing shoes at him when she was pissed off."

"That," he said, "does not surprise me."

"Yeah. My father's father died when my father was a teenager. There's some story my mother told me about him. He was a soldier in World War II, fighting for the Russians, but he was wounded and left for dead in a cemetery. The Germans picked him up and I guess he had a miserable time in the camps. He got into the US under a Russian name – Vialtov? Viatov? - anyway, he changed it back later. He was supposedly a mean drunk, like my father."

"Then he came by it honestly," Nick said.

"I wonder if I could find out anything about them here. If there's records."

"Better to look ahead," he suggested. He peered over her shoulder. "What are you thinking when you stare down there?"

"I'm wishing Vince could be here," she said. "I think this would do him good."

He receded, irritated. "You'll have to send him on your own. I don't do social work."

࿔

When the plane landed they had a car waiting for them, and someone to help with their bags.

"Do you want to find a hotel and rest before we look around?" Nick asked as they got in. "You didn't sleep much."

"Hell, no," she replied, unable to be still, completely incapable of resting. "I want to *taste* this place."

"Of course you do," he said, and pointed them toward Vilnius.

Once in the city, they walked through the Old Town with no goal in mind, just glad to be moving. At first, Stacey just absorbed with her eyes, taking in the artist's displays in shop windows and on the street, the old and new coexisting amicably. Angular modern sculptures stood next to statues of ancient gods with sagging faces, and thick wooden crosses intricately carved with burgeoning trees. She felt as if she'd been transported backward in time. They were surrounded by elaborate baroque architecture, with shadowy courtyards that might hold any angels, any devils at all. Nick pointed out various sights, acting the tour guide.

"That's one of the places where the Singing Revolution made its start," he said when they passed Cathedral Square. "Somehow, I imagine you had a few relatives present. Maybe we should go to Pauksciu Takas café, and read about the revolutionaries killed by the Soviets when they took over the TV tower."

"Fourteen," she said. "Fourteen were killed."

"Yes. And the soldiers should have known better than to make martyrs for the cause."

"I put the blame on the government. The soldiers were grunts, following orders," she said.

"Amidst a lot of noise. Still, they should have known."

"I wonder what they're doing now," she mused. "The ones who fired the shots."

His face knit into a frown. "Probably seeing the sights," he said, and they walked on.

For Stacey, the faces all looked familiar, people she'd seen in photographs all her life, or faces that surrounded her at family gatherings when she was young. The sound of the language was like a song, bringing back visceral memories of her grandmother telling stories, feeding trees, putting peppermint candy in her tea, the white and red swirls dissolving in the transparent gold-brown liquid. She was lost in family here. Lost in memory.

"Do you know how Vilnius was built?" Nick asked her.

"No."

"Gediminas, that great Duke, was hunting with a group of men. He tracked a huge bull up a hill and slaughtered it. That night he dreamt of an iron wolf, with the voice of a thousand wolves. He went to the pagan priest Kriviu Krivaitis and asked what the dream meant. Old Kriviu said the iron wolf was a magnificent city, and Gediminas had to build it here, where the rivers meet."

"Iron wolves and dreams," she said. "That's what the whole country's made of. Hard reality, and long nurtured mysticism."

"Yes," Nick agreed. "It's a place of deep shadow and frantic, brilliant light."

"You've been here before?" she asked.

"Many times," he said, and his tone was grim.

"Why?" she asked.

"Business," he said. "An ongoing business that remains incomplete. Let's go see Uzhupis."

"What's that?"

"The Jewish district before the holocaust, and after the war the realm of homeless people, drug dealers and prostitutes. Now it's the artist's area. In fact, they've declared it as its own republic, with its own constitution." He put a hand on her shoulder, turned her toward him. "Would you like to be a citizen?"

"Um, sure," she said. "How?"

"Follow me," he said.

He led her to the banks of the river Vilnia at a place where its swirling waters were shallow. He pointed forward. "In you go," he said.

She looked at him, looked up and down the river. "There's bridges, aren't there?"

"Yes, but the requirement for citizenship is wading through the water."

She considered her attire - shorts and t-shirt, flip flops. No problem there. Then she looked him up and down. "Your jeans'll get wet," she noted.

"They'll dry," he replied.

She saw mischief sparking in his eyes, and she understood. "Is this a test? To see if I want to be citizen of an artist's realm?"

"Ciurlionis once lived there," he said. "And there's some wonderful statues. Frank Zappa, their patron saint. Jesus with a backpack. An astonishing angel. A mermaid. A penis."

"I get it," she said.

She stared down at the water, thought of the night in the park with him, when she watched moonlight spin meaninglessness on the water. This, too, might be meaningless. A gesture. Yet, she couldn't cross this water unless she meant it. She didn't do metaphors.

"Maybe I don't want to be citizen," she said. "Maybe I just want to visit."

He held out his long, fine hand, made a noncommittal gesture. "Then we can stay on this side of the river, continue to see the sights here."

The waters moved at her feet, going forward. Going on. She observed the tones and undertones, its visual music. Green and tawny brown, with blue and an underpinning of brick red. Her hand moved as if she held a brush and was stroking its colors onto a canvas. Then, she laughed at herself. Hopeless. She was hopeless. She laughed again, and kicked off her flips.

"Let's go," she said.

The water was cool around her legs, and by the time they were halfway across, stumbling and laughing, she was glad she'd done it. As they emerged on the other side, clamored up onto the brick stairs and to the street, Nick took hold of her arm, pulled her to him, and held her close.

"Congratulations, Austeja," he said. "You're a citizen of Uzhupis, the artist's realm."

≈

They walked the narrow streets, with their abandoned and dilapidated buildings and cobblestone streets that hadn't been repaired in years, boarded up windows painted in wild colors, one of them with a mermaid statue hanging onto the ledge. Much of it was in disrepair, but it was all decorated. Stacey stopped to stare at a bridge, heavily festooned with padlocks.

"What's that about?" she asked. "They're afraid someone will steal it?"

"A Lithuanian custom. A groom carries his bride across the river Vilnia, and then they leave a padlock, engraved with their names and wedding date. They lock it, and throw the key in the river."

"That's - um. . . ."

"Terrifying?" he suggested.

"Pretty much."

"Have you no romance in you, Austeja?"

She turned to him. "What do you think?"

He raised a hand, ran a finger down the side of her face. "Maybe you have too much, and that's what really terrifies you."

She captured his hand, brought it to her mouth. "Where's that Jesus with a backpack statue? I want to see it."

After they admired the statue they continued to walk, stopping on Paupio street to read the constitution, which included the right to love and take care of a cat, and the right of the river to flow by everyone. Music wafted here and there - singing, a trombone, something that sounded like Lithuanian rap. On one corner, a young man who looked remarkably like Vince played the violin, his case open on the street for contributions.

Nick walked by, then stopped, looked at Stacey. He twisted his lips around, turned back and dropped a few bills into the case. Stacey smiled at the young man, and he winked at her.

"How much?" she asked Nick when he came back.

"Three," he said.

"He's worth at least a ten dollar bill, don't you think?" She reached into her purse, thinking she'd contribute to the cause, but he took her arm, led her forward.

"Three hundred," he amended.

"Oh," she said. "Well. Then that's okay."

"More than okay," he murmured. "Are you hungry? I am. Let's go to the Uzhupis cafe and eat, then head back to the airport. If we have time, we'll see more of the city on our way out. Are you ready to fly again?"

She brushed her hand through her hair, which she imagined was pretty wild. She still hadn't gotten to the hairdresser. "How do I look?" she asked him.

"Resplendent," he said.

"Then let's go," she replied.

Nick's plane took them to Palanga airport, where the pilot was set loose for a few days while Nick drove a rented car to the ferry, which took them to Nida, a place of ocean and forest and fields where scattered fishermen's houses still had thatched or tiled roofs. By the time he stopped in front of a smallish two story stone house it was dark, and thick low clouds scuttled on the horizon, moving toward them.

"The wind's picked up," Nick said as they lugged their bags out of the car.

Stacey nodded, staring at the house, its tiled roof and the circling weathervane, a tree superimposed on a radiant sun. It looked as old as the land, as if it had grown from this particular piece of earth a millennium ago. She felt the motion of a foreign place, with its own creatures and weather patterns and scents and life. Right now, in the interstitial light, it felt eerie and disorienting, her body uncertain what to make of all the new sensory input. She had the uncanny impression that she was being studied, the trees, the wind, all that lived here asking who and what she was.

Nick touched her arm. "Don't worry," he said. "They know you. You'll be welcome here."

He opened the door, flicked on the lights, and led her inside to a less watchful and mysterious place. She saw an open room that included a large kitchen and a living room, with a stone fireplace at one end.

He put a hand on her luggage. "I'll take that. Unless you prefer to struggle up the narrow steps."

"Won't you struggle?" she asked.

"I know the stairs."

She followed him up a steep staircase, to a bedroom with slanted walls and one large window that looked to the east. The walls were soft green, and the furniture simple oak. Someone had put a bowl of fresh flowers on the nightstand next to the bed, which was suddenly very inviting.

"Do we have to do anything? Change sheets or anything?" she asked Nick as he brought up the last suitcase.

"Are you insane? I had someone take care of all that. All you have to do is get in."

She did so, gladly, but she was restless at first, unable to fall asleep. Too many images shifted and twitched in her mind, too many feelings in too much motion. "When did you get this place?" she asked.

He pulled her to him, held her against his chest. "A very long time ago."

"Is that why it feels like home?" she murmured.

His hands moved gently over her hair. "To you, maybe. To me, it feels like home because you're here."

She sighed, and relaxed into dreamless sleep. All her dreams were around her now, and had no need to plague her in the night.

Chapter Fourteen

In the morning, Nick was up before her and brought her coffee and sweet rolls in bed. They took the ferry to Basanavičiaus Gatvė, determinedly lively at the tag end of summer, a good contrast to the medieval brooding of Vilnius and the mysteries of Nida the night before. They stopped at stalls where vendors sold amber, and watched street performers with the crowds of young people who roamed like raucous flocks of birds, playing, laughing, singing, and clearly drinking way more than was good for them.

When they'd had enough, they strolled the nearby Botanical gardens, then sat by the grotto at the foot of Birute Hill. The stone structure was overseen by a statue of the Virgin Mary, and seeing it, Stacey shook her head. "Birute wasn't much of a Catholic," she noted.

"Neither was Mary," Nick replied. "I don't think she'd mind sharing the space. They both had good sons."

"Huh," she said. "You're right."

"Do you want to sketch anything?" he asked.

"Not yet," she said. "There's something sad here. I wonder what it is?"

"The place where old and new met. The goodbyes linger on, I think."

They sat for a while longer, and then decided they were hungry. Nick found a small, obscure pub for lunch, about which Stacey was uncertain. She sniffed the air and smelled cabbage.

"You have a peasant side too, I see," she commented. "Ralph's, and now boiled cabbage."

"The food will all be authentic. Pickles from the cellar and bread right out of the oven," he promised. "And if we're lucky, good midus."

She remained skeptical. "My ancestors did many things well, but they ate a lot of boiled pig parts I'd rather not investigate."

Nick laughed. "We'll see if we can do better than that."

They did, getting cold beet borscht, kugelis and sweet cheese, and a platter of thick, warm bread with homemade pickles and sausages. An old lady with a round, wrinkled face waited on them, smiling broadly. "Anythink good?" she asked. "You need?"

When Nick answered in Lithuanian, her eyes lit up and she let out a stream of incomprehensible words.

Nick listened, responded, then turned to Stacey. "I explained we're American, but your family was from here. She welcomes you home, to your people, and asks what your name is."

Stacey smiled up at her. "Austeja," she said. "Austeja Vitautis."

The woman put a plump hand to her cheek, said something Stacey interpreted either as 'Austeja? Stay there, I have something for you,' or 'Austeja? Oh, no! I have to run away.' In either case, she scurried away and then returned quickly with a small jar of dark honey, which she put in front of Stacey. She turned to Nick and spoke.

He nodded, responding with short affirmatives and exclamations, then turned to Stacey. "She asked if you knew about Austeja and the bees, and I said you did. Then she told me she's been watching you, because you have the old eyes. The silver eyes. There's a story about a long line of women, all named Austeja, with those eyes. They say the first one lived near here, and she was murdered by a man – pardon me?"

The woman spoke rapidly, but Stacey caught one word. Vele. Nick turned back to Stacey. "I'm sorry. She was murdered by a man who then became a vele. He continues to seek her, and her soul lives on in the women with the silver eyes. She said such a woman appeared here in Birute's time, for a while. And her grandmother, who's from Kaunus, knew an Austeja with the silver eyes, but she thinks that one was killed during Stalin's rule."

"Oh," Stacey said. "Really? Huh. I think my grandmother was from near there. She was Geidre, but her grandmother was an Austeja."

"Small country," Nick commented.

"I guess. Other than that, I'm - I'm not quite sure what to say. Um – thank you? It's good to know my ancestors were also strange?"

Nick grinned, turned to the woman and spoke. She nodded a great deal, smiled, patted Stacey's hand. Nick turned back to Stacey. "I told her you were glad to hear the story. You were hoping to find out about your ancestors while you're here. "

The woman poked Nick in the arm and said something clearly provocative. Nick let out a good laugh and said something back that made her chortle wickedly.

"What was that?" Stacey asked.

"She said I looked like I could be a Velnias – that's devil, in Lithuanian - and she hoped I was being good to my Austeja. I told her you liked a Velnias now and then, as long as he kept your pockets filled. You catch the double entendre, of course."

"Yes," she said. "In any language."

The woman spoke more, patted Stacey's hand once again.

Nick said something to her, made a gesture with his hand that indicated a mild negative. The woman spoke more forcefully and gestured at Stacey, insisting on something. "You tell," she said in English, fluffing a hand at him. "Go tell."

Nick's face tightened. "She says the moon is full tomorrow night, and asks if you'll go to the field to sing, as Austeja did. To the long grass. I told her – "

" – Yes," Stacey cut in. She turned to the woman and nodded. "Yes," she repeated. "I will."

The woman seemed satisfied. A few more sentences, some expressions of gratitude from Stacey, and then she left them alone.

"What was that last bit?" Stacey asked.

He spoke hesitantly. "She said - well, she said you should be careful. But she thinks you'll know what to do, when the time comes."

Stacey felt an odd sense of time shifting around her. She saw her grandmother's wasted face, felt the long fingernails in her flesh. Nick reached across the table and took her hand.

"You did say you wanted to find out about your ancestors," he noted.

"Careful what you wish for?" she asked.

"Something like that."

"But that's not real," she said. "It's just a story. A local legend. Maybe she says it to a lot of Americans, only the eye color changes with the customer."

"Maybe she does," he agreed, but he wasn't having fun with it. He was regarding her seriously. "What if it was true?"

"It's not."

"Humor me. Imagine for a moment that it's true. What would that mean to you?"

"I guess," she said after some thought, "it would change most of what I believe about the world."

"Take a chunk out of that realist attitude?"

"Quite a chunk."

"But wouldn't it also explain a few things? The way you paint and can't stop? The angels and devils at your back?"

She chewed her lip. "What she said about Kaunus – my grandmother's grandmother was Austeja. And she had the silver eyes."

Nick was quiet, watchful and waiting. Stacey suddenly felt her skin go cold. Something in her gave a sharp command to stop, stop now. Don't go any further. "It's not real. Not any of it," she said. "Let's go back to Basanavičiaus Gatvė. I saw a pair of amber earrings I'm still coveting, so I might as well get them."

She did get the earrings – teardrop amber surrounded by a filigreed tree of life – and they found a café to sit at and watch the crowds. In short time, her hands began to itch, and she pulled her sketchbook out of her bag, but then let it sit on her lap while she stared at it.

Nick tapped her arm. "Go ahead," he said. "I like to watch you."

She smiled up at him. "I think I'm a little afraid."

"I'm here," he said. "I won't let you walk off any cliffs, or disappear into the forest."

"Promise?"

"Promise," he put a hand to her face, drew close to her and kissed her lightly. "I'll keep you safe this time."

She wanted to ask what he meant by that. She opened her mouth to do so, then stopped herself. It's nothing, she told herself. Just a figure of speech. She opened her sketchbook, got a pencil and started drawing what was in front of her. People walking by, gesturing to each other. A circle of teenagers, faces close together, expressions twitchy and alive. As she worked, Nick looked on, something careful in his eyes.

"What the old woman said, about the grassy fields. You aren't going, are you?" he asked.

"What grassy fields?" she responded, focused on her work.

He relaxed, leaned back in his chair. "Nothing," he said. "It wasn't important."

                                          ∽

That night, they made a fire in the enormous fireplace in the living room and relaxed on the couch in front of it while the moon came up. Whatever had changed in Nick since the bee incident included sleeping, because he was fast asleep long before her. She crept away from the couch and got her sketchbook to work out an image that wouldn't leave her alone.

It started with an open field of long grass, pine forest in the background, a full moon rising. In the foreground was a woman's hand holding a piece of a bee hive, dripping honey into a flame that burned beneath it. Bees crawled over the honey, over her hand. Near the trees, a man sat hunched on the ground, his back against a tree, his head lowered, his hands open on the earth. Next to him was a violin made of sap and honey, its neck a growing oak branch.

She was finishing this when Nick started making ghastly sounds, and she turned to him. He was struggling, caught in some dream. She went to him and touched his shoulder. He moaned out her name, then was silent.

"And you said you didn't dream," she muttered.

She roused him enough to get him to bed, and they both slept undisturbed.

In the morning, Nick's mood was brooding, and she chalked it up to a dream hangover. "Whatever was going on," she said, "it didn't sound like fun."

"It wasn't," he agreed.

"Tell me about it," she said.

"It's not worth talking about," he said. "Do me a favor, would you?"

"What?"

"Don't draw today."

She tilted her head at him. "Sure, but – any particular reason for that?"

"Like my dream. Nothing worth talking about. You know, today is August 15th."

"What's that?"

"Assumption Day for Catholics. In the old religion, it's Zoline, a day to thank Zemyne, the earth goddess. We could find a festival somewhere. It's still celebrated, by pagans and Catholics."

She considered, then shook her head. "No. Let's go exploring in the woods."

"That seems appropriate," he said.

They spent the morning walking the land around Nick's house, where he named plants and butterflies and birds that lived here. They heard warblers, thrushes and finches, whose song he knew. They saw no wild boar or elk, though he claimed they both lived here. They heard what Nick said were brown frogs and common toads, and they stopped to watch small Orange Tip butterflies, and fluttering Camberwell Beauties, their elegant black wings dotted with blue and outlined in yellow and god. A small grass snake slithered near Stacey's foot and she admired it, following its path while Nick laughed and called her Ragana, Laume.

In the afternoon, they walked to the beach, and sat on the sands by the Baltic waters, watching the sky change in the west as the afternoon progressed regally toward evening. Stacey collected amber washed up on the shore, rubbing it in her fingers and breathing in its ocean scent. She had no words to say what she felt, though part of it was contentment, or maybe completion. Like finding your mother, if you've never known her. It would feel this way. Quiet, and complete.

Yet, under the quiet, she felt a watchfulness, a sense of some impending event. She found herself listening carefully, as if she waited for a phone to ring or a doorbell to buzz. She wondered if it was a variant of jet lag, one she'd never experienced. It wouldn't bother her so much except that Nick was obviously feeling it, too.

As the afternoon waned, they moved back inland and walked the forest, then sat and ate sandwiches under the trees. She was glad she said she wouldn't draw, because she couldn't have focused on it anyway. She kept lifting her head, as if someone called her name. Someone she knew. She expected company at any moment.

The feeling stayed with them both when they returned to Nick's house, as the sun set and the moon rose, full and bright. Nick watched her carefully, and if she left the room he followed, or clearly waited for her return because she'd find him standing and brooding, his arms folded across his chest.

"Is something wrong?" she asked him at last.

"I don't think so," he said. "Do you?"

She was about to say no, then changed her mind. "I'm not sure," she said. "I just – I keep almost hearing someone. Calling me."

"That's me, calling you to bed," he said, and pulled her in that direction. But when they got there, they didn't make love. Instead, he held her close, as if he was afraid.

୨

She didn't realize she'd gotten up until she found herself in front of the house. She looked up and saw the moon. She looked down and saw she was wearing only a tank top and underwear, and her feet were bare. She began to walk.

The call she'd heard all day was more clear, but still distant, just on the edge of hearing. She walked into the trees where moonlight, lean and cool, made a different kind of shadowed land. She kept walking, her feet telling her where to go, until the forest dropped away and she stood in front of an open rolling meadow. In its center the grass grew tall, up to her waist. It glowed golden under the moon, and whispered constant encouragement to her.

Here, Austeja. Yes, here. Right here. She moved toward it.

Then, a hand clutching her arm. She turned. It was Nick, his eyes wide with fear.

"I woke up. You were gone," he said.

"I'm not gone," she said. "I'm here."

He kept his hand on her. "Come back to the house."

She shook her head.

"Where are you going?"

She pointed to the long grass. "There," she said, slipping his grasp and walking to it.

Nick stayed where he was. "Austeja. No!" he called. "Come back."

But she kept going, walking into the grass, her hands brushing softly against the tops of it until she was surrounded by its ocean. She turned to him and held out her hand.

He walked to the edge, then stopped. "I can't," he whispered.

She sighed, dropped her hand, and lifted her face to the moon. Its light shone down on her and entered her skin, filling her like a lucent bowl in human form. He bit his lip to keep from crying out. She was painfully beautiful, the revealed image of a soul at work.

And then, she started to sing.

Her voice rose weightless to the moon, as if the earth itself, all its trees and grass, rivers and small snakes and toads and dancing bees sang through her to the glowing face of Menulis and resting Saule, feeding them, returning to them what they gave to those who lived under their care. And in this, he understood who and what she was.

In spite of Razak's will, she continued to call out the soul. In spite of any death, any incursions against her, she remained that clear channel between flesh and spirit, containing both, connecting all. Her paintings were just another singing. She was made of song, and she nurtured all that was important in the world.

He'd waited more than an age to witness this, to feel its import in his blood and bones. He'd risked his continued existence, gone against his own best interests and the commands of those who owned him to do so. It was worth it. But he wondered at his own arrogance, that imagined he could control her. Like controlling a storm at sea, he thought.

"Dieve," he said quietly. "I had no idea."

He took a step forward, the need to be near her, to touch that hair, that skin, overcoming any fears. He had to be present. Nothing more than that. Just present at her side. But her song was interrupted by a grinding sound in his ear, like metal scraping metal. A hand fell on his shoulder and held him still.

"Ah, these women," a voice said. "What a nuisance they are."

Nick didn't turn. He didn't have to. He knew who it was.

"With few exceptions, I'd like to get rid of the lot of them," the voice continued. "Be done with their insistence on life and love, and their unpredictability and intuition, their stories and paintings and songs. Especially their songs. My master's had more trouble from one woman than from armies of men, who value power as it should be valued. You must agree with me, considering how much trouble this one has given you."

"You have no business here, Razak," Nick said.

"But I do. It's my business to remind you who you work for, and why."

"Not now," he said. "Not tonight."

"Because of what you feel? I warned you to be careful of her, didn't I? And you wouldn't listen. You've drunk her blood, tasted her. The damn bees saw to that, the little bastards. They always worked against us and protected her. We've done our best to get rid of them, and we're making progress, with this new pesticide everyone loves so much. They'll be gone soon enough, and in the meantime, everything you feel now will fade away. It's not yours, my friend. Not at all. It's a vicarious sip of her. When it's depleted, you'll remember what you really are."

Nick said nothing, only watched her. Only watched and heard her voice rise in the soft night air. Then, more noise in his ear, like nails on a chalkboard, like jackhammers.

"Listen," Razak continued. "The game has been amusing, but it's gone on too long. You see what she is. What she does. And she's singing again, after all our work to prevent just that. It's time to put a stop to it. If you don't, we will."

He heard both fear and threat in these words, and he ignored both. "I'll take care of her," he said curtly, wanting only for him to leave.

"It looks like you're taking too much care of her."

"I'll deal with it."

"How?"

"I have an idea. A plan."

"Is it along the lines of our conversation in Italy? Give her up and get the brother, the violin?"

"Let me alone and I'll work it out."

"You'd better. Because in spite of the spell you're under, nothing has changed. When her blood is gone from you, you'll still belong to me."

He was gone, and Nick knew why. While she sang, his powers had little sway. Her music, her light, was stronger than Razak would ever admit. Like her honeybees, she had not been, would not be, easily defeated. But neither would she be his, if what Razak said was right.

Nick closed his eyes. The thought of losing her now caused him pain worse than he'd felt when he lay here with grass peeling his flesh. Yet, overriding it was an impossible joy. It wasn't time to despair, not while Austeja sang in the moonlight.

When her song ended and there was only silence, he opened his eyes. She stood blinking at him.

"Nick?" she asked. She looked around. "Where am I?"

He walked through the grass to her. "You're with me," he said, and drew her close and kissed her, as if she was light, and he a thirsty star.

Chapter Fifteen

"Wow," Stacey said. "I had a crazy dream."

She rolled over in bed to see Nick lying face up with his hands behind his head and his eyes open, staring at the ceiling.

"Oh?" he asked politely.

"I wanted to take you somewhere, but you wouldn't go. It made me sad. Then I was singing. Standing under the moonlight and singing, in a field. Someone else was there. A – a devil, I think. He wanted to kill me. Or you. Maybe both.

"Not very pleasant," he said.

"That's the strangest part. I wasn't afraid. I knew what to do."

"Why am I not surprised?" He leaned up on an elbow and looked at her. "Anything else?"

"We were making love in the field, in this golden grass," she said. "Like the kind in the painting I made in Italy."

He reached up, pulled something from her hair and handed it to her. "Like this?"

She stared down at it. A thin blade of grass, gold at the edges, green at the center. "Oh," she said. "Right. That part was real."

"And the rest?"

She wrinkled her nose, shook her head. "Of course not." She rolled out of bed and made her way to the bathroom. Nick lay back down and stared at the ceiling some more while he listened to her brushing her teeth.

"You know what I think you need?" he called to her.

He heard her rinse and spit. "What?" she called back.

"A trip to the devil museum."

She came back and stood in the doorway between bathroom and bedroom, leaning against the frame, smiling at him. "The what?" she asked.

He let his gaze rest on her, savoring a happiness that was both simple and complete. Let me not forget how this feels, he prayed to himself. Take all the rest, even the Sibelius, but let me never forget this.

He smiled back. "The devil museum. In Kaunus. It has more than 260 devils, and you can bring your own and give it a permanent home there if you like."

"Had I known that," she said, "I would've brought quite a few."

They packed and put their luggage in the car, since they wouldn't return to Nida. They might go on to Trakai, or back to Vilnius, but they wouldn't be staying longer than a few more days.

The devil museum was more fun than Stacey anticipated, with the largest and most varied images of that creature in sculpture and drawing she'd ever seen gathered in one place. There were silly devils, sexy devils, frightened devils, fat devils, skinny devils, contemporary devils, ancient devils and more. Nick gloated over them, admiring or critiquing as he went. He was particularly fond of the greedy devil, counting his coins, and the smallish red devil with an enormous erection, chasing after a Pope.

"What about this one?" Stacey asked, pointing to a rather large and foreboding fiery-eyed devil bending over a man who crouched on the ground in front of him.

He looked at it, backed away. His face grew tight. "Where's the fun in that?" he asked, and they moved on.

He was right. That one, and a grotesque and sad devil's mask with its drooping face, were the only ones she couldn't poke fun at. Something in the melting face, the combination of sorrow and horror in it, made her shiver.

"Does it scare you?" Nick asked as they stared at it.

"A little," she said. "It's the only one I couldn't beat, I think."

"Because it's about despair, which even the Catholics knew was the greatest sin of all."

"The sins of the father," she murmured, then turned to him. "That's the thing," she said. "Real evil is relentlessly dreary. Without feeling."

Nick drew a lip through his teeth, took in breath. "But even that didn't scare your ancestors," he noted.

"Maybe they pushed back too many devils to see them as more powerful than they are," she answered.

"They've had more than their share," Nick agreed. "Like these two."

He pointed out a devil version of Stalin chasing Hitler across Lithuania.

"Yeah," she said. "I asked a priest how you beat the devil."

He gave her a sharp glance. "Whatever for?"

"It was right after I met you. Given our conversations, I wanted to know. He told me confidence and laughter, or tears and love. Especially love, he said."

Nick gazed at the Hitler and Stalin devils. "None of that worked on these two."

"Eventually it did," Stacey said. "The people who loved their country beyond all measure drove them out, right? And if anyone was in league with the real devil, these two were. That's what made my grandmother leave. I wonder if they have a hall of records or anything in town. Maybe I can find out things about her."

Nick shook his head "Wouldn't you rather leave your devils here, where they're safe among friends?"

"She wasn't a devil. And I'd like to find out more about her life."

"Are you sure?" he asked quietly.

Something in his tone disturbed her. "Why wouldn't I be?" He tightened his lips, said nothing. She put a hand on her hip. "You already know about her, don't you? What are you keeping from me?"

His expression showed sorrow, a deep and ancient river of it. He cupped his hands on her face, looked down at her. "Should I be as honest with you as you've been with me?" he asked with quiet intensity.

"Yes," she said. "Yes. I want that."

He drew in breath. "I had plans," he said. "Carefully conceived, every contingency accounted for. But they all flew away with a swarm of bees. Now I need a new road, in the oldest place my memory holds. I want it to be different this time."

"Different than what?"

"My past errors. And I'm afraid that's not possible. It's like evil – it just keeps going on and on, a force all its own. Once started, it can't be stopped. Austeja, do you believe in forgiveness?"

She glanced at the devils surrounding them and wondered what they'd make of this conversation. In her mind she saw a painting of a man kneeling, seeking absolution. She didn't yet know what figure would represent the priest.

"Yes," she said. "If someone's willing to change and do what's right, they should be forgiven."

"No matter what they've done?"

"I think so. Yes. If it's a real intent to do better."

"What if they're dead, like your father and his father?"

"That's different. Then you forgive them not because they need it, but because you do, to get on with your life. Because you want to put something better in the world."

"What if they're still alive, but struggling?"

"Then I guess it's like Vince. You help if you can, or leave them alone if you can't."

He gave a shuddering sigh and closed his eyes. When he opened them again, they were bright, and he was smiling.

"Do you want to know your ancestors, Austeja?" he asked.

"Yes," she said. "I do."

"Then I'll introduce you to them."

ℒ

They made their way into the heart of town, to an old library, where Nick already knew the librarian and the archivist. He spoke to them in Lithuanian, pointing at her frequently. They smiled at him, at her, and the archivist led them down a flight of stairs to a musty room that smelled of old books, old paper. A single light bulb hung from the ceiling and the archivist pulled the cord, revealing shelves of boxes, sorted by year and region. Nick offered thanks, in Lithuanian, and he left.

Nick turned to Stacey. "I have some older writings at my house in Nida you'd find interesting. Someday I'll show you those. But this is from your grandmother's time."

He took her hand and led her down an aisle of shelves, read dates and then reached up for a box, which he pulled down. He opened it and took out a manuscript, spiral bound, its Lithuanian title unreadable to her.

He ran his finger under the words, read them in Lithuanian, and then translated. "Survivor Reports, Trofimovsk Island, 1942-43. It's from people who survived Stalin's deportations. He killed millions, you know. More than 100,000 Lithuanians. A historian who survived contacted other survivors and had them write about their experiences, each in their own way. There's poems and letters, songs and straightforward reporting. The one I found most interesting is more like a story."

She touched the book. "It's in Lithuanian," she said. "I can't read it."

"But I can," he told her.

They found two metal folding chairs and pulled them under the bare light bulb. Nick opened the book, and began to read.

The Island

Trofimovsk Island, 1942-43

They'd done nothing wrong that Giedre Szaltaityte knew of. But one day the men in uniforms – the NKVD - came and pushed in the door of their old farmhouse and told them they were under arrest for crimes against the Soviet Socialist Republic.

Her father worked hard on the farm. Sometimes he went into town and drank too much and talked loudly about everything that was wrong with the world, but that was no crime. He was a good Catholic, and once he'd brought a priest to the house to say mass for them, but that had never been a crime before. And her mother was quiet, always quiet, pale and tense when the priest came to the house. Her grandmother was old, and she tolerated the priest, but preferred to say her prayers in the woods.

In spite of that, or perhaps because of that, they were under arrest, all of them to go to a work camp to compensate for their crimes.

"Why?" her father demanded. "What have we done?"

"You support the church against Stalin," one of the soldier's said. "Now you'll apologize with your backs."

They were allowed to take a small bag each, but they had no idea where they were going or for how long, so how could they know what to bring? Giedre's grandmother took 2 coats and scarves and stuffed food in her pockets. Her mother took jewelry and family pictures in silver frames. Her father took money and books and clothes. Geidre took her violin, a part of her family for many generations, which she'd always played in the house to amuse her grandmother, in the forest to amuse the bees. They danced around her when she played, and seemed to sing along. Sometimes, she played it just for the joy of feeling her fingers move on the string, pulling music from them, sweet and joyful and sad.

The soldiers laughed at her. "Do you think you're going to America?" one said. "To Car-nee-gee Hall?"

She didn't answer, but clutched it tightly under her arm.

They were shoved into a truck full of people, some of them neighbors, and brought to the train station where a line of such trucks poured out people. They were split up according to rules none of them understood. Giedre and her grandmother were pushed into one train car, her mother and father into another. Her mother looked at her as she was moved away, but there was no time for a goodbye, or a blessing or a kiss.

The train ride went on for days, and they were only allowed out once to relieve themselves. Soon the smell of urine, defecation, sweat and vomit, made her head swim. There wasn't room to sit so they stood the entire time, slept leaning against each other. Giedre felt her grandmother's hand on her shoulder throughout the trip. She was old, but she was strong from years of working their farm.

The train brought them to a barge, and the barge to docks where more trucks waited. They kept going north, and every moment it grew colder. The trees disappeared, leaving only small bushes. Then the bushes disappeared, and there was no sign of life at all. She tried to ask her grandmother questions and was hushed. "Say nothing, Giedre," she insisted. "From this point on, say nothing unless you absolutely must."

Finally, the truck left them on an island. This place, they were told, was Trofimovsk Island, their new home for as long as their sentences lasted. Giedre thought it was made of concrete, like the streets, but it was only so cold that nothing would grow here. Not even houses, for there were none at all.

"Where will we sleep?" she asked her grandmother, and was hushed again.

The Russian guards counted them – 400 Lithuanians and 100 men from Finland. Everything they'd brought was taken away, the guards gloating over jewelry, ripping pictures from silver frames. And of course, they took her violin.

They were set to work immediately unloading bricks and boards from barges at the dock. They had to dig a hole in the ground with their hands, and build their shelter with these bricks and boards. The bricks made a short wall around the top, and covered them with the boards, then covers the boards with moss that one of the women found.

As they worked, Giedre noticed a young man watching her. He was dark haired, and his eyes were not both the same color. The way he looked at her made her blush red. She was almost 20 and old enough to understand those kind of looks, but she couldn't understand how he dared, in this place, where the only feeling that made sense was horror.

At one point he worked near her and introduced himself, as if they were bringing in hay from the fields. "I'm Naktis," he said. "What's your name?"

"Giedre," she said.

"That old lady," he indicated her grandmother. "Is she your family?"

"My grandmother," Giedre said.

"She has the old eyes," he noted. "What's her name?"

"Austeja."

"You brought the violin, didn't you?"

She nodded, though she wondered how he knew about it. He stared at her for a moment longer. "We'll speak again," he said.

When they'd finished building, everyone was given a plank for their bed, while the guards slept in the warm rooms of the barge.

"How will we live?" a young woman moaned. "How will we live here, and winter coming on?"

In the night they huddled together, Giedre's grandmother holding her close, trying to share the warmth of her body.

The next day they were put to work building log houses for the guards. These were large, sealed tight against the constant wind. They had wood stoves, stacks of wood near them, brought by the prisoners who walked miles into the tundra to find logs carried down from the river. The prisoners hacked them out of the ice, harnessed them to their shoulders with ropes and dragged them back. The Russian guards would be warm when the polar nights began.

An older man named Aras tried to take a piece of a log for their barracks, but he was caught, and the next day everyone was brought outside while he was found guilty of stealing socialist property. He was sentenced to two more years, and when he heard that he went mad, attacking the guards and calling them beasts and devils. For that, he was sentenced to hang.

The guards made the prisoners build the gallows from wood allotted for heating their barracks. Then they all stood and watched while the rope was put around Aras's neck. He was calm, happy even. "I'm sorry to leave you here, my friends, but not sorry to leave," he said. "This place will soon be worse than any hell."

When he was pushed off the platform his feet twitched and his tongue stuck out. He danced for some time, his throat filled with choking, and then he was dead. The guards left him there as his face and tongue turned swollen and blue, and he began to smell.

∿

The polar nights began in November, darkness shrouding all. Blizzards blew snow into the barracks through the cracks and covered them as they slept on the floor. People died of cold and starvation and scurvy, and their bodies stayed in the barracks until the prisoners removed them, making a growing pile in the snow.

They could not be buried. The Evenki, who lived on nearby islands and were fishers and hunters, wanted to give fish to the prisoners, or bring everyone to their heated yurts, but the Russian guards said no. They were here to work for Stalin, because of their crimes.

They gathered wood to keep the guards warm, their feet wrapped in frozen sacks. Those who couldn't work lay on the planks bloated from starvation, their gums bleeding and joints and muscles filling with blood from scurvy. A woman named Ruta, who was beautiful when she arrived, had no teeth left and her blue joints swelled. She cried out that there were needles in her flesh, piercing her. Soon, she began to urinate blood, and shortly after, she died.

Some people prayed for a miracle, while some prayed for death. Others ceased speaking at all. Most thought only of food. When bodies were dragged from the planks to put out in the snow they were checked for the smallest piece of bread, which was eaten, no matter how lice ridden. People dug through frozen excrement in night pails for any morsel they could find.

During that winter, Geidre knew they would all die. Though the guards were dressed in furs, and ate bread and butter and canned pork sent from America, the prisoner barracks were unheated and people's hands and feet froze. They were infested with lice and riddled with disease. Even Giedre's grandmother grew weak, her hair falling out in clumps and her flesh melting from her face, making her silver eyes seem huge as oceans.

Only Naktis, the young man who stared at Giedre, stayed well. His job was to clean the guards' houses, work done in warmth. Then, the guards were bored, and Naktis knew card games, so they kept him at night to teach them, and amuse them with stories about the prisoners. Some said he told who was stealing, giving his own people away.

"Does he do that?" Giedre asked her grandmother. "Against his own people?"

"I would do the same, if it would save you," she replied.

When Naktis was in the barracks he still watched Giedre, though she was thin and sick, her joints aching and her gums bleeding.

"You didn't get your grandmother's eyes," he said to her.

"My daughter will, or hers. They always come back to the girls in our family."

"You think you'll live long enough to have one?" he asked.

One day the guards called those who could still walk into the office and gave them their salary - a three ruble note for each. Officer Petrov, well-groomed and wearing an elegant wool coat, made them stand while he gave a speech about their duty to the socialist party. Naktis sat at a desk, pen and paper in his hand, not quite as sleek, but in better condition than any prisoner.

"Your country needs your rubles to buy arms," Officer Petrov told them. "How many of you will donate?"

Giedre gaped in wonder. Didn't he see what stood in front of him? They were skeletons draped in thin yellow flesh. They had to buy their bread with their rubles. Without that, they would die. Still, when Petrov went around to collect, they all gave, and Naktis made marks next to their names on his paper. But Giedre closed her hand in a fist. What did she have to lose? Her life? Her grandmother's life? Both were forfeit if she gave the rubles away.

"I need bread for my grandmother," she told Petrov. "She's ill."

He stood still. His plans didn't include a girl who defied him. Giedre waited for him to hit her, or shoot her, not caring which he chose. Then, behind her, she heard the strangest sound of all. Somebody laughed.

There were gasps. "Velnias," the old man next to her murmured.

Yes, it must be, Giedre thought. Who would laugh in hell except the devil?

"Naktis,"someone hissed. He dared laugh. Everyone looked his way.

"Pardon me, Officer Petrov," he said. "I thought of a way to repair such insolence. Something you might find amusing. We can discuss it, when you're done here. And I think now the girl will give her rubles to you." He turned his strange eyes to her. They told her to be silent, to do as he said.

She lifted her hand to Petrov and gave him the money. What did it matter?

When the meeting was done she returned to the barracks, where her grandmother lay on her plank, the scurvy and a festering wound in her leg sickening her. Giedre was out of tears, too tired to even apologize for losing their money, their bread. She lay down, touched her grandmother's leg, and began to sing. Softly, she sang into the brutalized flesh. Softly, quietly, with no strength for more than a whisper of song.

Her grandmother sighed. "Aah, child. You make me see the forest again. I smell the honey, and hear the bees in the flowers."

Giedre was glad she could at least do that. Exhausted, she fell asleep.

That night, she dreamt she was standing in the long grass of a meadow near the forests of Nida. The sun was warm and the smell was sweet all around. But here, you weren't even allowed to escape into dreams.

"Get up," a voice commanded, waking her.

She opened her eyes, looked up.

Naktis stood over her. "What you did today was foolish. You're lucky I thought quick enough to save you."

She said nothing.

"I played for your life tonight, at poker. Of course, I won."

She wasn't sure the gift was a good one. "Why did you?" she asked.

"Your violin," he said. "Can you play it?"

"They have it," she said.

"Yes, and they can't play at all. Can you?"

She nodded.

"Can you play well, or like a schoolgirl?"

Geidre felt a hand clutch her wrist. Her grandmother, whose eyes were open. "She plays well," she said. "Very well."

Naktis looked to her. "You're not lying to me, are you?"

"If I was, you'd find out soon enough," the old woman said.

Naktis nodded. "Then she'll come with me. They want some music."

Geidre looked to her grandmother, whose grasp on her wrist tightened. "Give me a moment with her," she requested.

Naktis grunted. "One minute. I'll wait outside."

When he was gone, Geidre's grandmother turned her silver eyes toward her, and they were sparking with life. "Be careful of him," she said. "He is dead, in his soul."

Geidre nodded, understanding what her grandmother meant.

"But do whatever they ask. You must live, girl," she whispered. "No matter how. Your daughters wait to be born, and someone must remember what happened here."

She played for the guards every day after that. She played Russian tunes, Lithuanian tunes, songs they made her learn from the radio. Even more than the warmth of the guard's house, the music brought life back to her body, as if the violin fed her.

To her surprise, Naktis also fed her, making sure she ate as he did, which was much more than the other prisoners. He even had fish and meat. But he grew angry when he found her saving part of it to bring back to the barracks.

"This is for you," he said. "Don't let me see you giving it away again."

After that, she was more careful, hiding pieces of bread and meat in her shirt. She was amazed at how much food came to this island, though they were still starving. It arrived on the barges, in huge crates that said 'America' on them. She knew about America. It was a land of rich people who were never hungry or cold.

"Someday I'll go there," she said to Naktis.

"Why?"

"Because that's where the food comes from."

"It doesn't go to you. America feeds the Russians, and lets Lithuanians starve."

"Maybe it's different when you're where it comes from."

"I wouldn't count on that," Naktis said. "Like everyone else, they feed power, hoping it will feed them in turn."

But she knew better. She had cousins in America. They lived near a place called New York. She'd written their address on a piece of paper she carried with her, under her shirt. When they left this place, she'd take her grandmother there.

As the winter went on, more people died, and the pile of swollen corpses outside grew larger. She passed it as she went to her violin playing, and each day she'd see someone else she knew. There was Adomas, who ate the bread she snuck in yesterday and threw it up almost immediately. Jurgis and Audra had dug through his vomit to try and retrieve it. Now they were in the pile. Then Daina, who sang with her when they'd first arrived and who died screaming for God to save her. Others, Laima, Niele, Mykolas. One by one they joined the pile, eyes frozen open, still seeing horror.

She said she wouldn't play for the guards who did this, but her grandmother shook her hard. "Play," she hissed. "Sleep with them if they ask. You have an obligation to live. And when you leave here you have an obligation to live well, in joy."

She continued to play for the Russians, who ignored the bodies outside their doors.

After a while, Giedre noticed that one of the guards, Viatovsky, looked sad when she played Lithuanian tunes. Once she thought he hummed along, his lips barely moving. She asked Naktis about him, and he made a face. "He's Lithuanian, like you and I. But he joined the Russian army, pretending he was Russian because he was afraid."

She looked at Viatovsky with pity, until one day he took her aside. "Don't give me away," he pleaded in a whisper. "They'll kill me."

"No," she said. "They'll make you live with us, which is worse than death." She wouldn't do that even to him.

Throughout the long winter she played the violin and stayed alive, free of scurvy. Naktis fed her, but she placed no trust in him. He spent too much time laughing with the guards.

"I'm pretending," he said. "I must."

"You do it too well."

"Be careful Giedre," he said. "I may not always save you."

He slept on the floor in the guard's house now, but sometimes he'd walk her back to the barracks when she was done playing. In March, while winter lingered, he said to her, "Giedre, would you like to sleep where it's warm?"

Her body ached for warmth, but she said no. "I keep my grandmother warm."

"You won't keep her warm if you're a corpse," he noted.

"Then I must stay alive," she replied.

She turned from him, but he grabbed her arm. "Do you think that's up to you? And don't you think you owe me something, after all I've done for you?"

She'd waited for this. She was thin as a blade of grass, but she still had her teeth, she wasn't deformed by scurvy, and she had water to wash the lice away. "If you want that, you can have it," she said, remembering her grandmother's words.

He took a step back. "I wouldn't touch you. It's for Officer Petrov."

She shuddered. Could she? Her grandmother said she should, but could she?

"I see the idea doesn't appeal to you. Well, maybe I can get you out of it, but this time you really would owe me. How will you pay up?"

She ran her tongue over her lips. "I don't know," she said.

"I do. I'd want your violin. Or your soul if you think it's worth more."

Something about his confidence, his sleek assurance, sparked rage in her. She flung his arm off. "My soul? The Russians ate that long ago. The violin is all I have left, and I'll keep that. Tell Officer Petrov he can keep me warm."

She waited for the consequences to crash down on her, but nothing happened. She played for the guards and returned to the freezing barracks to sleep. She wondered if Petrov ever wanted her, or if it was a lie Naktis told to get her violin or her soul, or both.

He no longer spoke to her, but as winter continued on through March and into early April, she saw him whispering to Viatovsky, who began to show the whites of his eyes at her. Something was happening, and it was about her. She found Naktis as he cleaned the back office, and asked him what he'd done.

He scowled. "I've taken care of myself. Your grandmother is almost dead. If you give no daughters to the world, I'll be done chasing you through the centuries."

"I don't understand," she said.

"You don't have to," he replied.

Soon after, Viatovsky stopped her as she went back to the barracks. He pulled bread and three ruble notes from her pocket. "Stealing, are you?" he said angrily.

She looked at it in amazement. She'd taken nothing that day. "You put that in my pocket," she said.

He shook her hard. "You stole it. And now you'll pay."

He dragged her off to see Petrov, and on the way he whispered in her ear. "Why would you give me away?"

"I wouldn't," she said. "I never would."

"Naktis said otherwise."

She understood, then. Naktis wanted her violin, and would get it any ways he could She would be tried, and shot or hung. She would have no daughters, which seemed important to Naktis, though she didn't know why. And he would have her violin.

They made a great show of her trial, with everyone from the barracks forced to attend, including her grandmother. At least, she thought, she was buying them some warmth, and she could see they were thankful for it. The old Finnish man, Kimmi, actually mouthed the words at her, with tears in his eyes. For her part, she was grateful that someone here was still human enough to shed tears. Her eyes were very dry.

Officer Petrov asked her if she stole bread and money, socialist property.

"Yes, I stole it," she said, seeing no point in defending herself, and no point in giving Viatovsky away. Even if they believed her, Naktis would find some other way to kill her, and she was sick of this life, the dull evil in it. Though her body remained well, her heart was hollowed by what humans did to each other.

"Who did you steal it for?" Petrov asked.

"I just stole it. I was hungry."

He kept at her for some time, but she just repeated what she'd said. Finally he gave up, and instead gave a long speech about their duty to Stalin because of all he did for them. No one else said a word. They were silently praying to stay warm a little longer. At the end, she was sentenced to death by hanging.

Her grandmother cried out, but a guard hit her, knocking her down. She cried out again, and he hit her again, then he kept hitting her in some madness of rage, screaming, "Why do you make us do this? Why? Why?"

The other guards, including Petrov, looked on. Strangely, Naktis leapt up and pulled him off. "Friend, she's an old lady," he said. "Leave her alone."

The guard moved away, and her grandmother lay bleeding on the floor as Petrov, to show the mercy of the Soviets, asked if Giedre had a last request.

"Yes," she said. "Let these people sleep here tonight, and have extra bread."

"And you want to stay here with them?" he asked.

"That doesn't matter."

At this, Naktis hissed, as if something burned him.

Petrov was almost true to his word. The people slept on the floor in a back room of the guards' building, but they weren't allowed a fire. They had extra bread, but it was from the garbage. Still, they ate it, and were glad of it. All except her grandmother, who died in the night and was put on the pile of corpses with the others.

The next morning Petrov announced that her wrongdoing incurred the penalty of two days bread for everyone, since she would name no conspirators. Giedre hung her head, knowing what this meant to them.

Naktis walked her to the gallows, something he said he'd requested, though she didn't know why. "Is the violin your reward?" she asked him.

"I tried to help you," he said, as if he didn't care anymore, but she saw the muscles working in his jaw. "I thought you'd be grateful for that."

Anger filled her, and words came to her from some other place, perhaps from her grandmother's soul as it left the world. She stopped on the stairs leading to her death, turned her rageful face toward him.

"Stribas," she said, spitting the word at him, the word for those who helped the Soviets, the word that meant Destroyer. "You are Stribas. Your desire teaches you how to kill, but not how to live. Until it does, you'll *never* be free."

"You want me to live?" he hissed back. "Life leads only to death."

"But it offers hope, which you won't have after you kill me."

His grip tightened, and he pushed her up the steps. She was calm because she'd said all she needed to say. But halfway up, Naktis went insane. Naktis, always joking, always smiling, suddenly grabbed her hair and shoved her down on her face, held her by her hair and pounded her head against the wood step once, twice, three times. Then he released her and walked away as if he'd done nothing at all.

She lay there dazed, unable to move. She thought she dreamt of home, because she heard bees buzzing as they did in the summer. But no, she really did hear them. And she saw them rising from beneath the step, a nest Naktis woke too early with her head. She wanted to tell them to go back, they'd die here as everything did, but they were loosed, swarming the guards who didn't know enough to be still. They waved their arms and screamed, falling down the steps. She lay still, listening to the sweet song of the bees that sounded so much like her grandmother's voice.

A great commotion followed, and in it, Jecis, a big farmer who kept some of his strength, picked her up, carried her back to the barracks and untied her hands.

"They'll kill me tomorrow, I suppose," she said.

"Maybe," he said. "For now, you can rest."

But no one came for her in the morning, and rumor filtered back that a doctor had arrived, and he was arguing with the guards about how people here were treated. Someone learned his name, and they all repeated it, memorizing it as a shining, precious thing.

He was Doctor Lazar Solomonivich Samodurov. He was fighting for the hopeless residents of this particular hell.

They never knew how he convinced the guards, since they didn't have any conscience. Maybe he had powerful friends. Maybe he threatened to report them for misusing prisoners who were socialist property. No matter how, he saved their lives.

The next day instead of a hanging they all had a bowl of hot pea soup and a little frozen fish, which they ate raw to get all the nutrients from it. The doctor stayed and showed them how to germinate the dried peas and eat the sprouts. He had their clothes disinfected, made sure they had baths and some warmth as well as food.

Slowly, those near death crept back toward life. The prisoners couldn't pray enough good prayers for the doctor, whose presence healed their hearts as well as their bodies. He stayed a month, and everyone tried to be close to him. Only Naktis kept his distance, but he also stayed away from Giedre.

One day, at the dock, she saw the boat that brought the food from America. It occurred to her that she might leave. Her grandmother was gone, and she felt strong enough to take some action on her own behalf. That was the doctor's doing.

"Does that boat go back to America?" she asked him.

"Yes," he said. "Of course it does. Why do you ask?"

"I was just wondering," she said.

He gave her a funny look, and she wondered if she'd made a mistake. But no. He remained a hero.

"There are rooms at the bottom of it that no one goes into," he said. "A small, quiet person could hide there. But she'd need to bring some food. It's a long journey."

"When does it leave?" she asked.

"Tomorrow, before dawn," he said.

That night, she snuck into the guard's apartments and got her violin. Viatovsky was on duty, but he turned his back as if she was invisible. He was Lithuanian. He knew she had the protection of the bees. He knew what that meant. She put food in her pockets and walked to the great ship.

She stopped only once, where the pile of corpses were buried. She stood there, and recited the ancient death chant of her people.

"The green oak will be your father," she said. "The white sands will be your mother. The green maples will be your brothers, and the white lindens will be your sisters."

She turned away and snuck onto the ship, found the stairs and went down into the bottom. She wasn't afraid. She didn't think she'd ever be afraid again.

She found the darkest corner, put her head down on her violin case, and slept.

Chapter Sixteen

Kaunus, Lithuania, early 21st century

When Nick was done reading, he closed the book and looked at Stacey.

"My grandmother," she said, against a tight knot forming in her throat. "That was my grandmother."

"I know," he murmured.

She tried to say something else, but the knot was larger and tighter, and she had to gulp for air around it. She clutched at her throat, looked at Nick helplessly. Had she forgotten how to breathe?

Nick's eyes went wide, and he wrapped his arms around her, lifted her to standing and walked her up the stairs. She stumbled up next to him, terrified she'd pass out or maybe throw up because she felt nauseated, the walls swimming around her.

"Stay with me," Nick said. "We'll find the light."

Then, somehow, they were outside breathing fresh air and seeing people pass by, chatting happily. In the open air and bright sun, under the comfort of Saule, she hung on to him and waited for the world to right itself. Her breath returned and the world stopped its sickening motion around her. She breathed deeply and slowly, felt Nick smoothing her hair.

"That's what you didn't want me to know," she said.

"I was wrong. Or at least, overprotective. You have a right to all your history, and you're strong enough to bear it." He looked around, then pointed ahead. "There's a little church there. If it's empty we'll sit inside and be private. If not, we'll sit on the steps and be peasants."

The church was empty and quiet, soft candles glowing near altars that held statues of Mary and the saints. They went inside and sat down in a pew toward the back.

"Okay now?" he asked.

Stacey ran a hand through her hair. "It's the shock of connecting all that to her," she said. "She always seemed so happy. Well, happy in her own way. Lithuanians are serious people."

"Rimtas zmogus," he cut in.

Stacey smiled wanly, remembering the phrase. "Exactly," she said. "But she could laugh. When she saw birds or heard music, or when she saw me, her face would light up, and she'd laugh like a little girl. How could she, after all that? And knowing those men were never punished. She had all the consequences, and they had none."

"Some had consequences. The guard – Viatovsky. He ended up at the Russian front, and was left for dead by his troop. The Germans took him prisoner, which was no picnic."

Her brow knit down. That sounded familiar. "That's what happened to my father's father." And then, a new horror found her. She stared at Nick. "My grandfather, who got here under a Russian name, and changed it later."

"Viatovsky," Nick said. "Vitautis. He died young, long before your father met your mother. He really was a nasty drunk – there are jail records, in fact – and he passed that burden on. The domestic wars go on long after the foreign wars end."

She buried her face in his shoulder, too horrified to cry. The dreary and relentless evil stuck in her heart, in her throat. Ancestral grief filled her, and would not be released.

She felt him shifting, heard him take in breath. "Austeja, look," he said.

She lifted her head, saw that he'd turned around and was gazing up, pointing over the choir loft behind them. She followed his finger. The back wall had a large stained glass window, all golds and greens. But it didn't show a Catholic saint. Instead, it showed a honeybee, held within the center of a delicately rayed sun.

She stood and moved out of the pew so she could see it without craning. Horror had left her numb, but this brought the tears running down her face.

Nick joined her, and patted her shoulder. His hand reached out, holding a Kleenex. "Take this," he said. "Dry up and turn to something better, as your people always did. You see, the Pope got them, but they kept their bees. The communists got them, but they kept their churches. You have a long history of holding on to your souls, in spite of what the world can do."

"So it seems," she said. She wondered at the mysterious ways her past led to this present, where she stood in a church staring at a bee, with a rather strange man she suspected she was falling in love with.

"Austeja, I want to leave the old stories and talk about the new ones," Nick said. "Will you do that?"

"What are they?" she asked.

"They're about you. A very talented artist, who deserves the opportunity to fully realize her art. To take it on full time."

Stacey raised an eyebrow. "Fairy godmother?"

"Neither godmother nor godfather. Just someone who wants to support you, so you can have your own life instead of slaving away at a Marketing firm, however prestigious."

This wasn't what she expected. Not at all. And she wasn't sure if she was hearing it correctly. "Plain English, please," she requested.

"I'm offering to support you financially. You can quit your job and paint. I think your grandmother would be glad of that."

She felt the simultaneous tug of appeal and terror, both equally compelling. She responded from the fear first. "And you get – what? My soul?"

He shot her a look, then his face grew cool, neutral. "I think you'll need it if you're going to paint. Maybe I'll take your brother's, since he's not currently using it."

"That's not funny," she said sharply.

"I didn't mean it to be," he replied.

They were quiet, Stacey trying to absorb this, trying to determine how much was verbal jousting to rouse her from her tears, and how much in earnest. He let her wrangle it out with herself for a while, and then he said, "This is a serious offer, and you need it more than you know."

"I don't think need is the right word," she said.

His face twisted through some changes. "It may be. There are ways I can – take care of you. You clearly can't paint part time, and I'd like to give you the chance to explore your art. If you're worried about the money, I think you're more than talented, and I expect to realize a good profit."

"Then I'm an investment?"

"Not *just* an investment. Don't let the sex tangle up your thinking."

He was right. Being his lover complicated everything. Without that, she'd look at his offer as merely a patronage, like artists once had from dukes and kings.

"What happens if we stop sleeping together? The deal's off?"

"No. It remains good for as long as you want it, regardless."

She supposed that made a difference, if he meant it, but something about it still bothered her. A nagging resistance would not let her say yes.

"What's wrong?" he asked. "Is it the old immigrant work ethic? A need to do it on your own, through hard work? Most of the world runs on chance and connection, not work. Surely you know that."

She did. It wasn't that, not really. "It's – something else," she murmured.

He scowled, and muttered at her. "*Mano leituva bedale, Ar bijai.*"

"Speak English, for fuck's sake," she said, irritated.

"Are you afraid?" he asked sharply. "Do you lack your grandmother's courage?"

"No need to get testy," she said.

He backed off, folded his arms across his chest and scowled down at the floor, then took a deep breath and continued. "I apologize," he said. "But as I keep telling you, there's a great deal at stake here. And there's even more I can offer you later, if you'll trust me."

That was too mysterious for her liking, and she'd had nothing but mystery since they met, like devils and angels at her back, in her dreams. "There's a lot you're not saying, and I'd really appreciate it if you'd just spell it out," she said.

He uncrossed his arms, held a hand palm up. "Let's take it one step at a time. First, will you let me be a safe haven for you and your art? We can work it out any way you want – you can stay in your house, you can see sleep with me or not as you choose."

It was an opportunity anyone would sell their soul for. And something would not let her take it. Something. Many things. She knew what one of them was.

"You haven't said the magic words," she told him.

"Please? Thank you?"

She shook her head. "I love you."

He opened his mouth, and shut it tight again.

She felt a deep disappointment. "You're not going to say them, either," she noted quietly. "You can't, can you?"

"They're words, Austeja. Just words," he said. "In this context they're meaningless, as they so often are."

"But if you *can't* say them, that always means something. Besides, I think I want to choose my own destiny."

He laughed, a bitter sound. "You're thousands of years too late for that," he said.

Her emotions were in too many tricky places at once, and she'd had enough of his cryptic remarks. "Stop talking in goddamn riddles," she said angrily, and turned away, moving toward the church door.

"No," he snapped. "You won't walk away from this." He grabbed her wrist, whirled her around to face him. "All the reasons you've given me are smokescreen, Austeja. Say what really troubles you."

"I told you - "

"There's more." His grip on her tightened. "Name it, would you? Take it out of the dark closet and have a look at it, for pity's sake. You're terrified to claim the success your brother lost when Dad broke his hand."

She hadn't told him about Vince's hand, but of course he knew. And the arrow flew true, right to her heart. He saw it.

"That's not all, my queen," he said. "I know *why* you're terrified. The truth is, you rejoiced because your father broke *his* hand and not yours. Thank God, you cried out. Thank God I escaped. I can still paint, and draw and be who I am. Except now you're so wracked with guilt you won't let yourself be an artist. Your soul pursues you like an avenging angel, while you duck and cover at Accent marking. Isn't that so?"

"Let go of me," she said through clenched teeth.

"Why? You never let me go. All these years, and here I am, still trying to do what's right against my own best interests. I offer you your life and once again you refuse the gift."

She was frightened now. What the hell was he talking about, and where did this anger come from? Anger and desperation, as if he fought for his life. "I don't know what you're talking about," she said.

"Nor do you care to. You can't stand what that knowledge would do to your tidy worldview. What is it you *think* you want, Austeja? Tell me and I'll give it to you. To be above the human journey, never grow old or be hurt by love? I can give you that. You want your brother's hand healed? I can do that, too. You remember the bees. Or maybe you just want me to make your guilt to go away."

"Go ahead, magic man," she snapped back. "Make it disappear."

He laughed. "That's easy." He pulled her wrist up until her hand was in front of her face. "If I broke this brilliant, beautiful little hand so you couldn't paint you'd be just like your brother. Soulless. Lost. And all your guilt would be gone. Shall I do it?"

There was truth in what he said, a deep and piercing truth that hid under her unwillingness to commit and her ambition and her bright, sharp mind and her nights at Janus, wheeling and dealing. If her hand was crippled, would that even the score? If she took his patronage, would it balance a universe that sent her grandmother to hell, made her father into a monster, and stole her brother's heart if not his soul?

"Call it Austeja," he growled in her ear. "Name your desire."

He gave her wrist one more twist, and in the sharp pain that followed, she saw bright stars in a dark sky, and a woman who stood in tall grass, singing. Something more primal than her grandmother's blood stirred. Words emerged, not her own.

"First, name yours," she said, her voice guttural, foreign to her. "Say you have the courage to give your life to it."

He went still, his grip on her frozen.

"Would you be owned by what you love as I am, trusting it to hold you?" she demanded.

"You don't do that," he said hoarsely. "Not with me."

"You? You want only to control me – a thin desire you'd kill for. But will you die for what you love? Will you live for it? Or will you remain *Stribas*?"

She spit the last word at him like a curse, and it hung in the air, her ancient voice thrumming through them both. In response he cried out, a sound of immediate pain, and released her from his grasp.

They stood apart, staring at each other, his eyes sparking against hers. He raised his hands, looked at them, then at her.

"It's gone," he said. "The feeling. It's gone."

Chapter Seventeen

He walked away from her after that. Simply walked down the church aisle without looking back, walked out the door and kept going. She was a big girl, and she'd find her own way home. He'd make sure her luggage was sent back to her. Meantime, there was someone he had to see.

He went back to Nida and once more walked in the long grass at sunset, watching it turn gold beneath his hands.

"I wonder who's more restless tonight, Austeja," he murmured. "You, or I."

He could almost feel her bones turning in the earth beneath him, resenting his presence. Or maybe laughing at him.

"I think you are," Razak said, behind him.

Nick turned to him. He didn't waste time on pleasantries. He had none to offer. "You said there was another way," he said. "Was that true?"

"Another way to San Jose? What, specifically, are you talking about?"

"When you got my soul, you said I could get it back if I could undo my wrong. Was it true?"

"Of course."

"How?"

"Haven't you figured that out, after all this time?"

Nick thought of the attempts he'd made, all ending in failure. He shook his head.

"There it is. Most people don't figure it out," Razak said. "And the ones who do find they don't care to take the option after all. It's too painful, too much about what they were trying to avoid in the first place. Besides, you'd be mortal again, and you've seen how they die. Wasting away with age, eaten by cancer, mutilated by war, broken by an axe at their belly. It isn't pretty. Unless – do you want to die?"

Nick found both a yes and a no inside himself. He didn't crave death, yet, something of the moonlight on Austeja's skin lingered in him. The taste of her, still there.

"No," he said. "I don't. Neither do I want to be your slave anymore."

"Then let's move on," Razak said. "Let's end this tedious affair."

"What do you want?" Nick asked.

"Don't get that look on your face. I warned you repeatedly about her, and instead you encouraged her to paint, to tell her story, to *remember*. Then you take her to the very place where she can sing. My master's been patient about it – why not? He has eternity. But now there's some pressure on me to stop her. You understand. You saw her in the long grass."

Yes. He understood. Her very being put good in the world, against all odds. Her paintings were the beauty of the soul. Her soul itself was music. Her song could sustain the honeybees through a difficult time. Razak and his master were noise, looking only to destroy. They were both unbreakable forces, and what could not be broken must be slowly and meticulously dismantled. Razak and his master had been whittling away at her for ages, draining away what she knew of herself. They'd have her already except for his continued failures, and the persistent bees.

More than once he could have eradicated her. He'd get almost there, and then something inarticulate as wind in trees would stop him. Maybe his obsession to control rather than destroy her. His unwillingness to destroy something so beautiful. He couldn't say for sure. He had more questions than answers, and right now, he might as well ask one of them.

"Razak, perhaps this is all your own fault? Perhaps when you changed me, you didn't do a very good job."

Razak's eyes showed sparks of anger. "Don't try that on me," he growled.

"I mean it," Nick continued. "We've talked about it before. The phantom soul."

He'd once asked Razak if it was possible he'd done a bad job of soul stealing. He was new at it, didn't know exactly how to split body from soul, because in spite of his muted emotions, his muted sensations, he still felt longing for Austeja. As if he had a phantom soul, the equivalent of a phantom limb, part of him amputated but still sending messages along the old pathways.

Razak's anger dispersed, and he sniffed. "You may be right, my friend, but it doesn't matter now. Phantom soul or not, you'll have to do what we say."

Nick shrugged. Razak was right. It didn't matter anymore. "Just tell me what you want me to do," he said.

"That's a better attitude. And it's simple. Get us the violin and the brother and you'll receive your reward."

"Is that it? Then am I free of you?"

"Free? Nothing is free, my friend. Nothing and no one."

"What? You lied to me?"

"Please. Your righteous indignation is wasted here. If you paid attention, you'd remember I only said a trade would change things, and it will. You'll graduate from servant to master, and become a Razakel like me, since you've shown talent for corrupting others, our main task. You'll keep your immortality, and physical feeling will return, so you can enjoy your glass of wine."

"But not emotions."

"Haven't you had enough of those?"

The buzzing bees and an image of Austeja, naked and laughing, returned to him. A shadow of a shadow of feeling, a phantom limb that would not die.

"Was it sweet to you?" Razak asked.

He was going to say yes, but then the memory of the moment he turned from her, the wrenching away, also returned.

"That's one word for it," he said bitterly.

Razak laughed. "That's what I thought. But here's something else. If you do it right, she'll collapse, and then you can keep her, too. All for your own. To control for all of time."

A spark of hope in that. But he'd been robbed of his prize before, so he was wary. "Control, or destroy?" he asked.

"What's the difference? To us, nothing at all. Do as you like. But you'd better bring us something, or we'll have you on our table. Do we understand each other?"

"I understand you," he said. "I doubt you know me at all."

"If you fail I'll know you," Razak said. "Completely, and forever. I'll drink you, my friend."

He was gone after that. Just gone, the strange odor of burning he carried lingering behind. Nick stood in the grass for a long time, thinking little, and feeling less.

Chapter Eighteen

Upstate New York, early 21st century

Stacey returned to the US on a regular flight, crowded and uncomfortable. After that, she kept to herself. She did her work and went home, avoiding Janus, avoiding everything and everyone. When her luggage came back to her house, she didn't even open it, but just stashed it in a closet and closed the door.

Grant came by her office and after they'd worked a while on the I Love New York Account, he tapped her hand with his pen and said, "Hey. Are you okay?"

She blinked up at him as if he was a stranger. Had they really gotten naked together? It seemed impossible, somehow. "I'm fine. Why?"

"You're quiet. Haven't been to Janus in ages."

"I've been putting in some extra hours at home," she said.

"All about the work, right?" Then he shifted, opened his mouth, closed it again. She knew these signals. He was nervous about something.

"Spit it out," she said.

He shrugged. "I'm sleeping with Erin," he said.

Erin. Of course he was. "Okay," she said. "Have fun."

"That was our deal, right? That I'm supposed to tell you if something like that came up. Especially if it looked like it was. . .. going somewhere."

She raised her eyebrows. "Is it? That's quick."

"No faster than you and the rich man," he noted.

She took a moment to get her face under control. "We're not going anywhere," she said, trying to sound casual.

At this, he looked abashed. "I'm sorry to hear that. I was actually happy for you. You seemed different. Not as brittle. He softened your edges."

She was not willing or able to speak about it yet. "I have some calls to make," she said, shooing him away.

He got up, took a look at her, then turned to leave. "Hey," she said, and he turned back. "Congratulations. On Erin. I hope it goes well. I mean that."

"Thanks, Stacey. You were always a good friend."

When the door closed behind him she was surprised at the nothing she felt. She wondered if she'd caught that from Nick, his legacy to her.

≈

At night, she watched TV and ignored her paintings. She didn't answer the phone, and returned calls to Martha when she knew she was out, leaving chipper little messages about how busy she was and how everything was fine, fine fine. She had no idea how long she would have kept that up. A few weeks? A year? She was off her known map of relationship disaster recovery. Usually a few days saw her up and bouncing around again. Now she didn't feel like she'd ever return to standing.

Around the third week of her retreat she was surprised to hear her doorbell ring. At first, she hardly knew what the sound was. Then her heart beat hard, wondering if it was Nick.

She went to the intercom and pressed it. "Who is it?" she asked, finding it hard to catch her breath.

"It's me," a male voice said. Then, "me, Vince, I mean."

Her anticipation moved quickly to disappointment, and then turned to fear. Vince never came here. Was something wrong with Martha? With Alicia? She buzzed him in.

When he walked through the door she noticed he was sober. He'd gotten a haircut, a new pair of jeans, a new shirt. His eyes were bright and clear.

"Is something wrong?" she asked, wide-eyed.

He grinned. Something else she hadn't seen in a long time. His grin. "No."

"You're sure? Martha – Alicia?"

"They're fine. Really. I just – I wanted to come over and say thank you."

She sat down hard on the couch and caught her breath.

"You okay?" he asked.

"Yes. Just – give me a minute." She pressed a hand to her chest, felt her heart rate settle down underneath it.

Vince sat next to her, waited. "Let me know when I can talk," he said.

She took in air, let it out. "Go ahead. Anything you want."

He smiled again, folded his crippled hand in his good one and rested them on his knees, turned to look at her. "What you said last time you came over. I kept thinking about it. And I figured something out. I kept hearing the music, in my head, and it was making me crazy - to hear it and not be able to play it. Like I was filled with it, about to burst. It took a lot of noise to drown that out. Gambling, drinking, all that was just noise to drown out the music."

She thought of the quiet place she entered when she painted, what it would be like if she had the images but not the ability to put them on canvas. She understood. Vince kept talking.

"Then I thought of Beethoven," he said. "He was deaf, but that didn't slow him down. I started writing – working on some music I had in mind. I'm thinking of maybe trying school again, for theory and composition."

Tears of sympathy and relief stung her eyes, and her lip started to quiver. Vince, a little chagrined, put an arm around her clumsily.

"So it's okay now," he said uncertainly. "I mean, I think it is. Do you?"

"I think it's great," she said, and rubbed at her eyes. "I don't know why I'm crying. I just think it's a great idea."

"Good, because next I'm asking for help with tuition," he said.

"That," she said, "would be even greater." And she meant it. "Oh, God, I'm a wreck. Lemme go get a paper towel or something. Listen, you want anything? Coffee or tea or something to eat?" She moved off toward her kitchen.

"No. I'm good," he called to her.

"You sure?" she called back. "I can order a pizza."

"Really. I can't stay long. I just . . . ."

He stopped talking. She finished dabbing at her face with the paper towel and went back into the living room. When she got there, he was staring at her coffee table, his face blanched and tight. He pointed down at her sketch of the man emerging from the tree, which she hadn't finished yet except to fill in the man's face.

"What's this?" he asked.

"Just something I was working on. Why?"

"Who's the guy?"

"Someone I know. What is it, Vince?"

He tapped at the image, then looked up at her, his jaw tight. "He's the poker player. The guy who won the Amber."

Nick. It was his face. Unmistakably his. "Are you sure?"

"You think I could forget him? Do you know him? Do you know where he is?"

She tried to get her brain working. She had to think. Nick. He had the Amber all along. But he could be anywhere in the world. "I know where he might be, but I'm not sure if he's actually there," she said.

He grabbed at his bad hand with his good one, his face fierce. "You know him?"

"Vince," she said, "I had no idea who he was. . . ."

"Yeah, but you know him? How well?"

She let all the information sink in, let the implications and the possibilities make themselves clear.

"Well enough to give him hell," she said. "Maybe well enough to get the Amber back."

Chapter Nineteen

She told Vince to give her some time, and sent him away.

"Look, don't do anything stupid on my account," he said. "I mean that."

"This is between me and him, brother," she told him. "Just leave it that way."

She waited two days before she went to see Nick. She wanted to have her head on straight, her mind clear, and it took that long for her rage to settle down to a dull roar. She decided to go to his upstate house. If he wasn't there, maybe she could get Henry to talk, if she played it right.

But she didn't have to. She pulled up to the gate, pressed the button and waited. In a moment, Henry's archetypal voice spoke.

"Ms. Vitautis. Mr. Vecchio is expecting you."

"Is he now, the son of a bitch?"

"Pardon?"

"Nothing Henry. I'll go right in then."

And she did. Henry showed her to the dining room, where Nick was at table, drinking wine. He turned to her. "Austeja," he said. "What took you so long?"

When she saw his face, her words were stopped in her throat. He looked dead. His perpetually cool aspect had gone cold, and the mischief in his eyes was drained away. There was nothing of life in the aspect he presented to her. She lifted a hand, wanting to comfort him, go to him and hold him. Then she remembered what he'd done, and why she came.

"Where is it?" she demanded.

He swirled the wine in his glass. She waited for him to ask where is what, but apparently he wasn't playing games anymore. "How did you find out?" he asked.

"Vince saw a drawing I made of you. He recognized you."

"Ah," he said. "Of course."

"You haven't answered me. Where is it?"

"In a safe place," he said. "Do you want it?"

"You know I do."

He inclined his head, took a sip of wine and swallowed. "The price is high. I'm not sure if you'll be willing to pay."

She didn't respond. No more soul talk. She had questions of her own. "Did you know Vince was my brother when you took the Amber from him?"

"He didn't use his real name. Nobody there did. It's a private game."

"Why didn't you follow him? Try to find out where he got it from?"

"Oh, he told me that. He said he stole it from a drunk."

"And you believed him. I thought you were smart."

"But he spoke the truth. He got it from your father, didn't he? Besides, that wasn't important. I recognized the violin, and I wanted it."

"Why? You didn't sell it."

He smiled. "I wanted her song. Your song. I thought it would - change things. And it did. I played it the day you were lost in the woods. The day before we met. I played Sibelius."

She remembered what she'd heard, the singing, the violin. But it couldn't be. Couldn't be. "Did you follow me? To that bar?" she demanded.

"Not at all. I was there first, if you remember. Maybe you were following me. Called to me by the Amber's song." He raised a hand, brushing it aside. "It doesn't matter. We're here now." He took a long sip of wine, then looked at her directly, his expression complex and unreadable, his voice low and tense. "You should have taken my offer in Kaunus. I would have protected you. I wanted to protect you."

"From what?" she asked, and fear made her voice sharp.

"From what stalked you when you sang under the moon in Nida," he said.

Deep behind his bi-color eyes she saw fires burning in a darkened face, oceans rising. He made no sense. Some madness was in him. She opened her mouth to say something like cut the bullshit. To say he was just a rich guy with control issues, another crazy man she happened to sleep with. But in his strange eyes she saw a different truth.

A violin played Sibelius in the forest. The bees swarmed her, and she lived to tell the tale. An old woman in a foreign pub told her stories about who she was. An ancient song reached her over an open field, moving through forest. All her strange dreams, her paintings, more like memory than imaginings, what her grandmother had written about Naktis, merged into his words. Phrases and events from their past flicked like broken film through her mind, coming together to make a coherent whole.

"No," she whispered. "It can't be."

"You know better, Austeja," he said. He lifted a hand, and she saw it all.

His will to control a woman who sang, her gift giving life to her people. He strangled her, but whispering grass flayed the flesh off his tortured bones, laughing at a man who gave his soul for the poor and precarious recompense of control. Then his ages of following women with silver eyes, and ages of what would have been pain, if he could feel. The vast hunger he had for her flesh, for her soul. He showed her all of it, measured within a knowledge she'd tried to avoid. She knew who and what he was, and it was real. She felt the room losing stability around her.

"Jesus Christ," she whispered. "It's true."

"Jesus," he said calmly, "has nothing to do with it. And perhaps a better question to ask is what are *you*."

No, she thought. That was too much. More than she could absorb. Enough to know who and what he was. Anything else would tumble her to the ground.

She licked her lips. "You're – a devil?"

He grinned. "That would be a promotion in rank. For now, I'm just a man who made a bad bargain and wants to get back what's rightfully his. In that sense, you could say I'm like your brother, though I won't be the loser he is for much longer."

"You . . . sold your soul."

"Inadvertently, but that's generally how it happens. When you're thinking of something else."

"And you don't die?"

"I don't. Neither do I live, really."

"You can't feel," she said dully.

"Except for a brief time, when I drank from you. That's gone now."

"But you – you have -"

"Superpowers?" He lifted a hand over his wine, and it became clear as water. Moved it again, and it turned ruby red. He pointed to a corner of the room. A tree rose, and fire consumed it. Stacey stood her ground, telling herself she wouldn't run from this. She wouldn't run.

He saw her adamant stance and smiled. "I have some skills. Nothing compared to what I will have when I complete this deal. Well, you'll see for yourself."

"You were there with my grandmother," she said. "In the labor camps. Naktis."

"I found the record shortly after we met, wanting to make sure of you. To my eternal shame, I failed to kill her. If I hadn't, you wouldn't be here, and perhaps I'd be shed of you at last."

She shook her head. Something about that didn't make sense. Failed? No. He chose not to. Instead, he saved her, and then left her alone. He could have killed her, could have stolen the violin. Why didn't he? All those ages, and he'd failed to take her soul? Even this time?

"You saved my life, with the bees," she said.

His face darkened. "We don't need to revisit that. I've moved forward, and so should you. Our business is concluded, my queen."

"But you want my soul, in exchange for the Amber," she said.

He lifted a hand, let it fall. "You proved recalcitrant. I'll trade Vince's instead. It will please my masters just as well."

She stared at him, but the face she saw was her grandmother's as she lay dying. Don't be afraid, she'd said. The vele will find you, but you'll know what to do when the time comes. But she didn't.

He stood and moved to her, singing softly, "My wild love is crazy. She screams like a bird. She moans like a cat, when she wants to be heard."

"Stop it," she whispered.

He put his hands on her face. "Make me," he murmured, knowing she couldn't. "I would have given you so much, if only you'd shared what was yours. Now we're both out of time, and I won't accept the consequences of failure." He released her, walked back to his wine glass, picked it up and drank.

She stood in the warm room, feeling only cold. "They're your consequences," she said shakily. "Why should Vince suffer them?"

"Because I don't want to," he said dryly.

She tried to think of something sensible, practical. "Vince – he has to go along with it. Sign the papers?"

"There's no papers. He agrees to it, and means it. That's all. Then my master takes him, and I get my reward."

At this, she brightened. "But he won't. He's – something happened. He stopped drinking. He's going back to school."

"And when he saw the possibility of retrieving his violin?"

"He - he said he didn't care."

"Austeja," he said, "I believe that's the first time you've lied to me. No matter. Even if he didn't want it, I can talk him into it."

That, she did believe. Absolutely. But if Vince gave his soul for the Amber, he'd no longer feel, and so he couldn't play. The devil's bargain. She finally understood what that meant.

"Don't worry," he continued. "I can tell you from experience, it doesn't hurt. He may not even notice it's gone. There's so many soulless people in the world, and none of them feel a thing. Stalin. Office Petrov. Your own father's father. You see it all the time. Politicians, killers, and priests - do you really believe their sins are from bad genes, or an unhappy childhood?"

"But it doesn't have to be that way," she argued. "Not for you. We could find a way to help you," she said, thinking of what Father Pete said. "There's other ways to – to get out of it."

"And you of all people should know I've tried them all. Now what? Should I call a priest? The Pope? Is their salvation any different? Christians call it saving your soul, and Jews put a fence around the Torah and Muslims make Holy Jihad, and Presidents liberate countries, but it's all the same thing, isn't it? Control. Power. Greed and fear. Their God wants my soul just as much as any demon. How is what I do any different?"

The stubborn, steadfast voice of her ancestors spoke within her. She planted her feet more firmly on the shifting ground. "The difference is, I won't let you," she said.

"Ah, the rock-like mind of the Lithuanian. In spite of all you are, you can't stop me. Not this time."

His bitterness and anger were hurtful, a denial of what she thought they'd shared. She spoke against it, needing to affirm the truth she'd experienced. "You cared about me," she insisted. "You were kind to me."

He didn't deny it, or laugh. "That's what got me here in the first place. It's not a mistake I'm likely to make again."

"But you felt something. After the bees –"

"A temporary delusion, brought on by blood. Can I have you dancing at the edge of death just so I can feel for a little while? Do you really not understand your own precarious position, or are you being deliberately obtuse?"

Something desperate in his voice. Something. But it didn't matter. Not anymore. "If I can't stop you, I'll stop Vince," she said stubbornly.

"Not if he chooses it. Ever hear of free will?"

Her female ancestors beat on her back, telling her to do something. But they didn't tell her what. They merely demanded action, and she had none.

She put a hand out to him. "Please," she said quietly. "Leave him alone. Give them mine."

He stared at her, saw that she meant it. He turned away. "Leave, Austeja," he growled. "You don't know your own danger."

"Nick –"

He whirled back to her, and his face was changed, a thing of fire, with eyes that glowed like lit coal in a deep cave. His growl became a roar that filled the room with heat as well as sound. "I said leave! Now!"

She stepped back, stumbled, caught herself, and ran from the house.

Chapter Twenty

What followed was panic, and a sense of madness. What should she do? Call a cop? He'd done nothing illegal. An exorcist? She didn't know any personally, but she'd watched enough of the Discovery channel to know their process was way too slow. She got out the phone book and looked up the local ghost hunters group, but their website said they didn't do demons. Only ghosts. And which was he, exactly? He'd sold his soul, so he'd been human once. He wasn't exactly dead, though, so he wasn't a ghost. Whatever he was, it wasn't listed in the yellow pages.

She considered calling Vince, warning him. Hey Vince, she'd say. The guy that has the Amber, he wants to trade it for your soul. I wouldn't, if I were you. Vince would laugh and say why not, and that might be all it would take to seal the deal. A promise made lightly, in ignorance and disbelief. That was how Nick got there, wasn't it?

It was, if her visions were correct, because she remembered now, remembered events she'd never experienced as if they were her own. He'd told the demon he'd trade his soul for control of this woman who was and was not her, then he'd killed her, the ultimate control. But it wasn't. It wasn't.

Was that true? Was it real? Right now, it didn't matter. What mattered was saving Vince.

She went to the computer and did an internet search on *demons soul buying*. The first site she found told her there was no soul, and said a lot of things about theism she didn't understand. Another site said if she accepted Jesus and sent $350 she'd be fine. The third told her she could protect herself from the devil with a circle of salt or ash, or with tears. Tears, particularly, drove him away. The devil was apparently allergic to them, just as Father Pete had said.

The last site she tried was a series of postings on the question, "If you sold your soul to the devil, can you buy it back?" The answers were mostly facetious, as in, "I traded in my mother-in-law, and the devil sent her back to me."

She moved on, trying Lithuanian devils, and found mixed reports. In folktales, he was a trickster and usually lost because he was following a literal path while the farmers or their wives were playing with words and ideas. Devils were connected to humans, a part of the self that had to be dealt with through superior wisdom or wit. And they were invariably male.

"Doesn't that just figure," she muttered at the screen.

From reading, she decided Nick was technically a version of a vele or vaidila, a living ghost, never united with the earth, soulless and unable to find rest. Though these were usually benign, their tormenting form was a power to be reckoned with. This, she supposed, was what her grandmother warned her about. Good to know, but it didn't help much. Her research produced an awful lot of information, but no answers. She could think of only one more possibility. She picked up the phone, dialed.

"Campus ministry. Father Pete speaking," a deep, soothing voice said.

"It's Stacey," she said. "Stacey Vitautis. I need to see you."

"Okay," he said. "Is there . . . .something?"

"Yes. Are you free? Can I come see you?"

"When did you have in mind?"

"Um . . . now?"

He paused. "Right now?"

"It'll take me about 20 minutes to get there."

Another pause. He recognized panic when he heard it. "I'll be here," he said.

On the way there she thought of ways to ask him what she wanted to know without telling him what was going on. When she knocked on his office door she had her opening line figured out. "I need some help for a friend of mine who may be involved in devil worship," she'd say.

But the warmth of his greeting undid her. She sat down across from him at his desk and blurted out, "how do you stop the devil from stealing a soul?"

He opened his mouth, closed it again. "Well, now," he said. "That's not something I hear every day. You want to tell me more? Give the room some time to stop spinning?"

"Okay," she said. "I guess I should start with the dog."

He waved a hand at her, sat with his hands folded on his desk and she poured it all out, from the night with Tamsa, to Ralph's, to the bees and the field in Nida and the devil museum in Kaunus, and the Amber and Vince.

He listened attentively, his face moving through various levels of consternation, but never disbelief. When she was done she held her hands palm up. "That's all there is. I don't know if it's real, but if there's a remote chance he can actually do this to Vince, I have to stop him. Don't I?"

"Oh yes. I'd think so," he agreed.

She ruffled her hair, grateful for his matter-of-fact response. "You don't think I'm, you know, nuts?"

"You wouldn't be asking if you were. No. You're not delusional. All of this really happened. It's just a question of what it means. This man – Nick – did you say you were intimate with him?"

She couldn't stop the blood from rushing to her face.

"I'm not making judgments," he reassured her. "I just need to know. You cared about him?"

She nodded. "He's - he was good to me. Kind, really. And good for me. I was becoming someone I didn't like very much, all sharp edges and sound bites. He – he changed that. Put me on a different track."

"Really?"

"I started painting again because of him. Really painting."

"How very odd," he murmured.

"Yeah," she said. "My grandmother said it's a family curse. We're attracted to devils, apparently. But – anyway, the important thing is, how do I stop him?"

He drummed his fingers on his desk. "Like I said last time we talked about it. Tears, laughter, and confidence. And, of course, love. Understand, I'm not talking about romantic love, necessarily. I'm talking about the bigger love. Capital L. The love that asks you to meet human folly with compassion, and human wrongs by speaking the truth no matter what. Love that's more about what you do than what you feel. Love as a verb, and an energy all its own."

She chewed on her lip. Oddly enough, she thought she'd shared that with Nick. But how could he, if he had no soul, no feeling? She could not make sense of it. Could not make it fall into any logical shape.

"Tell me how I find that," she asked.

He sighed. "Have you tried praying?"

His words touched off an old, unexpected anger, deep as rivers. Her hand made a fist and hit hard against his desk, making him jump.

"I prayed when I was little," she said bitterly. "All the time I was growing up with a drunk father, I prayed. Please God, make him better. Please, Virgin Mary mother of God help me. Make him stop hitting my mother, Vince. Make him *good*. Who listened to me or Vince? Who listened to my grandmother? I think your God ought to go to confession. He's the one that needs forgiving."

"Stacey, humans did that," Father Pete said quietly.

She put her fist to her mouth and bit the knuckles to stop her tears. Maybe that was the problem. It was way too easy to blame human folly on God or the devil. Way too difficult to have any sense of control over what humans did.

Father Pete looked at her with all the compassion he'd talked about. "Maybe your prayers were heard, and answered," he said. "Maybe this man is part of that."

"I don't see how," she said.

"Neither do I. But I can't imagine someone who's totally evil bringing you back to your art. That - it doesn't make sense. And St. Paul was right once in awhile. We do see through a glass darkly, not really sure how to know the shadows from the light."

"Yes, but can't you do something? Throw some holy water at him? Some salt? Maybe an exorcism?"

"I'm sorry, Stacey. None of that would work. This isn't possession. It's - disconnection, I guess. Unfortunately, there's no ritual for that in my church. Maybe you should try the psychological approach. Think of this man as a reflection of something in you. Something that needs healing. Ask yourself what part of you is like him, connected to him. Love that part, heal that part of yourself, and you'll find your way. You and Vince."

She made a sound of frustration and he reached over, took her hand and patted it. "Okay, then. Try this. There's older churches than mine, and our ancestors knew them. What I call God they called something else, and they could hear it in everything that moved in the world. The trees, the toads, all that. You still carry that in you. Maybe you should go to them for answers."

She shook her head. "You're telling me go talk to the pagans?"

"I'm telling you go talk to the trees," he replied.

She took this in. Dreams she'd had of trees and the women who protected them recurred to her. She didn't think she was likely to get anything else here, so she thanked him and stood to leave.

"Don't be afraid," he said. "You'll know what to do when the time comes. Just remember, it's all about the love."

Talking to Father Pete made her less frantic, but no more informed. To clear her mind and see if there was any answer in the trees her ancestors worshipped, she went out to Martha's and asked to borrow Tamsa for a walk in the woods.

"Nice to see you, too," Martha said. "Now you want to tell me what the hell is going on? I got this phone call from Vince – something about you know where the Amber is, and have I heard from you because he thinks maybe you've been kidnapped."

"I have a lead," she admitted. "It's tricky, and I'm trying to figure it out, but first I have to - to exorcise a demon."

Martha's expression turned sympathetic. "Oh," she said. "Nick?"

"Yeah." She hadn't told Vince his name, so clearly Martha didn't know he was connected with the Amber. But she knew the face of heartbreak when she saw it.

"Turned out to be a bit of a devil, huh?" she asked.

"A bit," she admitted.

Martha sighed. "I'm sorry. He was, well, likable. I liked him, too. Well, you got some fun out of him, at least."

"That I did," she said.

"And then you fell in love?"

She bit her lip. "Just a little, maybe."

"Take the dog," Martha said. "I've got plenty of wine and a bed you can sleep in, if you need it."

She took Tamsa before she burst into tears, which seemed imminent. She supposed Martha was right. She'd fallen in love. But even worse, she liked him, and now she missed him. He'd brought out something in her that nobody else had, and she wondered if she'd find it again without him. And if he was what he claimed, did that mean everything he brought out in her was wrong, even though it felt so right?

But that was a different problem, and she had to put it on hold until she got the immediate one solved. She walked to the tall pines and sat under them while Tamsa sniffed about. She thought about what Father Pete had said. She had other ways of communicating with the divine.

"So, tell me what to do," she whispered to the trees, but if anyone answered it was in a language she didn't understand, perhaps the same way Nick didn't understand the language of feeling. What was it he wanted so long ago? A woman who sang. A woman who knew the language of the trees and stones and bees. Austeja.

"Who was she?" Stacey whispered. A goddess, in a woman's body. A woman who understood the song of the honeybees, and sang it back to the moon, to the trees. A Lithuanian woman, strangled but unsilenced, dead but undefeated, stubbornly returning again and again to see the lesson learned and the balance restored. A woman whose hands dripped with honey and amber.

She thought of Nick anointing her with honey and shivered with pleasure at the memory. She'd been tight, thin, full of noise before him. Would she be that way again, or would she go on to live like her namesake, her hands dripping with honey? At the pub in Palanga, the old woman said she was descendant of that murdered woman, containing her soul. That same woman in the fields, whose mysteries ran in her veins, lived in her heart. A part of her remembered, knowledge running in her most ancient DNA. But the Stacey who lived and worked in this world found it difficult to connect.

"Who am I?" she asked herself, and she found no answers outside her sorrow and her frantic fear. Around her, the trees whispered, moving with wind, speaking with a language that was far away and long ago.

She pressed a hand against one of them. "Okay," she said. "I'm listening. Maybe you can figure out how to get a translator to me."

She stood there, wrapped in whispers, until Tamsa nuzzled her nervously. She made her way back to Martha's house, and from there, to her own home.

༄

For a few days, nothing happened, and she began to think maybe it was all an extended delusion, a weird fantasy. Then, Vince called her.

"Hey," he said, sounding cheerful, hopeful. "That poker player – he called me."

She grabbed onto the wall to hold herself up.

"Stace? You there?" he asked.

"What?" she asked.

"I said, the poker player called me. Name of Nick Vecchio, right? He said he feels bad about what happened, wants to give the Amber back to me. Isn't that great?"

"I'm – really surprised."

"I figured it was something you said to him. Was it? What did you do?"

"I . . . appealed to his conscience."

"And he bought that?"

"I guess. When's he giving it to you?"

"He said tomorrow, at his place. You want to come?"

She thought fast. "Tell him to come here. To my house. We'll do it here."

"Yeah?"

"Sure. Tell him around eight, okay?"

"Fine by me. I mean, really, it's great. Stacey – thanks," he said, meaning it.

She almost said no problem, or it's nothing. Instead, she let his words and their warmth sink in. "You're really welcome," she replied.

Chapter Twenty-One

The day started out grey and damp, with intermittent drizzle casting gloom on everything. The nights were drawing in earlier now, and growing cooler. For comfort as well as warmth Stacey lit a fire in her fireplace. Arranging it, setting it up, helped her organize her emotions and her thoughts. It was blazing cheerfully when both Vince and Nick showed up, at the same time.

"Hi," she said, opening her door and gesturing them inside. "Come in."

Nick, dressed in what she knew was Gucci suit and tie, nodded coolly and went past. She resisted the urge to make a remark about the devil wearing only the best. Vince stopped, squeezed her shoulder, gave her a peck on the cheek. He hadn't done that in years. She touched her face when he turned away and saw Nick watching, his eyes sparking. She thought it was anger, then realized it was just the reflection from the fireplace.

She'd put out her paintings and sketchbook, hoping that would make Nick feel something, but he only glanced at them and then away. He put the violin case on the coffee table and looked from Vince to Stacey. "I want you to know I'm glad to do this. If I'd known what it was, I wouldn't have taken it. I don't get what I want that way."

"That's decent of you," Vince said. "Really decent." He ran his good hand over the case. "This is nice," he said.

"Proof against anything barring a direct nuclear hit," Nick noted. "I thought the contents were worth it.

Stacey gave a tight smile. "Let's look inside, shall we?"

Nick gestured to Vince. "It's yours. You do the honors."

Vince opened the case with his good hand. Inside was a shining thing, lighter in color than most violins, glowing amber in the firelight. They all stared at it, and Vince ran his crippled hand over the surface. Seeing that, Stacey winced. What it would be like to own it and not be able to play it? Torture, she thought, like having a woman you could never love.

Then she saw something neither of the men noticed. A dead bee, cupped under the violin's neck. A honeybee, dead and shriveled. The kind that had stung her. The kind Nick saved her from. She remembered what he'd said. He could heal Vince's hand, just as he'd healed her.

He could heal. That was something he could do. And in healing her, he'd begun to feel again. It was a way. A possibility. She worked to keep her face on as she tried to think it through.

"It's beautiful, isn't it?" Vince murmured.

"Gorgeous," she agreed. "Always was."

Nick ran a finger along the neck and scroll. "I had it tested for authenticity. The varnish was supposed to have special properties, and it did. It contains traces of tree sap, of honey and crushed amber."

"Huh," Vince said. "I didn't know that."

Nick nodded. "Part of its long story. There's also trace amounts of blood, which could be from the maker's hands, perhaps cut while working. Not enough to do a DNA comparison, but interesting."

"Or maybe," Vince said, "some of it's mine."

"Is that so?" Nick asked, perfectly cool. "Well, there's no telling if it has anything to do with the tone. Legend says it was finished by a girl who sang to it, and her voice was so beautiful it went into the wood, where it sings to this day. The 'A' signed under the Guarneri signature is supposedly hers."

Vince touched it lovingly. "She did sing," he murmured. "That's true."

"Yes," Nick said. "Well, there are title papers for you to sign." He pulled a sheaf out of his jacket pocket.

"You said there weren't any papers," Stacey hissed at him. Vince cast her a glance.

"It's title transfer, so he won't be accused of stealing it," Nick said calmly. He smiled at Vince. "I think your sister believes I'm trying to trade your soul for this."

Vince grinned back. "Sure. Right."

"Funny, isn't it? But – I wonder – would you do that? Such a beautiful thing. Is it worth that much to you, Vince?"

"I told Stacey I'd give hers, but I wasn't sober at the time," Vince said.

"And are you now?"

"Very."

"And stone cold sober, would you give your soul, or your sister's, for it?"

Vince opened his mouth to speak, but she cut in quickly.

"I have a better question," she said. Both men looked to her. She turned to Nick. "Nick, would you agree this deal wouldn't have happened without me?"

He cast her a suspicious glance. "Not necessarily. I would have tracked the owner. You know I have ways."

"But there was other unfinished business. With me."

He lifted his face, nodded once.

"Then I want you to do something for me. A little thing. It won't interfere with – with anything."

He narrowed his eyes. "When I was young you caught me in the fields, but I'm not a fool anymore, so don't trifle with me. Tell me what it is, then I'll decide."

She licked her lips, which were very dry. "His hand," she said, nodding at Vince. "Fix it."

He frowned, looked to Vince, then turned his head slowly back to her.

"You can do that," she insisted. "You said you could. And it won't prevent you from getting what you want."

He said nothing. She sweetened the deal. "You can have my soul instead of his, if you want it. And - and you can keep the damn violin. He can get another one."

"Hey," Vince cut in. "What the hell are you talking about?"

She moved a hand to silence him. "I know what I'm doing," she said. At least she hoped she did.

Nick closed his eyes, opened them again, stared at her. "I get your soul? Only me? You'll agree to that?"

"If you still want it," she said.

"What about your brother's?"

"That's his," she said. "If he wants to keep it, he gets to keep it. Just fix the hand first."

His smile brightened. "I accept your terms. Don't be alarmed, but I'll have to put him out for it." He moved toward Vince, who took a step back but never got further, because Nick raised a hand and he collapsed on himself like a cut reed. He lay on the floor, and Nick knelt beside him.

"Jesus. You didn't hurt him, did you?" Stacey asked.

"I'm doing as you asked," he said. He put his hand on Vince's. "A wise choice, really, because if I don't take you, the others will. And if you think this will have the same affect that healing you did, you're sorely mistaken. I won't even break a sweat."

No, she thought. He wouldn't. He'd agreed too easily. She'd made a huge mistake. Missed something. When he was done it would be over. All over. Her soul was gone, and for all she knew Vince would say the magic words and lose his as well. She'd placed her bet, and lost the whole pot.

She dropped to her knees next to him, searching for some way to make this right. But all she could think of was her brother's crippled hand, his perpetual fist clutching generations of anguish, generations of despair and fear and the whiskey it took to drown all feeling. It held the ragged and dogged persistence of the honeybees, of Lithuania itself, torn by war in the name of many powers, but still singing. Now Nick's hand moved over it, not feeling a thing, she supposed. Not feeling a thing.

And yet, he'd been able to feel, deeply. Nor could she forget that he'd saved her grandmother's life, making her own life possible. That meant he'd killed her once, but saved her twice. Three times, really, because when they met they were alike in their numbness. Without him, she'd be sharp and thin as glass, still sleeping with Grant and chasing accounts at Janus.

She thought of what Father Pete said, and an unexpected chill moved up her spine. How they were alike. What drew him to her. Yes, a small voice inside her said. Yes. That's what brought her to him. Her own refusal to love, deeply and truly. Then, for a little while, they'd each gone beyond their own limitations, diving into each other for the sake of love. Only a little while, but in that time she'd felt what most people spend their lives searching for. It had been hers, for a little while, and nothing could take it away from her again. She'd shared her soul with him, and in the sharing, learned her own worth.

She was an artist, a woman who crossed the River Vilnia to become a citizen of Uzhupis. A woman of vision and courage, whose body was a channel for light, whose voice fed the spirits and the earth. Moonlight filled her while she sang in the fields of Nida, feeding the honeybees who licked her with venom and joy. The sap of ancient trees ran in her blood. That was who she was, and nothing, nothing, could rob her of that.

She felt the sting and hiss of connection to all she'd ever been, all she'd known through so many lifetimes. In spite of what was happening now, that brought her immense joy. She'd found her past, healed the most wounded part of her soul. She feared no devil, because she owned that truth. And like her ancestors, she might be defeated, but she would not be silenced.

She put her hand on his.

Every cell in his body went still at her touch, his bicolor eyes sparking with unfathomable energy. "What are you doing?" he whispered.

She leaned toward him, her voice old and young, past and present, all her voices speaking. The scent of ocean and pine sap entered the room, and there was a singing of grass in the wind.

"I wasn't fair to you in Kaunus," she told him. "I never said it either. That I love you, I mean. But I did. I loved you from the minute you let me toss a drink in your face at Ralph's. I loved you when we walked under the trees in the park, and when you got me a Sue Wong dress. I loved your wit and your courtesy and the way you found all my scars, and the sorrow I saw in you. I loved you for Sibelius and Nida, and for speaking with the bees, and for you. Just for you, laughing and scowling and making jokes at the Vatican. And I swear as I sit here, I still love you. It's crazy, but it feels good just to touch you. Just that. It's all I want."

"Don't," he said quietly. A muscle in his jaw twitched.

She reached up and smoothed it. *Mano Lietuva bedale, ar bijai*, she thought. She understood the words now. My Lithuania, are you afraid? Perhaps he was, but she was not. Whatever wrong he'd done, her right was the stronger, and she would use it.

"I will," she insisted. "It's the end game, and I'll say it all. Make it complete. You took a life from me, but you've given it back, more than once. You helped me find my painting and my vision, and you showed me my soul. My wild soul, that you insisted on. Now you only have to know why you did all that. Know it, and name it."

His hand tightened on Vince's fist, which held all their pain, unreleased. Their ancestral grief, the clash of men and many armies for the illusion of power and wealth and control were all in Nick's grasp. She bent and kissed the hand that held so much.

"I absolve you, Nick," she said softly. "And now, we're both free."

She didn't know when she'd started crying, but she felt the tears on her face. One fell, coming to ground on the back of Nick's hand. As it hit he gasped in pain, and she sat back, saw the salt water sizzling into his skin, burrowing under flesh to the bone.

"Aah, Zemyne," he cried out. "Dieve."

She pulled in a sob, and another tear fell, and another. He moaned, time shivering along his muscles as his true intent ran through him, sending songs of sorrow and joy from the distant and recent past. He'd found her for salvation, not barter. And now he knew what that required.

He relinquished control, not valuing it anymore. To feel this was recompense enough for all kingdoms, all powers, all conquest. He lifted his hand to her face, touching the tears that burned him.

"Austeja," he said hoarsely, "Tell me what you want. Anything at all. I am yours."

A sweet voice from the past, the voice of a thousand honeybees, sighed with release. In the present, her own voice joined in. She heard the words, and knew he meant them at last. This was his redemption. To love completely regardless of consequences, to give himself to it without stint or bargain. Her ancestors crowded her, rejoicing.

No. Not rejoicing. Screaming at her. Look out. Look out.

She blinked, looked around. As she did, some hollow piece of wood in the fireplace whistled, screeched and popped, sparks flying out. One caught the curtains and they burst into flame. Within the flame a great shadow loomed, poised to strike. A wave of fire rushed over the ceiling like water, heat pressing her down.

"Nick!" She screamed. "What is it?" She crouched, terrified. How could this be happening? How could this be?

Nick sprung to his feet. "Razak, you cannot have her!" he roared. "Not now and not ever."

A fiery scarf of curtain floated away from the window and landed on her back. She felt it burning, then felt hands on her, beating it out. The hands lifted her, pushing her away from heat and smoke. Something was shoved in her arms. Her paintings, her sketchbook. Hands pushed her forward. She worked against them, struggling to go back. "Vince!" she choked out.

"Get out," came the rough reply. "I'll take care of him."

Hands shoved her from the room, down the hall through smoke that gathered at the ceiling and moved downward in lazy swirls, kept shoving her out the front door where she fell on her face on the front lawn, still clutching her paintings and sketchbook. She gathered her strength and raised herself on her elbows, dropped her burden on the grass. She pushed herself up to a squat and saw the front door open, saw Nick emerge, Vince's arm draped on his shoulder as he half dragged him from the house.

He clutched at Nick, saying something she couldn't hear, though she knew what it was. The Amber. It was still inside, the case open. Nick pushed him down, turned and went back to the house. She tried to scream at him to leave it, let it go, but no sound emerged. She tried to stand, but her legs buckled and she fell.

The front door opened again and Nick appeared, but now he was tightly embraced in fire. He tossed something onto the grass – the closed violin case, intact, cool and light. Then he stood there, a living flame. She stared, trying to understand, but it seemed to her that he was surrounded by the swarming of a thousand bees. All she heard, all she saw, were golden bees, reflecting some unnamed source of light.

The earth, she thought. Zemyne. He must be united with the earth.

"The green oak will be your father," she said, intoning the ancestral death chant through tears that kept falling. "The white sands your mother, the green maples your brothers, the white lindens your sisters." She scrambled to stand, ran to him, threw herself at him and pushed him onto the ground.

She hit something hard, and darkness swallowed all.

Chapter Twenty-Two

The devil was not a Botticelli but he did have horns, and his eyes were blood red, glowing like fire. He stood over a cowering figure who happened to be Nick. "He is mine," he gloated.

She wasn't afraid, but she was really pissed off. She held a piece of amber in her hand. Inside it was a small honeybee, caught in eternal flight. She tossed it to the ground, where rays of the sun bounced off its surface, breaking light around her feet.

"You loser," she screamed. "He belongs to himself."

He turned burning eyes to her. It occurred to her that she'd made a colossal mistake. Maybe, she thought, it was time to get out of here.

She woke with a gasp, sat up hard. She blinked, looked around.

She saw Martha and Vince staring at her. She saw white walls, monitors, and a small, cheap TV. Somewhere in the distance a voice spoke calmly over a PA system, seeking Dr. Rajid for Cardiology. A hospital, she thought. She was in a hospital.

She looked back to Martha and Vince. "Hey," she said wanly. "How am I?"

Martha leaned over, touched her hair. "You're fine. Just fine."

Memory of what got her here returned, though she wasn't sure how much of it was dream. There was a fire, though. That she knew. A smile twitched across her lips. "I'm not – it's not like my face is burned off and you don't want to tell me?" she asked.

"Oh, no, Stace. Not at all," Martha said quickly and convincingly. "No burns, except your hand, and that'll heal. You're just heavily sedated. Lean back, honey. You look a little drunk."

She looked down at her hands and saw that one had a thick bandage on it. She wiped the good one over her mouth. "I feel a little hungover." She looked to Vince. He didn't seem to be bandaged anywhere. "You okay?" she asked.

"I'm good," he said. "Better than good. Look." He held up his hand, no longer crippled. He opened it, closed it again. "Stace, it works," he said, truly amazed.

"Wow," she said, trying to sound surprised. "How'd that happen?"

"It's some kind of miracle," Martha said. "The doctors don't have a clue."

"Neither do I," Vince said. "You think it was all psychosomatic?"

She sighed, closed her eyes. "Maybe," she said. "Anyway, it works, and that's all that matters."

"And I have the Amber back," Vince added almost as an afterthought, a minor wonder.

Stacey opened her eyes and looked at him. His face shone with happiness. Clearly he was feeling, so she supposed he still owned his soul. And clearly what she remembered was true. Nick saved the Amber from the fire. But where was he?

"Nick?" she asked.

Vince and Martha exchanged meaningful glances. "I couldn't see anything," Vince said. "I passed out, I guess."

"He was on fire," Stacey said. "Or there were bees. I couldn't tell which. I thought I pushed him down."

Martha patted her arm. "You should rest. I'll call the nurse and get a pill."

"No," she snapped. "Tell me about Nick. The truth."

Vince ran his two good hands over his head, then looked at them. "They think he went back inside. That he was still inside when it collapsed. They're trying to find ... "

" – what's left of him," she finished. And she knew they wouldn't find a thing.

She didn't cry. She couldn't. Not yet. Now was a moment to be grateful for her life, and what Nick did to reclaim himself. Later, when she missed him, she'd cry. And she would miss him terribly. There would never be another like him.

≈

She stayed in the hospital another night, then went to Martha's while she found a new place to live. Her house was gone, but insurance covered it, and she had enough money to take care of herself. She decided to rent a cheap apartment, take a leave of absence from Accent. She could afford to, for a while.

She would paint. Let it own her. It was not such a bad thing after all, she thought, to give yourself utterly to what you love.

She sent Vince to collect ashes from the remnants of her house, and she put them at the roots of the oak tree in Martha's yard. Martha stood with her and they sang the old song, though tears instead of laughter watered the thirsty roots.

Epilogue

"I think it's a metaphor for corporate America, and the way the soul tries to rise above it," an endomorphic man in neon green t-shirt and black jeans said to a thin young woman draped in orange silk.

They were staring at a pastel of a little girl playing a golden violin, standing above the reach of gravity, in a space encrusted with light, the girl falling or flying toward a burning hand. Falling. Flying. Impossible to tell which was which.

Stacey didn't let them know she was the painter, or that it wasn't metaphor but vision, at white hot heat. Merely memory, translated to paper.

"The violin –" the young woman said.

"Exactly," the endomorphic man said. He ran his fingers lightly over the contours. "See how gold it is? Money, my dear. All about money."

Behind them, a heavily bespectacled man wearing a black turtleneck under his black jacket took notes. The art critic, she thought. Oh, Lord. She sighed and moved toward the open bar.

So this, she thought, was a New York City Art opening. Not much different than a night at Janus, as far as she could tell. Everyone looking for the main chance, even if they did it in designer dresses instead of Upstate knock-offs, and talked about theory instead of the bottom line.

Still, it was her opening, her very first. Vince, now full-time at Juliard, had stopped by earlier, and Martha called to congratulate her though she couldn't come because Alicia had a school play – she was being a chicken poc in the chicken pox dance, a tribute to a recent second grade epidemic.

Stacey's cynicism aside, it was going well, though it had come about in an odd way. About six months after the fire, the dealer she'd met with Nick called her. At some point between Vilnius and the fire, Nick had apparently sent him photos of her sketches. The dealer found them thrilling, and wanted to know if she was ready for a show, because he wanted first dibs.

As it happened, she'd been painting a lot. Just before he called she'd completed a watercolor of Trofimovsk Island, a pile of dessicated bodies contemplated by a very human devil, kneeling and weeping nearby. In her only self portrait, she painted herself with a hand on his head in a gesture of absolution. Her grandmother, an angel with leafy wings, poured honey on the bodies. Stacey called it *Daina*, Lithuanian for song. In spite of fear, she told the dealer she was ready.

That night, the internet news gave reports of miracles in Kaunus, Lithuania. An old woman's arthritis was healed, and an old man who was blind for many years could see again. A boy with Cerebral Palsy had his legs straightened, and a woman who'd lost her voice to cancer could sing. The only thing they had in common was a recent visit to the Devil museum. The Vatican was investigating, and they warned people against worshipping non-approved spirits.

That coincidence concerned her, until she recognized she could still feel, which was both a blessing and a curse. It probably meant she hadn't sold her soul, but it also meant she couldn't avoid the grief of knowing that the one person who would truly appreciate the situation wasn't here to share it with her.

Her complicated and profound feelings were in stark contrast with those of the people around her. They had only a lot of mind and the words to prove it. And she was still just a peasant, inarticulate except for her paintings, which she felt too deeply to be intellectual about.

The last visitors oozed away, leaving her with bids on every piece. She refused an offer of dinner from the ecstatically gushing dealer as courteously as she could, and made her way down the street toward her hotel. Halfway there, she stopped in front of a small bar named *HANK'S*, with the N missing from its neon sign.

Seeing it made her realize that in a few days it would be the summer solstice. Almost a year since she'd met Nick. Loneliness assailed her, a grief for which there was no cure. The only thing she could do was honor the moment, and the emotion.

"What the hell," she said, and went inside.

The bar was dimly lit, sparsely populated by men in flannel and denim. One of them wore a pork pie hat. A ball game played on the TV behind the bartender, who wiped glasses and took orders for beer. She took a seat at the darkest end and ordered a Jack and coke.

When the bartender brought it she pushed it around for a moment, pangs of grief gripping her throat. Then she lifted it and whispered, "To you, Nick. Wherever you are, I hope it's good."

Her drink was half gone and she was somewhere between sweet nostalgia and a persistent, piercing sorrow when she heard a voice at her back.

"You seem to like dives, Austeja," it said.

Her heart beat very quickly, a frantic bird caught inside her chest. All her defeated hope rested in that voice. But it was impossible, wasn't it? A trick of memory or longing. She paused, emptied the glass, and before she lost courage she turned.

Looming over her was a familiar face, with eyes that were both dark and light. Her hope, alive. Alive. She worked to regain her breath, and then she spoke.

"So do you, Nick," she replied as coolly as she could. "Why is that?"

He took the empty seat next to her. "I like to be among the people. Reminds me of home. What's your excuse?"

"The same." She looked him up and down. "I thought you were dead."

"You were wrong." He shrugged. "It was your tears. Razak couldn't touch me."

So, she thought. The internet was right about that. The internet, and Father Pete. "And you couldn't let me know? Where've you been?"

"Here and there. I had some business to attend to. Penance for an extended misspent youth. Or a gift of gratitude for a treasure regained, if you prefer. Maybe both. At any rate, I had to take care of it before I saw you."

She thought of the miracles in Kaunus. "I think I read about it."

"The media is everywhere. How was your opening?"

Of course he knew about that. He knew everything. But he was being courteous, old world and impeccably courteous as always, giving her time to know who he was, to choose what to say.

"Good," she said. "It went well. I sold all the paintings." She frowned. "That wasn't – you didn't –"

"I only bought two. Lady of the Grasses and Daina. Other people recognize talent when they see it."

"Then I didn't trade my soul or anything?"

"Not at all. It remains forever inviolable."

"That's good to know. So what brings you to New York? Art or business?"

"Not necessarily either," he said. He stared down at his hands, cautious and clumsy in his caution, being more accustomed to risk. She saw that his left hand bore a scar, where her tears had torn his skin. He signaled the bartender, who came over to them. "Whatever she's drinking, and a tonic with lime for me," he said.

"No rum?" she asked.

"No. I'm afraid I can't drink the way I used to."

A tingle of understanding ran through her. The bartender brought their drinks and she ducked her head down over hers. "You feel okay?" she asked.

His hand touched her hair and retreated. "I feel . . . . everything," he said quietly.

She sipped her drink, put it down and turned to him. She saw apprehension behind his cool exterior. He was afraid. He was capable of that now.

"I missed you," she said. "A lot. If I wasn't so happy to see you, I'd throw my drink at you and walk out."

He was momentarily at a loss. "Austeja," he started, then made a helpless gesture with his hand.

"Yeah. I know," she cut in. "Now tell me why you're here. Really."

He paused, waiting for the right words to make themselves known. "Maybe it's arrogant of me, but I'm seeking the greatest treasure of all," he said.

"What's that?" she asked.

"The human journey. Shared with another resplendent human soul."

She smiled. "What a coincidence," she said. "So am I."

He closed his eyes briefly, opened them again. Then he reached over and grasped her hand like a drowning man being pulled from a stormy ocean. He drew her to him and she was caught in his embrace, once more feeling the slow burn of his kiss.

It wasn't long before she heard appreciative noises from the men at the other end of the bar. Soon one of them would call out, 'Hey - get a room.' She didn't care because now he was kissing her neck, her hair.

"Aš myliu tave, Austeja," he murmured.

"In English," she requested.

"I love you, Austeja," he replied. "Afrikaans - Ek is lief vir u. Mohawk – Konoronkwa. Italian – Ti Amo. . ."

She pulled away from him, touched his face. She had to say something or she would drown in joy. "Then you're done with penance?" she asked.

"Yes, my queen," he crooned, kissing her hand, reveling in her skin. "Though I have more work to do."

"Work?"

He cast her a glance. "There's still a lot of soulless people around, and many honeybees to save. But we may be able to do something about it."

"We?" she muttered. "Hell."

"Not any more," he noted. He brushed a finger against her cheek. "Just the opposite." He leaned close, kissed her softly, breathed a small word into her ear.

"Paradiso," he whispered.

And this time, Austeja agreed.

Author's Notes

It's been my privilege and my honor to tell some of the stories of my Lithuanian ancestors, whose rich spiritual traditions, and whose strength and persistence have informed my life in so many ways.

In order to tell the story, I've drawn on the history of a small but important country, once the geographical center of Europe. Birute, Vytautus, Kestutis and more are all real figures in this history. Austeja, Saule, and the ghosts and devils of mythology inform the cultural soul of those who still live in Lithuania, and the souls of its children who sought refuge in other lands.

I learned a great deal from reading the works of Marija Gimbutas, a renowned Lithuanian archeologist who wrote a lovely book about the imagery of her country's artifacts. I also learned a great deal from reading about Stalin's deportations of Lithuanian Citizens. If you want to know more, I refer you to *Lithuanians by the Laptev Sea: The Siberian Memoirs of Dalia Grinkeviciute*. Believe me, my fictionalized version of that experience has much less horror than the real thing.

In my version, I did include the very real name of Dr. Lazar Solomonovich Samodurov, because it's important to remember the names of our heroes, even beyond the names of our enemies.

Many thanks are due to those who told such stories, and those who saved the people. Thanks also are due to my father, who lived in such a way that I absorbed a very LIthuanian sensibility about the importance of the land, of the trees, of the small toads and snakes, and, of course, the honeybees.

Made in the USA
Middletown, DE
13 May 2017